MADDY MADRIGAL MYSTERIES BOOK 1

BARELY MAGIC

DEBRA CASTANEDA

SHADOW CANYON

— press —

ISBN: 979-8-9903956-4-0
Edited by: Lyndsey Smith, Horrorsmith Editing
Cover design by: Jacqueline Sweet

To Teri.
You have the BEST ideas, my friend.

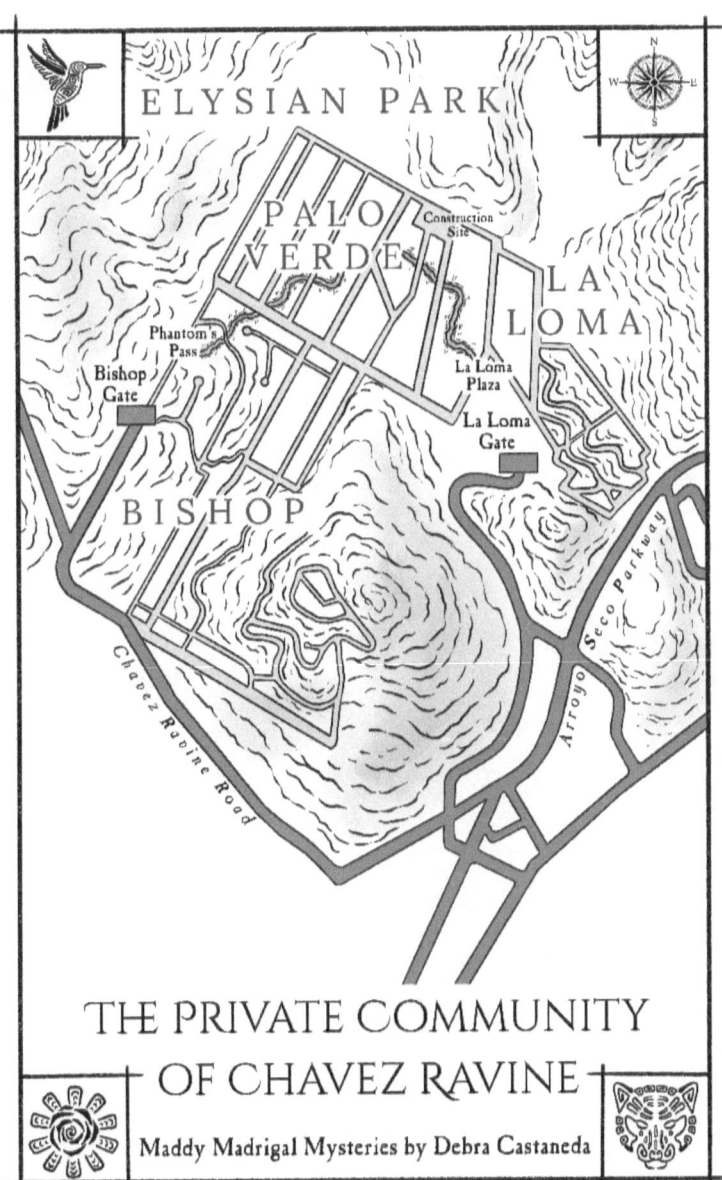

ELYSIAN PARK

PALO VERDE

Construction Site

LA LOMA

Phantom's Pass

Bishop Gate

La Loma Plaza

La Loma Gate

BISHOP

Chavez Ravine Road

Arroyo Seco Parkway

THE PRIVATE COMMUNITY
OF CHAVEZ RAVINE

Maddy Madrigal Mysteries by Debra Castaneda

Chapter 1

No matter how many times I walked into a first encounter with an entity, my thighs tingled, and my palms would go sweaty.

I had taken all the usual precautions. My radio was on my belt in case I needed to call Jo for backup, and I was towing an empty entity crate. But I was still on edge.

This wasn't something I was supposed to do solo, but we were shorthanded. The rest of the team was on a call at the La Brea Tar Pits, so there I was, alone.

I walked slowly down the cobblestone alley, past the trinket shops and food stalls of Olvera Street.

Movement in my peripheral vision. Something gray flashing through the air. A flyer.

Crap.

Flyers were always bad news. I preferred my entities with feet, tentacles, or whatever firmly on the ground.

Another streak, this time on my left side. And just ahead, a sombrero from a souvenir shop came soaring toward me. Not even a tourist trap like Olvera Street sold flying sombreros, so there had to be something inside it.

"Stop, please!" I warned politely.

The sombrero did not comply, and I had to jump out of the way to avoid it. It crashed into a fountain. I sprinted toward it and snatched up the cheap straw hat, revealing the thing beneath it flapping in the shallow water.

It could not possibly have been uglier. The flyer had a wrinkled head with gray skin. A hairless body about the size of a chunky chihuahua. Enormous, clawed hands at the end of long skinny arms. But the face—its pinched mouth was turned down in a permanent scowl.

Yuck.

This was no water sprite, not the clumsy way it was flailing around in the fountain. And it had no wings, so how had it managed to fly?

I unclipped the gloves from my belt and pulled them on, then grabbed the nasty-looking thing around the waist.

We locked eyes.

There was always this moment with new entities, their first encounter with a human. That lost and overwhelmed expression in their gaze. No matter how big, bizarre, or intimidating each appeared, they all seemed bewildered. At least, at first.

I tried my soothing voice—the one that usually worked best with newcomers. "All right, all right. Everything's going to be okay. My name is Maddy Madrigal. I'm not sure if you can understand me, but—"

"It's from Mexico, pendeja! Try speaking Spanish."

Okay. I have an audience.

My critic hung out of a second-story window.

"How do you know it's from Mexico?" I asked.

The middle-aged man with the mustache pointed at the souvenir stand nearest the fountain. "Because I sell little statues of those things. I buy them from Mexico. They're from the Aztecs or something."

"What are they?" I shouted.

"Chaneques. Like, Mexican fairies."

Well, that would be a first. We had never logged those before.

I glanced at his stall, and sure enough, there they were. A whole shelf full of ugly. Dead ringers for the one in my hands.

I sighed and turned back to my captive. If this creature dated as far back as that—before the Spaniards came to Mexico—it probably didn't speak Spanish, but it was worth a try.

"How many friends are with you today?" I asked.

That didn't go so well. The creature hissed, then spat in my face.

Gross.

I gave the thing a little shake. "All right, enough of that. You've left me no choice. Into the crate you go."

It was a struggle getting the chaneque inside the container, but I managed it. All while maintaining a neutral and professional expression, of course, just in case my second-story friend was recording me.

I had just finished latching the crate when something hit my back. The impact was like a wet sandbag slamming into my body, and I went tumbling to the ground. My cheekbone glanced against the lip of the fountain.

Upstairs, Mr. Helpful shouted, "Watch out! They're behind you."

I scrambled to my feet.

A pack of the things was closing in. But they weren't flying. They were jumping—straight at me.

Then I noticed their strange feet. They had three: two for standing and an extra one protruding from behind, which seemed to propel them into the air.

The damn things were spring-loaded.

I instinctively covered my face with my hands while they bounced toward me, claws out. But they flew over my face, right for my scrunchie. My loose bun gave way under the assault.

Their claws got tangled in my hair, and they started dragging me across the path. Strands were being yanked out with each painful tug, and my scalp felt like it was on fire.

A door banged open, and feet thudded toward me.

The last thing I needed was a civilian coming to my "rescue."

"LAPD, Occult Affairs Division. Please don't approach!" I managed to shout.

That worked. People tended to stay away from Occult Affairs officers, especially when we were grappling with entities.

I really needed to get the little monsters out of my hair, and I had something perfect for emergencies like these. At least it worked on gnomes, so I hoped it would be effective on these things too.

I slammed my fist against a rubber pouch dangling from my belt. A cloud of purple smoke shot out and filled the air.

God, I love that stuff.

The purple haze performed like a charm. It was one of our best tools for close combat—a scientifically formulated powder that sapped the energy out of most entities, even if only temporarily.

The bad-tempered nasties collapsed into little heaps of gray. Even in their sedated state, their downturned mouths made them look disgusting.

After a quick search, I found two more hiding under a bench and hit my pouch again. I sent an update to Jo in the command center. She was obviously relieved I wasn't asking for backup because she really didn't have anyone to send.

I packed up the entities and put them in the crate. By the time I dropped them off at The Dump, our nickname for the downtown L.A. Entity Receiving Center, my arms ached.

When I got back to the squad room, I sank into my chair and started typing up my report. Not two words in, I got a message on my screen:

Officer Madrigal, report to the chief's office immediately.

Here we go again. I knew what was coming before I even walked into the office.

"Did you respond to another incident without a partner, Madrigal?" the chief barked.

I sure did, and not because I had a choice. But I couldn't say that. Instead, I cleared my throat.

"I thought I'd assess the situation and call for backup if needed, sir."

The chief scowled. "You make sure to include that in your report. That it was *your* choice. Got it?"

I resisted the urge to rip out his hair plugs. Instead, I pasted a smile on my face, nodded, and backed out of the door.

In situations like those, it was best to keep one's mouth shut. If I had tried to defend myself, I would have gotten Jo into trouble, even though the staffing shortage had nothing to do with her and everything to do with the chief.

A normal boss would have congratulated me for handling the chaneques quickly and with almost no disruption to the public. But that wasn't this guy's style. I long ago gave up hoping for an "Attagirl" or even a "Glad you're okay." Instead, I got a scolding.

The chief really made it hard for a girl to drag her butt into the squad room every morning.

No wonder we were chronically short-staffed.

Between the fights with entities and my jerk of a boss, this job was starting to get old.

Chapter 2

In the past month, I had been shoved into a pool by a shape-shifting water sprite and almost drowned. Then, I was hit with an iron chain by a foul-smelling ghost who was wandering near an old, deserted jail—maybe the spirit of some criminal. And there was the nixie incident at the water park. I had arrived while she was trying to lure teenage boys into the deep end of the wave pool. It was our first encounter with a nixie, so I had no idea how unpredictable they could be. When I asked her politely to come with me, she grabbed a seashell ornament from her hair and scraped it across my face.

What I'm saying is, all this stuff took a toll. Five years previous, getting dragged by the hair across cobblestones would have left me a little sore, but the morning after my encounter in Olvera Street, I rolled out of bed feeling twice my age, more like eighty than forty. Not even a long, hot shower eased the aches and pains.

At least the things hadn't bitten me. That had happened before, and it was never fun. First, I would have to see an entity specialist, then wait for test results to find out if I was infected with something. If so, I would have been looking at a round of painful shots. So yes, things could have been worse.

I winced through my morning workout in my small living room. It was furnished with a rack of free weights, an adjustable workout bench doubling as a coffee table, and a couch. If I'd had more space—and friends to see it—I would have decorated. But what was the point?

While I swung my kettlebell, my eyes raked across the sad little room. My apartment was beginning to annoy me as much as my job. I'd had both for six years, a personal record.

Maybe it was time to look for something else. With a new job should come a bigger paycheck. Maybe I could afford a nicer place—a two-bedroom. I might even hang a picture or two.

The more I thought about it, the more optimistic I felt. It was time for a life upgrade.

The workout and the shower that followed helped. Perkier, even refreshed, I sat down with my coffee and a piece of toast with peanut butter to check my email.

What a great way to ruin a nice morning.

A message awaited in my inbox:

Dear Madeline Madrigal,

I am writing to inform you that the building in which you currently reside has been sold. The new owner plans to make changes that directly impact your tenancy.

Unfortunately, this means that your current lease agreement will be terminated in accordance with section 8.3. You must vacate the premises within 60 days of the date of this letter. Please remove all your belongings and return the keys to the management office by that date. Your security deposit, less the cost of repairs, will be refunded within 30 days…

Blah, blah, blah.

It ended with a request for me to contact the management company if I had any questions or concerns.

Well, I had plenty of those. Like where the hell was I going to move on such short notice? And did they have any suggestions for a place I could afford on my salary?

I closed the laptop and went into the bathroom to put on my makeup.

Maybe it was time to accept the offer in the small hill town ninety minutes southeast of Los Angeles. The rent would be cheaper, but I'd had my fill of small towns while growing up.

The last I'd heard, my mother was living in Palm Springs, which would be a little too close for my liking. And I couldn't move and keep it a secret. My mother had an uncanny way of knowing where I was. She didn't need a phone call or a message. My mother would…sense it.

By the time I got to work, over-caffeinated as usual, my optimism was gone, and my heart was beating fast. I wondered if I might be having a cardiac thing, the stress of that place finally getting to me. But surely, I was too young for that? And if it *was* a heart thing, what was I supposed to do, quit? I was on my own, hadn't married, and never had a job that covered more than rent and a few bills, so no savings. Quitting was not an option.

Such was the life of an Occult Affairs officer.

I pulled into the uncovered parking lot. One would think the city would provide secure parking for its staff, but no. I put on the lanyard with the alarm button on it—Jo's idea after an unfortunate entity attack on the command center—and headed for the door.

A woman appeared from behind a palm tree, startling me. If she hadn't been so respectable-looking, I might have actually used the alarm.

I stepped back to put some space between us, just in case, and then smiled. My soothing voice worked on people too.

"Ma'am, I think you might have ended up in the wrong area. This is the officer entrance. The public entrance is around the corner and down about half a block."

"Yes, I know." She cleared her throat and continued. "My name is Cora Bernal, president of the homeowners association at Chavez Ravine. I was hoping you had a chance to read my messages?"

So *this* was Cora Bernal. She was older and more elegant than I had expected. And she was persistent. Over the course of a few weeks, she had sent several messages asking if I would be interested in a security job with the Chavez Ravine HOA. Obviously, I was thinking about getting a new job, but that one sounded awful.

The ritzy enclave in the hills above downtown Los Angeles made a big deal about being "entity free." I wasn't ready for a demotion that would have me wearing an even dumber uniform and patrolling the pristine streets of a gated community.

Besides, I had issues with Chavez Ravine. Serious issues.

I did my best not to roll my eyes or allow my face to make any of the expressions it usually did when I was caught off guard. "Yes, sorry I haven't responded. It's been pretty hectic here lately. And to be honest, I'm not sure I'd be a good fit for the job."

Cora gave a little sniff. "You don't know what the job is."

"Mmm. Security guard? Something like that?"

Cora wrinkled her nose. "Nothing like that. We have plenty of security guards. No, what I have in mind is much more involved and requires a certain expertise."

"I see…" Although I did not. My expertise was in entity encounters and containment, and the folks up at Chavez Ravine swore they had never had an entity problem.

"I should mention, we pay twice what you're making now, and we have a generous benefits package that includes a two-bedroom condo."

"It does?" My voice went all high and squeaky. So much for the cool cop act.

A car pulled into the lot, and a male voice shouted, "Hey, Madrigal, you better get your ass inside if you don't want to get chewed out by the chief."

Cora continued hurriedly, "I'm sorry to ambush you like this, but I thought if we met in person—and if I could convince you to come with me to Chavez Ravine—I could give you a little tour and tell you more about what we're offering. I think you'll see we are a good fit, after all."

The woman had word skills. But she also had something more—an affordable place to live. *Better* than affordable. Free, by the sound of it. I would have been an idiot not to consider it. Boring might not be so bad. Hadn't my body taken enough beatings? And I wasn't getting any younger. The optimism from earlier in the morning started to make a comeback.

"What is your timing to fill this position?" I heard myself ask.

"As soon as possible."

I thought for a moment. The chaneque attack gave me the perfect excuse to take a few hours off. I would just tell the chief I needed to get my wounds checked out.

"Does first thing tomorrow morning work?" I asked. "As long as I'm at work by eleven."

"We can do that. Eight o'clock. You know where we are. I'll leave your name with the guard at the gate, and they'll give you directions to the community center. I'll meet you there."

She turned and walked back to her car, leaving me to wonder which of us was more surprised by the outcome of that little chat.

And there might be more surprises ahead. The HOA president didn't seem to know about my history with Chavez Ravine, and I certainly wasn't about to tell her.

Chapter 3

Everyone in LA had heard of Chavez Ravine, but few people had been there. One couldn't just drive in and check it out.

Over the years, while the three original neighborhoods in the Ravine had grown ritzier, the residents became sick of all the looky-loos. The villages got together and turned the whole place into a gated community. Now, there were two guardhouses: one leading into the village of Bishop and the other into La Loma. The swankiest of the three neighborhoods, Palo Verde, sat in the middle.

In all the time I had worked in the Occult Affairs Division, we had not had a single call from Chavez Ravine. So, it was special, and in more ways than one. The community had its own zip code and was home to the highest concentration of wealth in Los Angeles County. Most people could have only dreamed of living high in those scenic rolling hills above the crowded streets of the city below.

So why did the president of the Chavez Ravine HOA need a security specialist, and why did she want me in particular?

When I drove up the long and meandering road toward La Loma, my nerves began to jangle.

The landscaping on either side consisted entirely of cacti. I didn't know much about plants, but they seemed aggressively large and a brighter green than normal, their fruit and flowers nearly neon under the warm sun.

The weirdness didn't stop there. The sky appeared bluer. Below, the air had been hot and still. Up here, a cool breeze ruffled my hair. I glanced at the temperature display on the dashboard. Seventy degrees. It was at least ten degrees cooler than down in the city. How was that even possible?

The guardhouse at the top of the hill was as big as my apartment but better furnished. And fancier too. White-painted stucco with a red tile roof.

"Nice place." I handed over my driver's license. "Got a jacuzzi in there?"

The young man with wavy brown hair winked. "No, but I've got a nice cot in the back room if you'd like to check it out."

Oops. Hadn't meant to sound flirty. He was at least ten years younger than me, and if I decided to take the mysterious job, the guy might report to me. Not a great way to start off a professional relationship. I made a note of his name. Ron Mendez, according to his badge.

I caught him staring at my uniform, and his mouth dropped open.

"Occult Affairs?" His voice had gone up an octave. He looked around wildly, as if expecting a troll to emerge from behind the prickly pear cactus next to the guardhouse. "Did the board call you? Is there something going on?"

Ron looked panicked, and I didn't blame him. If Chavez Ravine had truly been spared from the entities annoying the rest of the city, Ron had a very cushy job.

"Nothing like that," I said. "Just here to meet with Cora Bernal."

The mention of Cora's name had an immediate effect. He cleared his throat and straightened, suddenly all business. He ducked inside and checked a screen. Moments later, the security gate lifted.

"Señora Bernal is waiting for you at the HOA office in Palo Verde. Stick to the main road down through La Loma. At the bottom, take a left at the green sign shaped like a saguaro and follow it until you hit Palo Verde Plaza. That's where you want to be."

When I drove off, I looked in the rearview mirror. Ron was standing outside, talking into a walkie-talkie, presumably letting Cora know I was on the way.

It was my first time visiting Chavez Ravine, and it was even more upscale than I had imagined. The houses lining the road probably started out modest decades before, but they had been remodeled and added onto over the years. All had fresh paint and lush, well-tended gardens. Beyond them, the homes got progressively bigger and more opulent. All the houses were either Craftsman style, with wide porches and gabled roofs, or they were patterned after Mexican haciendas, complete with thick adobe walls, arched doorways, and red tile roofs.

And the landscaping was immaculate. The red and purple bougainvillea growing on trellises were so bright, they made my eyes hurt. Jacaranda trees, with their delicate violet blossoms, and exotic-looking birds-of-paradise accented perfect lawns, while tall palm trees lined the boulevard.

This early in the morning, there weren't many people outside, just a few women—probably nannies—pushing fancy strollers. A group of older ladies were out for a power walk, swinging their arms, and a man paced on his front porch, talking on his cell phone. His yard had a fountain worthy of a Las Vegas hotel.

But there was more to Chavez Ravine than money and good gardening. The place had a serious past. And out of it had come some very unusual rules about who could and who couldn't live there.

There were only two ways to live in Chavez Ravine. Either you had a historical connection to the old neighborhoods—and the paperwork to prove it—or you were rich enough to afford the astronomical asking price when a rare property came on the market. Oh, and if you bought your way in, you would also have to survive an interview with the HOA.

And the truth was, I should have been living there instead of my crappy apartment.

But no. My family had missed their chance to document their connection to the old neighborhoods. Call it unfortunate timing, horrible planning, or just bad luck, but everyone from my grandparents on down had ended up poor. Well, except for my mother, but that was another story.

Driving through the ravine and seeing how people lived was tough. I had never quite understood what I had lost before, and witnessing the wealth made me clench my teeth so hard, my jaw ached.

Palo Verde Plaza was straight out of Beverly Hills, minus the gnomes. Which I thought was weird, since all the gardens and statuary around the plaza made it the sort of place gnomes loved.

Of all the entities we had seen so far, gnomes were the most difficult to round up. Once entrenched, they took over yards and refused to share them with the homeowners. Gnomes weren't dangerous to people, though they sometimes attacked dogs, but they were notoriously stubborn and uncommunicative.

I wondered if Chavez Ravine had *ever* had a gnome problem. If so, the HOA must have done everything in its power to get it under control quickly and discretely. Nothing lowered property values faster than those pests. One could just ask the unfortunate residents of Beverly Hills.

My Jeep was the smallest, oldest, and dirtiest vehicle in the parking lot. I was almost embarrassed to leave it among all the gleaming luxury cars.

The community center obviously served as a gathering place for the residents of Palo Verde. In addition to a large hall, there was a small bar, a restaurant, and a library with historical records. I peered through the glass doors. The walls were lined with old black-and-white photos, and I longed to have a look, maybe check if I could find my grandmother. She had bought her home in La Loma less than a year before the City of Los Angeles sent eviction notices to all the residents of Chavez Ravine. Talk about bad timing.

I followed the signs to the HOA offices on the second floor and went up the stairs.

Cora Bernal was waiting for me. She was wearing a gray dress and a yellow shawl.

"I'm so glad you could make it." Cora took my hands in both of hers, like I was a lifelong friend instead of a job candidate.

"Thank you for inviting me. I look forward to our conversation." I glanced not-so-discreetly at the clock on the wall. There was a lot to discuss, and I had to get to work by eleven.

Cora smiled, her teeth very white against her brown skin. "So do we. I thought you should meet with the rest of the board."

"The board?"

I had thought it would just be the two of us. She hadn't said a word about meeting with anyone else, let alone an entire board.

We walked into a large room with a bank of windows set high on the wall. A long, dark wood table was lined on both sides by leather chairs, which looked like they belonged in a fancy Mexican restaurant. A huge vase filled with flowers sat in the middle.

Five sets of eyes stared at me. Cora sat at the end of the table closest to the door and motioned to the empty chair next to her. There were four board members besides Cora, and their collective gaze judged hard. I sat down, a smile plastered to my face, my stomach all fluttery.

Cora could have warned me. The day before, she had made it sound like the job was mine for the asking, but it appeared not to be the case. By the hostile expression of the blond woman sitting across the table, the plan to hire me had some opposition.

Cora pulled a folder from a tote bag and flipped it open. "We're very lucky to have Madeline Madrigal here with us today. She's an officer with the LAPD's Occult Affairs Division and has spent most of her career in law enforcement. As you know, I've been advocating for a full-time head of security to join us, and—"

The blond woman held up a hand. Late forties, I guessed. Bob haircut, an upturned nose, and light blue eyes ringed with black eyeliner.

"I still don't understand why you think this is such a good idea, Cora. We don't have any crime here to speak of—no burglaries, very few car break-ins—and we certainly don't have any issues with entities. We already spend a fortune on the guardhouses and patrols, so what is your justification for adding an unnecessary, ongoing expense that will just increase our dues?"

A deep, melodious voice chimed in from the opposite end of the table. "Cora's always been a bit *nerviosa*."

The voice belonged to an imposing-looking older gentleman. Early seventies. Craggy features but handsome. A head full of black hair shot through with silver. A V-neck sweater over a skinny black tie and crisp white shirt.

When I glanced at him, he smiled and added, "Cora and I go back years. She knows I'm just teasing."

Cora didn't seem to think so. Her nostrils flared. She opened her mouth to reply, but the man spoke first.

"I'm sorry. We haven't been introduced. I'm Hernan Frias, a founding member of the board. I'd like to thank you for making the trip up here. Cora has shared your qualifications with the board, and they are quite impressive. It's my opinion that you'd make an excellent head of security, but I'm afraid I'm with Eileen Simpson on this one." He nodded at the blond across from me, who shot him a simpering smile. "I just don't feel we should take on the expense of a full-time head of security when crime is not an issue here."

Cora hurriedly introduced the other board members. Charlie Perez was a man of maybe fifty or so. With his scrunched face and square head, he resembled a bulldog.

A man with a long face and a welcoming expression was Dan Berman. He had gray hair tied back in a ponytail.

When the introductions were done, Hernan continued. "But Cora feels we need a head of security, so maybe she knows more than she's telling us?" His dark eyes were penetrating.

Hernan's attention shifted away from me to Cora, who was exchanging worried looks with Charlie Perez. It appeared there was, indeed, something they weren't saying. And whatever it was, if they needed someone like me, someone with experience containing entities, it was serious.

Chapter 4

I blinked my eyes slowly and took a beat. Obviously, if I wanted a shot at the security job, I would have to think fast. I needed a sales pitch, a story, something I could say to help these overconfident board members realize how difficult it was to keep entities out of a neighborhood. And how hard it would be to get rid of them once they had settled in.

So, I cleared my throat to cut the tension and started my spiel.

"I have to be honest with you, this isn't the first time I've heard people say an entity infestation can't happen in their neighborhood. Then we get a call a few weeks later from those same people, complaining about sprites in their plumbing and—"

The conference room door burst open, and the receptionist rushed in. "There's been an attack!"

Chaos ensued.

The board members forgot all about their little power struggle and jumped to their feet. Chairs fell over. The color drained from Cora's face, and she clutched the edge of the table.

I wasn't head of security yet, so I kept my mouth shut.

Hernan Frias was the first to recover. "That doesn't sound good. What do you mean...*attack*?"

The receptionist had reddish hair in a pixie cut. The freckles across her nose seemed to dance above her skin. "I just heard from the guard at the Bishop Gate. One of the residents called him. A woman. Said a naked man had broken into her house and she'd locked herself in a panic room."

Cora gritted her teeth and exchanged another long look with Charlie Perez. Both seemed distressed by the news but not totally surprised, which was pretty darn suspicious.

"Has someone called the police?" Eileen asked.

I had to give her credit. That was a very reasonable question.

The receptionist shook her head. "I don't know."

It was time to take charge. After all, I was a cop. An Occult Affairs cop—more than capable of handling a situation like this.

I stood and reached for my cell phone. "I'll check the status of the police response." To the receptionist, I added, "Give me the address of the woman's house."

There was no status. Dispatch had no record of the disturbance, so I called Jo. There was a serious incident at a college in the valley, and she couldn't talk long, but she had not heard about anything happening in Chavez Ravine either.

I turned to Cora. "Do you know why the police didn't get a call?"

She went all tight around the eyes. "That's not how it works here. If someone sets off an alarm or has any trouble, the guards respond first."

Charlie cleared his throat. "We don't like to involve the police if it's not necessary. And it hasn't been necessary, not for a long time."

Mmm. Another LA community trying to hide its dirty laundry.

I looked at Cora. "Do all the houses have panic rooms?"

Before she could respond, Eileen piped up. "No, just a few of the newest ones."

I stared at her, wondering why she felt it necessary to butt in. Which she obviously sensed.

"I'm a real estate broker," she said. "I handle most of the listings that come up in Chavez Ravine."

I should have guessed. Some people just looked like real estate agents. Eileen, with her perfect blond 'do, was one of them.

Before she could hand me a business card, I grabbed my purse and headed for the door. "Is the intruder still in the house?"

"We don't know. The surveillance system in the panic room isn't wired up yet, so she can't see out."

At the very least, the woman was safe. Presumably, the door was strong enough to withstand an assault by a determined naked man, who I suspected wasn't a man at all.

And if that was the case, Chavez Ravine had just experienced its first contact with an entity.

———>·→·||||·◄·◁·———

As an Occult Affairs officer, I don't carry a gun. Traditional weapons don't work against most entities. I have something better than bullets—my standard-issue anti-entity rubber pouch. Two of them, in fact: one in my purse and one in my glove compartment. I grabbed both before heading to the house.

Ron Mendez, the guard I had met at the gate, was waiting for me on the porch with two of his coworkers. They had already checked the grounds and discovered the intruder had scaled the backyard fence and walked through wide-open French doors leading from a patio, which looked like something out of a magazine.

Actually, the whole house looked like a showplace. It was enormous, with three levels. Spanish tile floors everywhere. Cream-colored stucco. Modern leather furniture. Bright paintings of desert landscapes.

The guards had checked every nook and cranny. The intruder was gone, but I got whiff of something funky, like unwashed socks stuffed in the back of a closet.

"Smell that?" I asked Ron.

He gave a tentative sniff and frowned. "No. What?"

The smell was stronger in the hallway. More potent still on the short set of stairs leading to the industrial-sized door to the panic room. The intruder had probably spent some time there, trying to figure out how to get inside.

Ron introduced me to the owner of the house, who was younger than I expected. Mid-thirties, at most, though it was hard to tell with all the cosmetic procedures she'd had. Her eyes were red, and tears ran down her cheeks, but otherwise, I would never have known anything was wrong because the rest of her features were frozen.

"Katherine, I'm Madeline Madrigal with the LAPD." No use mentioning Occult Affairs. "Are you all right?"

Katherine Morris had long hair dyed silver with purple tones. She wore faded jeans and a white frilly tank top.

Katherine clutched an embroidered pillow to her stomach and nodded. "Yes, I'm fine. Thank God my husband insisted on having the panic room put in when we built the house. At first, I thought it was ridiculous. I mean, we could have used it in the Hollywood Hills, with all the crazy stuff that's happening over there, but here? I thought he was overreacting. But it saved me today."

More tears.

I sat down across from her and patted her knee. "Did you get a look at the intruder, Katherine?"

She pressed a hand to her mouth. "Just out of the corner of my eye. I was in the kitchen, and I saw him on the patio. Oh God, he was so weird-looking. Not very tall, but huge. Wide. And totally naked and really, really hairy, and…" Katherine seemed to be swallowing a scream. "And he had the most enormous dong I've ever seen."

That made me sit up a little straighter. When logging entity descriptions, we rarely encountered private parts. There had been the occasional randy juvenile nixie, but that was it.

Instead of replying, I made sympathetic clucking noises and tapped a note onto my screen.

"I'm serious," she continued. "It was terrifying. Like a bull."

My heart skipped. "You didn't happen to get a look at his feet, did you?"

"His feet?" Katherine echoed. "I was too busy freaking out by what was hanging down to his knees."

I coughed to cover the alarm bells ringing between my ears. No, it couldn't be. It was something we had talked about in occult affairs. Joked about. But never really expected. "Yes. Did it have cloven hooves?"

"Like a horse?"

"Yeah. Something like that." More like a minotaur, but there was no need to get mired in details.

Katherine shook her head. "I don't think so. I mean, when I saw him, I started running for the panic room, and he chased me. If he had hooves, I would have heard them on the tiles. It was just feet. He didn't have any shoes."

"Hairy feet?"

"He was hairy everywhere," Katherine replied. "But not enough to cover…you know." She gagged. Whatever she had seen had been burned into her brain.

I picked up my screen and swiped through. When I found the image I was looking for, I held out the display. "All right, Katherine. If you can just take a quick look at this for me."

It was a picture of a troll. We'd had lots of encounters with them. Usually, they appeared farther north in the foothills, but it was hilly enough here, one might have gone astray.

"Does this look like your intruder?

Katherine regarded the display warily, then leaned in slowly, frowning. She blinked at the screen before falling back against the pillows with a heavy sigh. "Not really, no. That doesn't look like a person, does it? The intruder was definitely a person."

She paused for a moment and moaned.

"I can't believe this happened. We bought this place because it's supposed to be so safe up here. My in-laws gave us the down payment because where we used to live got really bad after the last quake, but I don't think I can stand living here anymore. I'm not from here, you know. New York has its problems, but they're nothing like this."

So, the intruder wasn't a troll, and it wasn't a minotaur. I couldn't think of another entity matching Katherine's description, so we were dealing with something else. Something *new*.

There was nothing left for me to do at the house, so I asked the guards to take over and returned to the yard, where I took photos of footprints in the flower bed lining the back fence. They were about double the width of the average human footprint, but they had five toes. Not a troll, but it didn't mean the intruder wasn't still an entity, though.

I stood next to the in-ground hot tub, called Jo at the command center, gave her the address, and asked her to check the heat map for the latest entity eruptions.

Jo grumbled about how busy she was, but her fingers tapped away. A moment later, she asked, "Are you in Chavez Ravine?"

"Yeah. Don't ask. Long story. Whaddya see?"

"Nothing."

"Are you sure?"

Jo snorted. "Yes, I'm sure. The closest thing I'm seeing is in North Hollywood. Three more of your chaneques showed up at a strip mall. Why? What's going on up there?"

"Probably just a freaky-looking burglar. Listen, I'll log what I've got and head in, but I might be late."

"Not a problem."

I wasn't sure how I would explain why I was in Chavez Ravine when I was supposed to be visiting a doctor, but I'd think of something if the chief questioned me.

When I returned to the community center, I gave Cora and the other board members a quick update. While I couldn't confirm whether the intruder was an entity, everyone looked decidedly nervous, especially Cora and Charlie Perez.

"Then what was it?" Eileen demanded.

"A home invasion?" I said vaguely. "You have your own security up here. You can choose to call the police if you'd like and have them look into it further. At this point, there's not really much I can do. Katherine Morris was scared but unharmed. No property damage to speak of. She left some doors open, and someone walked in. And he didn't attack her."

Realizing I wasn't helping my chances of getting hired, I continued.

"I said I couldn't confirm it was an entity. But it *might* have been. It certainly had characteristics that would be pretty unusual for a human. It could be a variety of entity we haven't seen yet. We see new entities all the time, unfortunately."

Cora stared at me in a pleading sort of way. She obviously wanted me to go on, but I had to be subtle.

"I think I should let you know that Katherine Morris was very upset about the incident, and I wouldn't be too surprised if she convinced her husband to sell their place so she can move back to New York."

Eileen gasped. A bejeweled hand fluttered to her ruddy chest. "Oh no. Oh, please, no. Katherine's a beauty influencer. She has a huge social media following. We can't have her bad-mouthing Chavez Ravine!"

Cora rearranged her yellow shawl. "Then we need to get in front of this, don't we? Show we're taking it seriously? We need to do what I've been suggesting for the last year: hire someone to oversee security before we have a problem we can't control."

The nods weren't exactly enthusiastic. More like resignation. The suspicious cop in me wondered for a moment if Cora had staged the whole thing, just to make a point.

It seemed like the perfect time for me to make my exit. You know, leave 'em wanting more.

"I'm sorry, but I need to get going. I do hope you can agree on a solution for what could become a very serious problem." I turned toward the door.

Charlie Perez took the bait. He made a big show of consulting his phone. "I think we should meet again at our first opportunity and continue talking about this. Everyone?"

To my surprise, Eileen did not object. They all agreed to meet again the next morning at eight o'clock.

And I was invited.

Chapter 5

After the spotless streets and lush landscaping of Chavez Ravine, my crappy apartment seemed smaller and sadder than ever. Had I really lived there for six years? I opened the ancient fridge and winced. Had it always smelled so moldy, or had my standards gone up in the past few hours?

I grabbed a club soda and drank it straight from the can.

Though I was feeling uneasy, I couldn't pinpoint why. Because a cushy job in a fancy enclave had been dangled in front of me? One that wasn't a sure bet after all? Or because I was conflicted about leaving my job with the LAPD?

I had been a cop working out of the LAPD's Rampart Station when the department started the Occult Affairs Division. The new division's recruiting efforts were a bust—nobody wanted to come anywhere near entities, let alone wrangle them into crates. And then there was the salary. Way too low to tempt civilians.

But for me, taking the job had been a no-brainer. I had always been easily bored, and car break-ins and petty crime got boring fast. Plus, I was curious about entities. They had emerged minutes after a massive earthquake rocked Los Angeles. A small chimera had crawled out of a hole in Griffith Park, stumbling around on wobbly legs. It was so disoriented, animal control was able to capture it.

More things soon appeared: selkies at Venice Beach, ghosts at an amusement park already thrown into chaos by the quake, trolls in Angeles National Forest. Since there was such a wide variety of supernatural beings, no one word could accurately describe them all. Eventually, some bureaucrat had come up with the catch-all term "entity," and it stuck.

I had been excited to be a part of something new, to be on the front lines of this new era in Los Angeles history. And I really felt I could make a difference, both for the people of the city and for the entities themselves.

My biggest surprise, once I hit the streets as an Occult Affairs officer, was how pathetic newly arriving entities seemed. No matter how scary they appeared, there was no ignoring the lost look in their eyes. Assuming they had eyes, of course.

They might not have been human, but it was impossible not to feel sorry for them. The entities didn't choose to be in LA, and the moment they arrived, most of them were captured, taken to The Dump, and packed off to a preserve in the desert.

Maybe that's what I was beginning to feel: my optimism had turned into sadness. I could sense the hopelessness of their situation. Which just gave me one more excuse to leave.

I called Jo. She was driving home and put me on speaker.

"Hey! Want to meet me for a drink somewhere? Holly's working late."

"I've got laundry and stuff. But if you have a moment, I'd like to talk about something."

"Oh, I have a moment." Jo chuckled. "The 101 is a parking lot."

"Remember when I mentioned I was up at Chavez Ravine?"

"Yes. You want to tell me what that was about?"

"I was there for a job interview."

A long silence followed. A horn blared in the background. Jo muttered a curse, then exhaled loudly. "All right. What kind of job?"

"Head of security."

Jo barked out a laugh. "Security? It's the safest place in all of Los Angeles. No crime. No entities. What do they need you for? HOA enforcer? 'Hey, you over there, get that pink flamingo off the lawn, or I'll fine you.'" She laughed again.

"Jo, this is serious." I threw the empty can across the kitchen into the recycling bin. "They actually had an incident today while I was interviewing with the board, so something's going on. They're very cagey about what, but just the fact that they're recruiting *me* says things aren't as rosy up there as we think. Jo, the salary is amazing, and the benefits include a place to live, so it's pretty attractive. I honestly don't know what I'll do if—and it's a big *if*—I get the offer. Should I take it?"

Jo whistled. "A place to live in Chavez Ravine? Wow. Look, Mads. I know you've not been happy for a long time, and I'm not judging you. It's one thing to sit in the command center like I do, and it's another thing being out in the field. Let me ask you something: on a scale of one to ten, how unhappy are you?"

"Good question. An eight? Eight and a half? Ever since we got the new chief? And we thought the last one was bad. Hah! Who thought it was a good idea to hire an insecure, misogynistic ass-kisser? I've applied for promotions, but the jobs always go to his golfing buddies.

"When I moved to Occult Affairs, it was all new and exciting. Like, a calling. We were a special team, doing important stuff, keeping citizens safe, and treating the entities humanely. But people don't care that we put ourselves at risk. It's like they blame us for the entities or something. They just want the problem taken care of and then want us to get the hell out as fast as possible so they can pretend life is normal. It's really messed up. I might as well be a dog catcher."

Jo sighed. "Okay. That's a bit of an exaggeration, but I get it. I'm trying very hard not to freak out that our best officer is considering leaving. You're right about one thing. The chief is going nowhere. He's not going to change, and you're stuck in the job you've got. That is the unfortunate reality. As much as I hate to say it, Mads, the only way to go up is to get out."

I wasn't sure what I was expecting, but it wasn't Jo agreeing with me. *Damn.*

I stared outside. The older man across the courtyard was fixing a broken window by taping a piece of cardboard over the opening. Classy. Though I didn't blame him. The landlord wasn't going to fix it anytime soon.

"They're offering a two-bedroom condo." I sounded positively wistful.

Jo gasped audibly. "Hell, if you don't take the job, I will, Mads. Look, worst-case, even if the job sucks, you'll be living in Chavez Ravine."

When we hung up, I continued watching the man across the way. He was writing something on the cardboard. When he stepped away, I read:

FIX THIS SHIT NOW.

My throat was closing. I had to swallow and take a deep breath to get some air into my lungs. The message seemed like it was just for me. I had been presented with a chance to fix my life, and I needed to go all-in for that job in Chavez Ravine.

Chapter 6

I woke up early so I could put extra time into getting ready. The red lipstick and wing eyeliner were a bit much, but the woman in the bathroom mirror staring back at me looked like a boss lady, so I went with it. Instead of my usual uniform of black pants and white shirt, I slipped on a dress. V-neck but not too low, hitting just at the knees.

It showed off my legs, which I had worked hard for. Thousands of squats and lunges.

I checked the results of my efforts in the full-length mirror and hardly recognized myself. The navy blue dress was professional but just the slightest bit sexy, and my caramel-colored hair was doing its part by lying flat instead of poofing out.

Damn, I'd hire me.

I had plenty of time, so I decided to check out the Bishop entrance to Chavez Ravine. That approach to the gated community was entirely different. The LA neighborhood below Bishop was congested and gritty, which was a nice way of putting it.

Storefront windows were covered in garish ads and security bars. Sidewalks were littered with trash, and there were clusters of sad-looking people sitting on plastic tarps. Even entities seemed to avoid the area. In fact, I could only think of one previous event: a dog with scales and red eyes had tried to herd people living on the street until it was tranquilized and taken to The Dump for processing.

Chavez Ravine Road climbed up the hill, leaving all that behind, and eventually ended at a guardhouse. The gate at this entrance was taller and more elaborate than the one outside La Loma. It was made of black wrought iron and was practically Gothic in its design. The guardhouse looked more imposing too, with black shutters and a peaked black tile roof. It gave me the impression of a small, haunted house. If the HOA was trying to send an outsiders-not-welcome-here message, they were succeeding.

The guard, a man with a fleshy face and deadpan expression, checked my ID against a portable screen, then waved me in.

"This first gate is going to open," he said in a gravelly voice. "Go through and stop at the second gate. Another guard will meet you there."

Two gates and two guards? Was this typical, or was it a response to the naked intruder? I was curious, but I didn't want to waste time asking questions. It didn't matter unless I got the job.

The second gate, a few yards ahead, was even taller than the first one. I was boxed in on both sides by tall wooden fences. Somebody had thought this through.

The young man I recognized from the day before, Ron Mendez, had second-gate duty. No guardhouse, just a small kiosk to shield him from the sun. He sauntered over to my window, a smile on his face, told me how to get to Palo Verde Plaza, and opened the gate.

The road to Bishop climbed high into the hills. A green space was visible up on the ridge, but before I got there, I hung a left and was greeted by a street filled with what appeared to be townhouses in the Mexican hacienda style. Smaller than the homes in Palo Verde, but nicer than anything I could ever afford.

Was this where I would live if I snagged the job? Suddenly, I wanted it very, very badly. Not only would it solve my personal housing crisis, but reporting to Cora Bernal would sure beat dealing with the chief. Eileen Simpson and the rest of the board might get a little tiresome, but at least they wouldn't spit on me, try to scratch my eyes out, or smack me around with an iron chain.

Plus, not saying it would be easy, but my duties would be confined to just three neighborhoods.

And not just *any* neighborhoods. The nicest and most charming neighborhoods in Los Angeles. All those gorgeous properties. The pretty little parks and amazing landscaping.

While I drove, I noted the geography. The community had come by its name honestly. The three neighborhoods spread across a ravine, so there were plenty of beautiful hills and gullies.

I crossed a bridge over a dry creek bed. A pedestrian on the walkway, a dapper man wearing white sneakers and a baseball hat, gave a friendly wave.

When I arrived at the association offices in Palo Verde Plaza, the redheaded receptionist greeted me. Her eyebrows shot up. She had obviously noticed the upgrade in my appearance and was trying not to show it.

"I'm so sorry, but they're running a bit behind this morning," she said. The nameplate on the desk read "Caitlin Dubois."

"No problem, Caitlin. I'm a little early." I perched on the edge of a leather chair and glanced at the wall clock: 7:45 a.m. The board was hard at it already, so I wasn't the first item on their agenda. They were probably trying to iron out their disagreements before I arrived.

I crossed my legs and picked up a copy of *Chavez Ravine Magazine*.

"Would you like some coffee?" Caitlin asked.

"No, thank you." Honestly, I would have loved some, but then I would have had to pee. Not good if the interview dragged on.

I flipped through the magazine, one eye on the clock. The glossy pages showed plans for a new development up near Elysian Park, with homes designed for people fifty-plus who were downsizing but still wanted all the luxuries and amenities, including lap pools.

The time hit eight o'clock, and still, the door did not open. At 8:05, I checked my phone to see if I had missed a message from Cora saying they would be late, but nothing. After another several minutes, I cleared my throat and cast an inquiring glance at Caitlin, who got the message.

She smiled sweetly, if a little awkwardly. "They should be done soon."

Finally, at 8:17, the door opened, and a tall man strode out, followed by a pink-cheeked Cora. She gave me a little wave.

"I'm so sorry we ran long, Maddy. I'll be right back out to get you." She returned to the conference room and closed the door behind herself.

I didn't know Cora that well, but she appeared frazzled. And a little embarrassed. What the hell was going on?

The tall man stopped for a chat with Caitlin. They obviously knew each other. He wore a tailored blue suit and had brown hair and twinkling blue eyes a little too narrow and close together. Serious vertical lines framed his mouth. He was handsome in an unconventional way. But there was something almost smug about him.

The man cast a quick look in my direction, and I thought he was going to wink. Instead, he flashed me a smile, and my belly went warm. The magazine slid off my lap and onto the floor. When I reached down to retrieve it, my eyes took it upon themselves to check for a wedding ring. Either the man was unmarried or he was one of those guys who refused to wear one.

When the mystery man left, Caitlin stared after him and sighed, as if she was sorry to see him go. Was he a vendor there to meet with the board or a builder with the new housing development?

Cora darted out of the conference room and motioned for me to follow her into her office. She quickly shut the door behind us. "Maddy, I thought it only fair that I should warn you. After everything that happened yesterday, Eileen decided to get involved in the hiring, and I have to allow the process to play out. The fellow you just saw is Stu Wells. He's a resident, but he also runs a security company that specializes in celebrity clients. Yesterday, Eileen asked him if he would consider taking over security for us in exchange for his monthly dues, which are substantial, given the size of his property, and he said he would consider it. So, we had him come in this morning."

Whatever I had been expecting, it wasn't that.

I had thought the job was mine to lose. Now, I had a competitor with an inside track. Cora didn't need to spell out his advantages. He already had a place to live, so the board wouldn't have to provide housing, and they would save on my salary.

Shit.

Cora hurriedly said, "Maddy. There's a reason I want you for this job. You're the right person for it. And you belong here. But I can't deny that Stu Wells *is* qualified for the job, and he's presenting a very attractive option for the board members concerned about keeping our costs down."

Cora sat down behind her desk, crossed her hands in front of her, and looked me in the eye.

"Now, there is one way I can be sure you get the job. If you claim legacy stakeholder status, it's yours because stakeholders get priority. *Top* priority."

My ears started ringing, and I became a little lightheaded. Somehow, Cora knew about my family history in Chavez Ravine. Did she know the whole sad, pathetic story?

I shook my head. "I can't. It's complicated, but my grandmother never responded to the letters the city sent her. She never returned the payout they gave her, and she never reclaimed her property. My mom says she didn't see the letters because she'd moved to Salinas, and by the time she heard about the city changing course, it was too late. The offer had expired."

Cora held her hand up, like she was stopping traffic. "Yes, I know about all that, but it's not the end of the story, Maddy. Unclaimed properties reverted to the Chavez Ravine Association, which eventually became the HOA. We own it. Well...technically, we're holding it for the family. And that's you. Legacy status is available to you. I know I mentioned a condo would come with the job, but if you're legacy, then your grandmother's house goes to you. All you need to do is claim it."

For about five seconds, I was happier than I had been in a long time. But then my elation faded, and I stared down at my feet. "I changed my last name. I wasn't always a Madrigal."

Cora cleared her throat. "I know that too. When I first heard about you, I asked Stu for a favor, and he helped me track down your background."

Great. Stu knew all my secrets. Big and small, including the string of crappy places I had lived and probably even the inferior pay I had received over the years.

There was more to this story than Cora was telling, and I had to know what it was. "Why me?"

Cora threw up her hands. "You're the granddaughter of Liliana Bantacorte, for one thing. She didn't live in La Loma for long, but as a curandera, she was a well-respected member of the community."

A witch, my mother had insisted, but I wasn't about to say that.

Cora continued. "And then there's your mother. If she tried to file her claim for legacy status, she'd never qualify. The board can block legacy stakeholders under extreme circumstances, and because of your mother's close associations with entities, even I would vote against her. We couldn't take the chance of them following her here. But you're not your mother, are you?"

God, no.

The idea of changing into my drab uniform and walking into the Occult Affairs Division, with its dirty linoleum floors and oppressive, dangerous workload, brought a sour taste to my mouth. Any worries I'd had about switching jobs had disappeared. In its place was only the certainty that the time had come for a change. A big, whopping life change.

"What do I need to do?"

Cora smiled and clapped her hands. "This is marvelous! Just marvelous." She crossed to her desk and rummaged through a drawer. Moments later, she waved a paper in the air, then set it on the desk. "Just fill this out, and we'll get the process started."

The form was printed on high-quality paper. At the top it stated: "CHAVEZ RAVINE ASSOCIATION: APPLICATION FOR LEGACY STAKEHOLDER STATUS."

When I had read it, I wrote my name in my best cursive on the signature line and dated it. I'm not sure what came over me, but I felt like crying.

Chapter 7

The board was stunned, to say the least. Apparently, Cora Bernal had never mentioned my legacy ties to Chavez Ravine. After a few minutes of discussion and some accusations about Cora having been less than transparent—which, I had to admit, seemed to be legit—everyone calmed down. They didn't really have a choice. My connection to the old neighborhoods didn't leave a lot of wiggle room.

Though, Eileen Simpson seemed less concerned about *that* connection than my other one.

"Your mother is Malena Bantacorte?" Eilleen gasped. "Malena B?"

Oh, God. I hated it when people called my mother that. Like she was some kind of pop star. She *was* famous, and her appearances *did* sell out, but "Malena B" sounded ridiculous for a woman pushing seventy.

"That would be correct," I replied stiffly.

Eileen got a bit wild-eyed at that and appeared genuinely panicked. "But…but…we can't have her here! She steps one foot in this place, and anything can happen. We'll be—"

"Invaded," Hernan Frias interrupted. His voice was positively thunderous.

These people had no right to know I had been estranged from my mother for several years, but I needed to reassure them. They weren't wrong to be concerned.

I held up my hand. "Don't worry. My mother will not be visiting Chavez Ravine, for obvious reasons. As your new head of security, I will be just as concerned about that as you are, if not more so."

Cora followed the exchange closely, eyes narrowing, lips pursed. She would make a terrible poker player. Hernan Frias still seemed displeased at this turn of events.

"What about that intruder yesterday? What are you going to do to find him and make sure something like that doesn't happen again?"

I refused to allow the man to put me on my heels when I wasn't even on the payroll yet.

"I'll be investigating as soon as I get my feet under my new desk," I said pleasantly.

That shut him up, but the bad vibes continued coming from his end of the table. I shuddered, wondering what it was about the guy making me feel so uncomfortable. Not even the chief, with all his erratic moods and temper tantrums, had that effect on me.

I asked Cora about him later when we were alone. "Is there something I should know about Mr. Frias?"

"Hernan?" Cora's voice rose. "Don't mind him. He termed out as president and thinks he knows more than everybody else about what's good for Chavez Ravine. He can trace his family back to the very beginnings of Palo Verde, and they were instrumental in organizing the protests that got the city to reverse the evictions. But between you and me, if something isn't his idea, it takes him a while to warm to it. And that includes hiring you."

Cora fussed with papers on her desk instead of looking at me.

"There's nothing else?" I pressed.

She looked up, brows narrowing. "Like what?"

I shrugged. "I just get a funny feeling from him."

Cora's tongue clicked against her teeth. "Well, he was a big mucky muck at the college where he used to teach. He was the chairman of a department. He tends to treat younger people like students. Maybe that's what you're sensing."

"What did he teach?"

"Mystical studies," Cora said briskly, then busied herself with her papers.

Well, that was interesting. It explained his reaction toward my mother. Because she was the queen of mysticism. A queen with an unfortunate attraction to entities.

It was sad how little time it took to pack up my tiny apartment. A day, all told. After donating everything that was out of style, my entire wardrobe fit into a medium-sized cardboard box. Wearing a police uniform had saved me a lot of money on clothes, but it meant I had almost no professional-looking outfits. I would need a suitable selection for my new job.

What would the Chief Security Officer of the Chavez Ravine Association wear anyway? I would have to figure that out, then go shopping.

But I hated shopping. All those badly lit dressing rooms with three-way mirrors…My pathological fear of those was one of the reasons I worked out as hard as I did. But still, there was always something to ruin your day. The patch you forgot to shave. The weird pooch that could be the start of a menopot. Or was it just bloating? For some reason, my knees always freaked me out—they looked, I don't know, *saggy* in those dressing rooms.

Ugh.

I remembered those mother-daughter shopping trips when I was a teen. My mother's sense of fashion was as dramatic as her personality, and all I had wanted was to wear jeans and T-shirts.

I supposed I would have to tell her about my new job sooner or later, but I wasn't sure how she would take the news about me living in her mother's old house in Chavez Ravine. That I had managed something she had always wanted to do but couldn't.

I shoved pots and pans into a couple of boxes, did a quick cleanup, and dropped off my key at the leasing office.

And that was that. A quick, unceremonious ending to my old life.

I climbed into the Jeep and headed up to Chavez Ravine to begin my new one.

—⟶·⟶· ⫟⫟⫟⫟ ·⟵·⟵·⟵—

Cora had an appointment she couldn't get out of, so Charlie Perez—the HOA's vice president—met me in La Loma to take me to my new place. I got there a little early, so I decided to walk around and scope out the area.

The address I had been given was in the middle of a long street at the bottom of a steep hill. At the top was the new housing development under construction, surrounded by a chain link fence. The faint but steady roar of heavy machinery sounded in the distance. Beyond that was Elysian Park. I could barely make out a wooden fence separating the public land from Chavez Ravine, but it wasn't that tall. Anyone determined enough could hop over it.

Maybe that's how Hairy had gotten in—scaling the fence, lugging the package we had heard so much about. Hopefully, he had earned a few well-placed splinters for his troubles.

I made a mental note to inspect the perimeter for weaknesses, then come up with a plan to fix them.

While I was pacing up and down the sidewalk, Charlie pulled up in a green sports car. He was wearing gray pants and a melon-colored polo shirt with the Chavez Ravine logo. If "preppy" had still been a thing, it would have described him perfectly.

"Bienvenido!" Charlie's grin widened, and he dangled a set of keys in the air. "And here we are! Home sweet home!"

He kept chattering as we walked up the brick path to an old house much smaller than the others on the block. I liked it immediately.

"And can you believe it? Your grandmother paid six thousand dollars for it back in the day. How about that?"

I nodded, too distracted to respond.

The Bantacorte house was a compact structure that looked as though it had been empty for a very long time. The tall windows seemed to stare unblinking at the northern and southern approaches to the property. It wasn't half as nice as its neighbors, and it wasn't in great shape.

But it felt like my destiny.

Chapter 8

The appliances in my grandmother's house were old, and there were only one and a half bathrooms—and those needed updating—but it had wide, gleaming plank floors, lots of windows, and three bedrooms. That meant I would have a room dedicated to my workouts, and my weight bench wouldn't have to hold nachos and wine glasses any longer.

On move-in morning, the place was spotless. Even the insides of the refrigerator and oven had received special treatment. Most importantly, the house radiated good vibes, especially the enclosed sunroom at the back.

My mother had said my grandmother Liliana practiced curanderia, and I guessed the sunroom was where she met her clients. She had learned the art of healing from her aunt, Lencha Bantacorte, who had been Chavez Ravine's most famous bruja and, as far as I knew, the only real witch in the family.

The sunroom had a practical terracotta tile floor and a built-in counter made of dark wood planks. I ran my hand across the counter. My fingertips tingled when a surge of electric warmth ran up my arm.

I snatched my hand away and searched for something that could have caused it, like a wire sticking up between the planks. There was nothing. I warily touched the wood again, and the same thing happened.

My mother would probably remember whether the sunroom was where Liliana had done her healing work. I really wanted to be the grown-up and reach out to her, end our estrangement, but I wasn't quite ready to do that. Even though I kind of missed my mother, I also needed my own time and space. Malena Bantacorte took up a lot of energy, which meant less for everyone else.

There wasn't much of a backyard. A patch of brown grass separated the house from an ivy-covered hill. Charlie had said something about sending over a gardener. I had a black thumb, so that was a relief. The front yard was in better shape, but it would still take a professional and a lot of money to bring it up to Chavez Ravine standards.

I wandered around the empty rooms, wondering what kind of furniture I would buy to fill the place. For a forty-year-old woman, I was a late bloomer when it came to home decor. Anyone seeing my gray couch and mismatched chairs would be excused for thinking they had walked into a bachelor pad. And actually, hitting the furniture stores sounded fun. Images of brightly colored cushions and throw rugs flashed before my eyes.

When my stomach started grumbling, I made my inaugural grocery run. I drove to Palo Verde Plaza and the enormous grocery store next to the community center.

Palo Verde Market was every bit as nice as Cora had described. To my surprise, it wasn't much more expensive than the sad market with the permanently stained linoleum in my old neighborhood.

The market had vaulted ceilings, soft lighting, and trendy industrial shelving. The produce was so perfect it looked fake. The butcher counter had all the usual offerings of meat, poultry, and fish but also carried the kind of stuff found in a good Mexican market, like freshly made chorizo, carnitas, al pastor, and flank steak.

I bought some flank steak to make machaca for dinner.

There was also a head-spinning choice of tortillas and hot sauces. Chavez Ravine might have gone through some serious gentrification, but I was heartened it had not forgotten its humble Mexican-American roots. I was really starting to like it.

When I got home, there was a pickup truck parked in the driveway. The bed was filled with plants, which meant the gardener had arrived.

I found him below the living room window, digging a hole for a large fuchsia, with its bell-shaped flowers in eye-popping shades of pink. In the short time I had been at the store, he had already managed to get five of them into the ground.

"Wow, those are nice," I said, setting the grocery bags on the porch steps.

The man sat back and regarded me with serious brown eyes under a cap of curly dark hair. He wore a Chavez Ravine-branded T-shirt and faded jeans.

"I heard you're related to Liliana Bantacorte." His tone was edged with wariness.

Wow. News travelled fast. "Granddaughter." I stuck out my hand. "I'm Maddy Madrigal. Nice to meet you. You must be the gardener."

His chin went up a little. "Master landscaper. I'm Ben Tomas." He stood up and shook my hand. Mid-thirties. Not much taller than me, which put him at around five ten, tops. Barrel-chested. Ben had the physique of a man accustomed to hard work outdoors. Either that or he lifted weights. Maybe both.

"Sorry. I'm new here." Which was kind of a dumb thing to say, but I hadn't intended to offend him, and I had to say something. "What does it take to become a master landscaper?"

"I studied landscape design and horticulture in college, then did a bunch of certifications."

"Well, the place looks amazing. Are you legacy, by any chance?" As soon as the words left my mouth, I realized it might have been a rude question. Who knew how sensitive the whole legacy thing might be?

He wiped his forehead with the back of a hand. "Yeah. My family's from Bishop. We've had the same house on Paducah Street since 1935. Most of the good jobs around here are offered to us legacy stakeholders first." He pointed toward the other side of the porch. "I put some fuchsias over there too. They should do well with the morning sun."

I stepped back to get a better look. There were at least three more, so large they didn't even look newly planted. The flowers reached to the bottom of the windowsill of the small room I had designated as my office.

The yard already looked a million times better.

"It'll probably take me a few days to finish up with the front. I've got some guys coming in to do some prep work in the back. It's a mess. Is it okay if they start early tomorrow?"

"Not a problem." I picked up my grocery bags. "Thanks for all this. I'm sure it'll all be great when you're done. Knock on the door if you need anything, like the bathroom."

He dipped his head. "Thank you. Oh, and by the way, I put your cat inside."

That stopped me. "I don't have a cat."

Ben laughed. "You do now." He pointed.

There, in the kitchen window, sat a giant feline staring back at me with green eyes. It was the color of cinnamon, with spots all over its coat. The damn thing looked like a small leopard. It licked its paws, but its eyes never left my face.

"That is *not* my cat," I said firmly. "Can you go and get it or something?" I cleared my throat. "Sorry. I know that's not your job. But I don't like cats."

Ben tilted his head and studied the animal. It gave an enormous yawn in response. Ben shrugged and disappeared inside. I heard him say, "Okay, party's over, gatito. Let's get a move on." Then he clapped his hands.

The cat glanced over its shoulder at Ben, then back at me again. Could cats roll their eyes? I swore it did.

Ben stealthily approached the cat, who seemed to be intentionally ignoring him, then picked it up by its mid-section.

The cat wasn't having it. It exploded out of Ben's grasp, managed to get in a few mid-air swipes, then bounced out of view.

When Ben appeared in the doorway, scratch marks on the side of his face and neck were bleeding. Not a lot, but enough that I dug out the first aid kit from a box in the kitchen.

"Where did it go?" I handed Ben an antiseptic wipe.

He pressed the square against his cheek and winced. "Living room, I think."

Which is exactly where it was, lounging on the couch, licking a paw. The cat paused long enough to give me an aggrieved sort of look. I darted past him, into the sunroom, and threw open the door to the backyard.

With a clap, I said, "Shoo!"

It blinked. I stomped my foot, then again. Nothing. It didn't budge. I inched closer to it. The cat wasn't wearing a collar, but it was well-fed and groomed, so it had to belong to someone.

"Does the HOA have a way to report lost pets?" I asked, joining Ben in the kitchen and taking a closer look at his wounds. The cat had gotten him good.

He shrugged. "Not that I know of. I really should get back to work."

The front door closed behind him. I wasn't sure what to do about a cat that refused to leave. It's not like I could use an entity smoke bomb to knock it out and take it to The Dump.

There was nothing else to do but put away the groceries. Maybe something would come to me. In the meantime, the cat had fallen asleep on the couch, not a care in the world.

It slept on while I unpacked the dishes and the pots and pans and then through all my cursing while I hooked up my television and laptop. At four thirty, I cut up vegetables for a salad and realized I had forgotten to buy salsa to make the shredded beef. I also forgot wine. A pinot noir would be nice. So, I grabbed my keys and drove back to Palo Verde Market.

While heading for the salsa aisle, I passed the pet food.

Should I? It has to eat too, right? If I fed it, I would never get rid of it. But if I didn't, it would probably start howling or something. I decided to get some cat food.

Because I knew nothing about cats, I spent way too long trying to choose between dry food and wet food. The wet sounded more delicious and looked tastier, if the packaging was to be believed. I bought both, just in case, and some small stainless steel bowls.

Back home, my little guest watched me from the kitchen doorway while I poured a glass of wine and popped the lid on a can of Salmon Delite. He began yowling as he hurried over and brushed against my legs. I shoveled the food into the bowl, and he slowly began to eat. To my great surprise, he looked up at me, lifted a paw, and placed it on my foot.

"Weirdo."

Most of the next day was spent unpacking and putting things away, but by three o'clock, I was ready for a break. I thought I would go check out my new office, so I called Charlie and asked if he could meet me with the keys.

Charlie was his usual talkative self, but he seemed worried about the intruder incident. So far, Katherine Morris hadn't blabbed about it on social media, but that didn't mean she wouldn't, and there wasn't a damn thing we could do about it.

Charlie had a theory about that, and it wasn't a bad one. "If they really want to sell their place and move, they'd be idiots to talk about it publicly. If potential buyers think that house is an entity entry point, they'll never unload it."

"We still don't know that Naked Hairy Man was an entity," I reminded him.

Charlie shrugged. "Well, I'm not sure it matters. We didn't catch anyone, and the description makes him sound like a troll. And no offense or anything, but Occult Affairs has been wrong before."

True. Not that many times, but it had happened. Especially in the beginning, when entities first began to emerge and the heat map technology was new. Once, a seven-foot creature with pale skin and long flowing hair had gone on a rampage in a theater. The heat map didn't pick it up, so the chief had gone on the record, denying it was an entity.

"An illegal immigrant from Eastern Europe," he had said in front of the cameras.

Wrong. Turned out, it was a type of giant known to frequent eastern Russia. At least, that's what he had told my mother when we brought her in to communicate with the entity.

After that, things went rapidly downhill. Evidently, the giant had a thing for the ladies, and the attraction was mutual. We put him in isolation, but that didn't really work. A few months later, we had the first entity-human offspring. It was still being studied at a secret location.

My office was above the Chavez Ravine Association gift shop—which sold branded polo shirts, sweatshirts, hats, and key chains.

My door was unmarked, which was just the way I liked it. It had a little vestibule with two chairs, a table, and a second door with a keypad. My office was through there.

It was larger than I expected, with a modern ergonomic chair and a heavy wooden desk that looked like it belonged in a hacienda. A computer was ready to be set up, but that could wait until I started work the next morning.

My mind was already assembling a to-do list:

- Check out the surveillance system and location of the cameras. Why hadn't they picked up Naked Hairy Man?

- Get a list of all residents and whatever information was available on them. I wanted to know who our high-interest individuals were, like billionaires, celebrities, and politicians. And sooner rather than later.

- Inspect all three neighborhoods for likely entity emergence points. This is where my particular expertise would come in. If I found any candidates, we had some options for containment, but it wouldn't be cheap. Or foolproof.

My to-do list was pretty long and didn't include getting spit on or being assaulted by a flying griffin.

After locking up, I checked out the pottery shop. It was still closed, but through the window I could see a nice variety of mugs, baking dishes, and terracotta pots decorated with simple line drawings of birds and animals. Everything looked expensive, but I decided I would come back when it was open and check out a small statue of a woman holding a molcajete.

It reminded me of a photo I had once seen of my great aunt, Lencha Bantacorte.

Chapter 9

While I cleaned up after dinner, the cat sat inside an empty box and stared at me expectantly. I had no idea what it wanted—I did not speak cat—but then realized I hadn't bought a kitty litter box. It didn't have a place to do its business.

Great.

I went into the sunroom, opened the door into the backyard, and called, "Hey, gatito, do you have to go to the bathroom?"

The dusk sky was painted with strokes of crimson and amber. The yard was framed by a few palm trees, their fronds gold in the fading light. I couldn't wait to see whatever Ben Tomas had up his sleeve. If it was half as nice as Katherine Morris's landscaping, I would be thrilled.

It struck me in the fading light that I had just experienced a big life upgrade, and I felt nothing but gratitude.

The cat brushed past me, his tail flicking against my bare legs. He sauntered over to the dilapidated garden border wall and neatly jumped over it. A few moments later, he reappeared and dashed past me into the house, where he took his place in the middle of the couch. I poured myself a second glass of pinot noir, dug out a crime thriller, and read until my eyes began to close.

It was ridiculously early to go to bed, barely even ten o'clock, but why not? I would wake up early, get in a good workout, and be ready and refreshed for my first day in the job.

When I went into the bedroom, I left the cat on the couch, hoping he would stay there.

Of course, he did not.

Since the cat spent most of the afternoon and evening sleeping, he had saved all his energy for night explorations. He jumped on and off the bed, knocked over the lamp on the nightstand, and sent a tube of lotion to the floor. The cat then batted it all around the room.

I righted the lamp and flicked it on.

He gave the lotion tube another swat, sending it skittering under the bed.

"Will you please stop?" I shouted.

The cat froze and seemed to consider my request, obviously rejecting it.

A few swats later and both he and the lotion tube were in the hallway. And on it went. Eventually, despite the racket, I drifted off to sleep.

A strange noise woke me up. An insistent *bang, bang, bang* coming from the sunroom.

Had I forgotten to close the door? For sure, I did not set the alarm system before going to bed. In fact, I had forgotten I had one.

Bang, bang, bang.

What was making the noise? The odds were in favor of cat rather than entity, so I wasn't too scared. I crept down the hall toward the back of the house and hit the light switch.

The cat was on its hind legs, batting the rattan room divider between the living room and the sunroom.

"Excuse me!" I shouted.

The cat remained standing. I had no idea cats did that, and it was weird. *Really* weird. It pummeled the divider a few more times, making the whole thing rattle, then stopped and stared at me, pleased it had my full attention.

"Would you care to explain?" I asked, hands on my hips.

His mouth opened, and for a moment, I thought he was going to talk, but instead, he howled. The unearthly noise made the hair on the back of my neck rise and sent prickles up my arms.

I stomped my foot. "Stop that this second."

Over the racket, my cell phone rang. *Now what?*

I dashed toward my bedroom. The time on my phone read 3:10. My mother always said 3:00 a.m. was the devil's hour, and I dearly hoped there wasn't anything to it.

The caller was Cora Bernal.

Heart racing, I punched the answer button. "Are you okay?"

"I am so sorry to bother you like this, Maddy. I'm fine, but one of the guards called me, asking what to do…" Her voice drifted off.

"Did something happen?" Had Naked Hairy Man returned?

Cora hesitated. "Well, it's a little unusual. One of our residents reported she'd seen a ghost—or something like one—outside her place. The guard said he thinks she's been drinking. He did a drive-by but didn't see anything, so he called me. And I called you."

Ghosts had been among the first entities to emerge after the earthquakes forever disrupted Los Angeles. We called them "ghosts" because it seemed like the best term for them, but they weren't the woo-woo type. Most looked like people, just in odd clothing and with weird, blank expressions. In past years, their numbers had tapered off, but they still appeared from time to time, mostly in the Hollywood Hills and near the city's old cemeteries.

My contract had kicked in at midnight, so I was officially the new head of security for Chavez Ravine. If we'd had our first appearance of a spirit, I needed to check it out for myself.

"I'll go," I said. "Please send me the woman's name and address."

"Her name is Becca Tey. She's in La Loma, not far from you." Cora texted me her address. "And thank you, Maddy. Thank you so much. Please let me know what you find."

The name sounded familiar, but I couldn't figure out why.

I quickly pulled some clothes on. The cat jumped onto the foot of the bed, flopped onto its side, and began licking its paw.

"You better be back on the couch when I get back, mister."

Cora was right. The woman who had seen the ghost lived a mere four blocks and four million dollars away. The homes on her street were nearly three times as big as mine. Her massive Craftsman-style house was situated next to a gully, and lights blazed from every window.

I knocked on the front door. A woman opened it almost immediately.

I hardly knew where to look because there was a lot going on. Her head was swathed in bandages, and what little skin was visible beneath her eyes and mouth was purple with bruises. Then there were her boobs, which were impossibly large and firm for her small frame. She had long, silky black hair.

Becca Tey wore an elegant blue and white kimono. She looked me up and down. "You're the new head of security?"

"First day on the job," I said with a smile. "I'm Maddy Madrigal. Would you like to tell me what happened?"

"Well, it's nice to get such prompt, personal service." Becca pulled me inside. She was slurring her words, but I understood her well enough. "My husband is on a golf trip, and we're empty nesters, so I'm all alone." She gestured at the bandages. "I just had my face done, and it hurts like a motherfucker—" Becca interrupted herself. "Where are my manners? Can I get you some coffee? Tea?"

I shook my head. If I had either, I would never get back to sleep. "Just some water, thanks."

She wobbled toward the kitchen. It was a mess: bowls piled in the sink, empty carryout containers and plastic bags on the counters. And there, in full view on the modern glass dining table, was the reason for the slurring. A half-empty fifth of vodka and a collection of pill bottles.

Becca caught me glancing at them. "Don't judge me," she warned, shoving a glass beneath a spigot in the fridge door. "I've had a rough go. The doctor said it would be a breeze, but it's been hell."

I sipped my water. "So, what did you see, exactly?"

Becca sighed. "I'm sleeping downstairs in the guest suite so I don't have to go up and down the stairs. So, I went to the bathroom that overlooks the gully, and there was something white and glowing below the window. At first, I thought I was imagining things, but I wasn't. I'm sure of it. There were three of them, and they were really weird. Tall and skinny, with small heads and long arms. There were just...walking."

"You said they were in the gully. Where did they go?"

"The gully runs all the way to Palo Verde. They walked that direction."

"I see. Were they wearing clothes?"

Becca sank into a chair and gave me a funny look. "I don't know. I didn't get the impression they were naked or anything. Is that important?"

She touched the side of her head. Her hand was shaking slightly. Despite her calm demeanor, the woman was clearly frightened by whatever she had seen.

"I'm just trying to get a full picture." Some ghost entities arrived with outfits suggesting the period during which they had lived, but honestly, knowing that didn't help us get rid of them. It was primarily used to describe them on the logs: the Wild West cowboy, the Victorian-era lady in the glowing green dress, the Civil War-era nurse with a cap.

"It looked like they were maybe wearing long-ish coats?" Becca said uncertainly. "But they were ghosts. For sure, they were." She groaned. "My husband is going to shit when I tell him. We just refinanced, and if we have an entity outbreak and Chavez Ravine goes downhill, we're totally screwed. Fuckity fucky fuck."

Despite the pills and booze, Becca Tey understood the scenario quite clearly.

"Do you work, Becca?" It wasn't any of my business, but I was curious.

She gave a little snort. "I'm an actor trying to stay in the game. Why else would I do this to my face?"

That's why I had recognized her name.

Becca tipped her head back. The movement must have hurt because she gave a little moan.

"Is that why they hired you? To help us deal with an outbreak? If so, the board really should have brought this up during the last meeting. I make sure to attend every one, and no one said a damn thing about entities in Chavez Ravine. I mean, they're obligated to notify us, aren't they?"

It had always been a part of my job to reassure a nervous public, but it suddenly dawned on me my duties had shifted. No longer was I speaking for the city of LA—I represented the

HOA board. Now I needed to calm jittery residents and assure them the board had their best interests at heart. Whether that was true or not was another question.

"The board's top priority is protecting our property values, and part of that is making sure we have a safe community," I said. "That's why I'm here now to take your statement."

I sat down opposite her at the table, took out my tablet, and proceeded to ask her the standard list of questions for entity encounters. It was a perfectly good list I had brought with me from the LAPD. No use reinventing the wheel.

When we were done, I stood. "I'll be launching an investigation. Entities rarely enter buildings—for some reason—but just to be sure, please keep your doors locked."

Becca stared at me. "You've got to be kidding me. They're ghosts! Can't they do whatever they want?"

I shoved my tablet back into my tote bag. "Generally, yes. But they seem to have trouble with locks." No one had ever said ghosts were smart.

After we said goodbye, I walked to the back of the house and peered into the gully. No glowing ghosts. I scanned the brush with my flashlight. An animal with glowing eyes darted among the bushes. A coyote, probably.

I sat in the Jeep, called Cora, and gave her the update.

"What do you think they were?" she finally asked. Cora sounded nervous. It was interesting she hadn't concluded the ghosts were entities, but I was suddenly too tired to explore that further.

There was nothing else to do but go home and try to catch a few hours of sleep before I was due in at the office at 8:30. I had just turned onto my block when something caught my eye near the new housing development.

Something white. And glowing in the moonlight.

Even from a distance, it was tall and skinny, its head too small for its ghostly frame. There was only one of them, there in the middle of the street. I hit the gas and roared up the hill. By the time I reached the top, it was gone.

A chain link fence surrounded the construction site. It was too high for me to scale easily, so I made a quick call and asked the guard on duty if he had a way inside. He said he had a code, then agreed to meet me.

The new development was bigger than I expected, and since the property was at the top of a hill, the whole place was easy to view from just inside the fence. The brush had been cleared, and no walls had gone up yet, so there was nowhere to hide, if our glowing white friend was so inclined. Though, in my experience, ghost entities didn't bother with that.

I walked deeper into the property, scanning the shadows for movement, but found nothing. The only sound was the distant hum of Los Angeles traffic far below. My mystery phantom was gone.

Chapter 10

I s it just me, or does the best sleep happen right before the alarm goes off?

When my phone blasted on the nightstand, I felt like I had been drugged. After I stopped the horrible noise, I propped myself up on one elbow and glanced around the room, wondering where the cat had gotten to.

Not far, as it turned out. He was sprawled near my feet. The cat raised his head and blinked his green eyes at me.

I sighed. "You again."

That was his cue to leap off the bed and saunter toward the kitchen, where he began meowing. And I knew what that meant. I blindly grabbed a can of cat food, popped off the lid, and immediately regretted my choice. The smell of tuna filled the air. Before I had even had my coffee, mind you. What little appetite I had disappeared.

The cat meowed louder and flicked its tail against my bare calves. Apparently, I wasn't moving fast enough.

"Give me a break." I scooped the foul mixture into the bowl and rinsed out the can with hot water and dish soap.

Warm morning light poured into the kitchen. I looked out at the front yard and, for the first time, wondered who my neighbors were. When I had a free moment, I would have to introduce myself. Maybe they knew the cat's owners.

I thought about the work ahead. There was to be no leisurely honeymoon for me. I would start my first day on the job with trying to figure out where the entities were coming from. Cora had probably notified the other board members about the call from Becca Tey, and they would be clamoring for answers. And results.

The pressure was on.

My three-month probationary period loomed before me. Entities were unpredictable. Capturing them and tracking down their entry points involved much more art than science. My job was not only to solve Chavez Ravine's entity problem—if that's actually what it was—but also to set the board's expectations appropriately. If they expected me to come into town like Annie Oakley, blasting away at all the pesky varmints, they were mistaken. I needed them to understand it took time to track down entity problems, and results weren't always perfect.

If they didn't get that, the board could let me go after three months and maybe even claw back my house. The idea made my skin go clammy. I had been in my new place all of one day, and already, I couldn't imagine living anywhere else.

A strange noise from the windowsill caught my attention. It sounded like "*ek, ek, ek.*"

The cat was standing up in the space between the kitchen faucet and the window, chattering away. And then I understood why.

A hummingbird hovered midair right outside the window. It seemed to be looking past the cat and straight at me. It was a big one, larger than any hummingbird I had ever seen. It had the usual, vibrant iridescent feathers, and its head and body were mostly red, green, and white. But as a whole, it was the size of a baseball.

The hummingbird and I were locked in a stare-off contest. Certainly, this wasn't normal avian behavior. Maybe it wasn't a hummingbird at all. Perhaps it was some sort of new entity. I jumped to my feet and raced outside.

The damn thing waited until I was practically on top of it before it zoomed away. *Cheeky.*

A truck rumbled up the street. Ben Tomas arrived with a small crew to work on the backyard. My hair was a mess, but at least I was decent. I waved hello, then went inside to start a fresh pot of coffee for the gardeners.

Correction. Master Landscapers.

The cat greeted me in the entryway, and a thought hit me. I had left the front door open, and he hadn't followed me outside to chase the bird. *Weird.*

Three men piled out of the truck and immediately began tilling the brown grass. A fourth man arrived in another truck and scaled a palm tree, sawing off dead fronds and dropping them to the ground.

I showered and got ready for work. There was no time for a workout, but I could always squeeze one in before dinner.

Before I left, I let the cat outside. Unfazed by the activity in the yard, he did his business in the same spot as the day before, then dashed back into the house and gulped down water as if he were dying of thirst. With a sigh, I mopped up a puddle of water next to his bowl. I had spent an extraordinary amount of time with an animal that was not my own.

It was too early to go knocking on doors and asking my neighbors if they were missing a cat. I told the crew I was leaving the back door open so they could use the bathroom, then headed to work. If the cat got out, so be it. Easy come, easy go.

It took less than ten minutes to get to my office. I had never had a shorter or more pleasant commute in my life. Sure, there had been other cars on the road, but there was no real traffic. With a fresh, invigorating breeze coming through the open windows of my Jeep, I drove through rolling hills and past brick pathways weaving through the trees.

The gritty streets of Los Angeles seemed a world away. And instead of the dread I used to feel when I got closer to the squad room, I found myself looking forward to the day. I had my work cut out for me, but it wasn't anything I couldn't handle.

Hopefully.

My first official act when I plopped down in my chair was to set up an account with the independent forensics lab I had used with the LAPD. They handled the overflow from Occult Affairs when the in-house lab got too busy, and they were good.

True to form, they came out that morning and gathered what samples they could find from Naked Hairy Man and Ghost Dude. They took soil and a few hairs, and by afternoon, they had a preliminary analysis.

I loved those guys.

The report was a blur of numbers and jargon, so I flipped to the end, and my jaw dropped.

There was a ninety-six percent chance Naked Hairy Man wasn't an entity, or if he was, it was one we had never seen before. But it wasn't human either. Or, at least, not Homo sapiens. The report noted the possibility it might be Neanderthal and said the company had sent the results to a paleontologist.

Holy crap.

If it was a Neanderthal, it would be the first time anyone had seen an extinct human species emerge. I hoped like hell that wasn't the case—there would be no keeping it out of the news. Chavez Ravine would make headlines for all the wrong reasons, and the board would foul their collective pants.

I poured my second cup from the gleaming coffee maker sitting on a credenza behind my desk. Did I mention how much

I loved my office? It even had a small refrigerator and a giant TV. Sure beat my gray metal desk with sticky drawers in the middle of the noisy squad room.

While I sipped my coffee, I reviewed the security cam footage from La Loma, hoping to see which direction the ghosts had come from. Sometimes cameras can pick them up. Most often, they don't. I was hoping to get lucky.

One thing was for sure: watching the footage on the small screen of my computer monitor wasn't going to work, so I filled out a form asking for the security camera system to be hooked up to my big TV, just like we'd had at the command center in Occult Affairs. Which reminded me…

I called Jo.

"Good morning, traitor," she said. "Miss us yet?"

"Nope, but I have a favor to ask."

"Hold on." Jo put her hand over the receiver. Then, muffled, "Quit arguing and get to the scene, will you?" And back to me, "Sorry, Mads, you know how things are here. So, I gotta ask. Is this going to be a regular thing? You asking for favors?"

I thought about that for a moment. It was a totally legitimate question. Civilian security operations did not have heat maps. How the hell was I supposed to do my job without access to that most basic of technologies? Crap.

Then I had an idea.

"You know how we always wondered what was up with Chavez Ravine? Why they never seemed to have trouble with entities? Well, between you and me, that might be changing. If it does and this suddenly becomes a hot spot, it's going to mean more work for your department. Sure, I'll be able handle some of it, but you guys are going to be up here all the time, dealing with angry rich people. Now, if I had access to the heat map, I could be a lot more effective. Hell, I may even be able to take care of the whole place on my own."

I let that sink in before continuing.

"See what I mean? If you help me, I can help you."

Jo sniffed. "That remains to be seen."

"I'm serious, Jo. With my background, I'll be able to cut down on the number of responses up here. Assuming we have an outbreak, of course." That sounded a bit optimistic, even to me, but I was sure of one thing: that's exactly what the entire membership of The Chavez Ravine Homeowners Association would want. Deal with the entities as discreetly as possible and avoid the sirens, lights, and publicity that came with the Occult Affairs first responders.

"All right, what do you want to know?" Jo finally asked. Grudgingly.

I gave her Becca Tey's address. "Can you check the heat map and see if you have anything within a mile of there between midnight and five a.m.?

"If anything popped up in Chavez Ravine, I'd know about it from the overnight shift."

"Yeah, I don't trust them."

The people on overnights were mostly part-timers working without benefits—the department's devious method of keeping down costs. Turnover on the night shift was even higher than the day shift, and that was saying something. Plus, they were surly and resentful. And they missed entity appearances. All. The. Time.

"Point taken," Jo said.

I imagined her putting on her red glasses and swiping through the heat map records. There wasn't anyone who could read them better.

A long silence followed.

"Not a thing," she finally said. "Is there anything I should know?"

I filled her in about the possible Neanderthal, and she gave a long, low whistle. Then I told her about the ghosts in the gully and the one I had seen on my street.

"That doesn't sound like typical ghost behavior, though," she mused. "When they first appear, they're usually in your face, like they want to be found."

"True." I drummed my fingers on my desk. None of it made sense. Something was off.

After lunch—a chef's salad from the deli at the far end of the plaza—I reviewed the map of surveillance cameras and sensors installed around Chavez Ravine. It looked like an effective system.

The cameras were strategically located around the periphery of the three neighborhoods, with the highest concentration in Bishop, closest to the problematic streets of Los Angeles. They were also near park entrances, along stretches of isolated fencing, and at major intersections. The guard stations had both cameras and license plate readers. The area bordering Elysian Park appeared to be the weakest link in the system, with not nearly enough cameras to adequately cover the long stretch.

No matter. It was easy enough to fix. Before I chatted with the board about my findings, a walk-through was in order. But with so many other things to do, I would leave that until tomorrow. It would probably take the entire day.

Besides, my head was pounding. Which was odd since I wasn't prone to headaches. It couldn't be a hangover. I had felt fine earlier in the morning. But since I got to the office, I had been increasingly hot and sweaty, and my stomach felt queasy.

Maybe I was coming down with something. Not great timing, being my first day on the job and with a ton of work to do. I started thinking about how Eileen Simpson would spin it: evidence the board should have hired Stu Wells.

My chair wasn't helping either. Something must have been wrong with the height adjustment because I kept slowly dropping and had to raise it back every few minutes. Finally, I knelt next to the chair and began fiddling with the lever, which appeared to be stuck. I felt around the base of the lever, and my fingers brushed something under the seat. Something crinkly.

I peered under the chair. A brown paper bag had been taped to the underside, secured with black duct tape. An electric prickle ran up my spine.

The chair was brand new. Why would someone tape a bag to the bottom of it? And what was in it? Extra screws or something? There was only one way to find out. I ripped off the tape.

The small paper sack was too heavy for just a few screws. It seemed to contain something else, like sand.

I dumped the contents onto my desk. It appeared to be a mixture of coarse salt, which glittered under my desk lamp. A pungent, smoky, and familiar aroma filled the air. I leaned down and sniffed.

Cumin.

What the hell?

I pressed a finger into the stuff and felt a tiny stab of pain. Something was sticking to the fleshy pad of my index finger.

A shard of glass.

I had no idea what it meant, but somebody had put that bag under my chair. My headache intensified and moved from my temples to the backs of my eyes.

The bag was all wrong.

Then it hit me.

I carefully scraped the mysterious salt back into the bag. After washing my hands in the bathroom, I held the sack in front of me, like it was a bomb about to explode, and took it outside in search of a dumpster. I spotted one at the far end of the parking lot, but that felt too close. Instinct told me anywhere in Palo Verde would be, so I drove to the guard gate in Bishop and asked Ron Mendez to dispose of it at least a mile away.

"You're kidding?" He stared down at the bag suspiciously. "What's in it?"

"A hex," I replied. It just sort of popped out.

Chavez Ravine was more than it seemed.

I could feel the heaviness of it in my bones.

Chapter 11

D on't ask me why because I can't explain it, but on the way home from work, I stopped by a pet store in Bishop. I spent way too much time trying to choose between kitty litter trays and ended up buying one with high sides made of BPA-free plastic. The cat wouldn't be around long enough to splurge on one of those ridiculous robotic self-cleaning models.

He didn't greet me at the door. I followed the sound of frantic scratching to my bedroom, where I found the cat under the bed, pawing at the underside of the frame.

"*Now* what are you doing, weirdo?" I called, changing into shorts and a light sweatshirt.

Underneath the bed, something dropped to the floor. The cat howled, and paper ripped.

My bedroom suddenly reeked of cumin.

I froze. My stomach dropped.

No. It couldn't be. I crouched and looked under the bed.

It was another paper bag, but this time, the salt, glass, and whatever other stuff was in there had spilled onto the floor. I straightened, breathless.

How long had the bag been there? And who had done it?

The cat came skidding out from under the bed, jumped high into the air as if spring-loaded, then bounced from the top of the bed to the dresser, where he stood on his hind legs and hissed. His fur puffed out, making him look twice his size.

"I get the message," I said.

The cat didn't seem to believe me. He launched himself off the dresser, landed at my feet, and proceeded to whip his tail against my legs.

"Okay, okay, okay." I went into the kitchen, found my broom and dustpan, and returned to the bedroom to clean up the mess while the cat circled the room.

"Am I doing okay, Mr. Supervisor?" I poked the broom under the bed to sweep out the salt and glass.

By then, my shock had given way to rage. Leaving a hex in my office wasn't enough. Whoever had done it had wanted to make sure to get me where I worked *and* lived. When had they been in there?

I had left the house open for Ben Tomas and his crew, so any of them could have done it. Then there was Charlie Perez, the keeper of the keys to the house, so I couldn't rule him out. And who knew who else had had access to the keys?

I hadn't changed the locks yet, but I hadn't been in a rush either. It wasn't like crime was a serious concern in Chavez Ravine.

I dumped the hex materials into a garbage bag, tied it off, and marched it out to my Jeep. Maybe my mother knew about hexes. I could call her and ask, but it all sounded too exhausting.

When I drove back to the Bishop guardhouse and repeated my request from the day before, Ron Mendez was surprised, but he agreed to get rid of the second bag too.

"Someone's got it in for you."

I stared at Ron, not really seeing him. He was right, but who? And why? I was so new to Chavez Ravine, I hadn't had time to make enemies. Which meant someone really, really wanted me out of my brand-new job.

When I got home, the cumin hit my nostrils the moment I opened my front door. Down the hall, the cat sneezed repeatedly.

I found him in the second bedroom, prowling around unopened boxes. The spots on his red coat seemed more distinct, like a small leopard stalking prey. The cat didn't even bother to glance my way. I got the clear impression he was looking for more paper bag bombs.

"I'll leave you to it, then."

In the kitchen, I filled a pail with warm water, squirted in some soap, and mopped the hardwood floor in my bedroom. That helped, but it didn't totally get rid of the cumin smell. I threw open the windows and allowed the fresh breeze to rush in. As an extra precaution, I stripped off the bedding and tossed it all into the washer, then mopped the hallway and continued through the rest of the house. Just in case.

Back in the kitchen, I ran into the cat. He had somehow figured out how to open the cabinets, and he was pawing through them. I'd have some good stories for his owner when I found out who that was. The cat had a future in detection services.

Which reminded me. It was time to introduce myself to the neighbors.

I changed into jeans and a T-shirt and started with the house on my left. It looked like a cute cottage in front but had a less charming addition in the back. How had the owner managed to avoid the HOA's architecture rules, which were very clear about "upholding the appearance and ambience of our distinctive community?"

I knocked on the door and was greeted by a guy sporting shoulder-length black hair with a pronounced silver streak.

Good-looking. Dressed in a white button-down shirt, which contrasted nicely with his olive skin.

"Oh, hi!" he said. "Are you our new neighbor? Okay. I'm being ridiculous. I know you are because we've been spying on you." He laughed.

Normally, hearing that would set me on edge, but he was so friendly and jovial, I couldn't help but laugh too.

From another room, a voice said, "That didn't sound creepy at all."

The guy at the door made a *whoops* face. "That's my husband, Toby. I'm Leo. And look at me, keeping you standing outside like this. We hit the G&Ts a little early, so you have perfect timing. Come in and join us!"

Any other time, I would have. But if I started drinking, I would miss another workout.

"Oh, thank you, but I have so much unpacking to do. I'm Maddy Madrigal. I just wanted to ask if, by any chance, you're missing a cat? A large one. Reddish. With spots?"

"Not ours," Leo said.

Toby appeared in the entryway. Medium height, bald, scruffy beard. He wore a black-and-white chef's apron and looked quite dapper in it. "Oh! You're the new head of security for the HOA!"

Leo turned to Toby, eyebrows raised. "How do you know?"

Toby sniffed. "Because I read the HOA emails, unlike other people in this house."

"I'm a lawyer. All I do is read emails. And those people on the board send too many. I can't keep track of them." Leo slung his arm around Toby. "But I'm glad you're on top of it. So, wow. We lucked out. The head of security lives right next door! We can call you any time, right, if we have a problem?" He winked, just to show he wasn't serious.

I asked—because I really wanted to know. "Have you? Ever had any problems here?"

Toby shook his head. "This is Chavez Ravine, so no. Because if we had, Leo would blast off emails to the HOA and demand something be done. The worst thing is what's happening up the block with the new housing development. We're not too excited about it, but there's nothing much we can do because it was in the works when we bought our place. We *are* a little concerned about the rumors the developer wants to expand and buy us out. We're not legacy, and neither are most of the people on the block, so if the HOA decides it wants us out, it can *eminent domain* our asses. It was in our disclosures and—"

Leo interrupted. "And I read them, of course, but we wanted in so bad, and this was one of the few places we could afford on just one salary. Toby's opening a new restaurant, and there's more money going out than coming in, so we make do on my income. That said, if it happens, I'll fight it.

"The membership has to vote on any project that requires evictions—for obvious reasons—but most owners don't really care. Something like this wouldn't affect them, just people like us who live on this block. And it doesn't help that our properties are a little down-market for Chavez Ravine, so I think most people would be happy to see tidy new homes going in."

Wow, Leo was a talker. But the conversation had taken a very interesting turn. Good to know my neighbor was a lawyer with the same interests as mine.

"I'm legacy, so I'm hoping that makes a difference."

Leo's eyes widened. "Oh, thank god. Then you may save us, Maddy."

It was Toby's turn to laugh. "Wait until the developer hears *that*. They have the big bucks, but around here, legacy trumps money. You sure you can't come in for a quick drink?"

I shook my head. "I'm tending to a fifteen-pound cat, and I need to figure out who he belongs to. But thank you. Another time."

We said our goodbyes, and I accepted their invitation for drinks over the weekend.

I continued knocking on doors. Everyone seemed very nice. There was a young couple with two small kids and an adorable pug, a family with young teenagers who crowded around their parents, asking if they could have the cat, and an assortment of couples ranging in age from their early forties to middle seventies.

Nobody was missing a cat, and they didn't recognize the description either.

But I did learn something interesting from a young woman with short dark hair who lived in the townhouse complex across the street.

"When I got my rescue dog, he jumped the fence and ran off. I freaked out and called the animal shelter, but they said they don't handle Chavez Ravine because it has its own group. Dan Berman on the board runs it. They send out an email blast to all the residents anytime there's a missing pet."

"You're kidding!"

She shook her head. "I'm not. And it works, too, because Cooper had made it all the way to Bishop, and someone there found him. I got him back in like three hours."

When I returned home, I discovered the cat in the back of my clothes closet, face in my sneakers.

I began tapping out an email to Dan, got to the end, then deleted it.

It was arguable the cat had earned his keep. Who knew what would have happened if I had slept in the bed while the salt bag was underneath? And the truth was, I liked the idea of a little extra security myself.

Even if it came with four big paws and strange green eyes.

Chapter 12

We—the cat and I—had a good night's sleep. My phone was silent, and the cat was tired. All the prowling around, inspecting every nook and cranny, must have wiped him out. He actually snored.

Was it normal for cats to sleep with people? Wasn't there such a thing as a cat bed? I doubted he would consider it anyway. And why should he? I had splurged on a plush mattress topper and a light down comforter. The furry guy knew quality.

After I showered, I put on comfortable clothes and hiking boots. I planned to spend my day checking out the more challenging and remote areas of Chavez Ravine. Places where entities were most likely to appear and hide.

While I sipped my coffee, I checked messages.

The paleontologist's report on Hairy had come back. I set my coffee down, took a deep breath, then opened the email. The report concluded the samples did *not* belong to the Neanderthal family.

Well, that was a big relief. My fears about news crews and university research teams invading our idyllic valleys—and everyone's real estate values plummeting—faded away.

One crisis averted. For now, anyway. We—*I*—still hadn't identified Hairy or Ghost Dude and how they had managed to get into the community.

I shot off a quick note to Cora Bernal with the update on Hairy and also let her know I would be out of the office, inspecting the property.

After grabbing the tote with my notebook and hi-rez camera, I went outside to greet the landscaping crew. I explained I needed to leave the house locked because of the cat, which, of course, was a total lie. The cat wouldn't abandon his cushy lifestyle, but I would be an idiot to leave the place unlocked again.

I set up the kitty litter box under an alcove in the sunroom and said goodbye to the cat.

The cat. Guilt nibbled at my intestines like tiny fish.

I had asked my immediate neighbors if they were missing a cat, but I hadn't gone much farther. Besides, if someone's furry companion was absent in Bishop or Palo Verde, wouldn't they have notified Dan Berman?

Notifying Dan Berman was the right thing for me to do.

But the truth was, I didn't want to do the right thing.

I wanted to keep the cat.

What the hell was happening to me?

Armed with a map, I decided to start my walk-through in La Loma, where the ghosts had appeared two nights before. I knocked on Becca Tey's door and she answered, wearing a gray velour tracksuit, her face still swathed in bandages.

I figured, given her condition the other night, I had better reintroduce myself.

"Hi, I'm Maddy Madrigal, the new security chief in Chavez Ravine."

"Yes, I remember you. I slept well after you left."

"Any more…activity…since then?"

"No, everything's been quiet. Though, I'm not sure I'd have noticed. Last night, I took enough sleeping pills to knock out a horse."

I pointed at the gully. "I'm going to take a look down there. Just didn't want you to be alarmed if you saw me wandering around in the yard."

She didn't answer, just stared at me through her bandages. "I heard Stu Wells was up for your job. I wouldn't exactly have minded if he'd showed up at my house in the middle of the night. But I must say, you do seem to be on top of things. I can't imagine Stu tromping through the gully."

Was that a smile? Couldn't tell.

"Just remember, if you see anything, please call the emergency number and tell them to contact me immediately. I live nearby and can get here quickly."

"Really?" The woman seemed genuinely surprised.

"Really." Entities often developed a routine, and it wouldn't have surprised me if Ghost Dude showed up again. Becca was my best shot at catching him.

The side of the gully was steep, and I half slid, half walked down. I reached the bottom where it narrowed, then started walking along the gravel bed, pushing through clumps of scratchy shrubs. Occasionally, I snagged my hair in tree branches. I passed under two small bridges, then climbed up an embankment, finding myself heading up a hill.

The gully continued all the way to Palo Verde, branched off to the left, and angled up to the new housing development. Bulldozing and hammering came from the top. The walk was steep, so I walked backward up the hill for a little extra exercise. By the time I reached the development, my thigh and calf muscles were burning.

The gully became wide and shallow, so I easily walked out to the street. I went past the construction area up the road, which turned into a dirt path zigzagging toward Elysian Park. The streets were empty except for a couple of workers sitting on upside-down buckets, eating burritos, and a stocky guy with a hardhat walking from the path toward the construction fence.

When entities first began to emerge in Los Angeles, they had made their debuts in parks and wilderness areas, but eventually, they got bolder and shifted to more populated places. Lately, Elysian Park had been pretty calm. When I was working for Occult Affairs, we had only had three calls about incidents within all its six hundred acres. Still, it was possible Hairy and Ghost Dude had popped up there, eluded heat map detection, and crossed over into my community.

I walked up the path to the wooden fence separating the park from Chavez Ravine. As I had suspected, it wasn't tall enough for my liking, and there weren't enough cameras. Both problems could be fixed.

If I could get the HOA to loosen the purse strings.

I had the distinct impression certain board members wanted to keep the dues down, but I was confident the prospect of an entity-induced property value bloodbath would turn them around.

While I was up there, I decided I might as well check the cameras. I grabbed a cord from my backpack and plugged one end into the closest device, the other into my handheld monitor.

Nothing.

The camera wasn't working. I fiddled with it for a while. It had power but wasn't recording video. *Odd.* I made a note of the location, then wrapped a piece of blue tape around the base of the pole so the repair person could find it.

My inspection along the breezy ridge turned up three more bum cameras. I was surprised nobody had noticed before. It was almost as if someone didn't want them to do their job.

I returned to the first malfunctioning camera. If it was working properly, the motion sensor would trigger it to start recording. I waved my hands in front of it.

Nada.

How long had they been disabled? They were relatively new. Four malfunctioning cameras didn't sound like a coincidence to me, considering how nervous Cora Bernal was about security. It was hard to imagine they had bought a cheap system.

My watch showed it was nearly ten thirty. Time for a coffee.

I decided to check out the shopping center in La Loma. It was much smaller than the one in Palo Verde but just as nice—built to resemble a Spanish-style courtyard with red decorative tiles, blush-colored stucco, and fountains. There were various boutiques, a hair salon, a few galleries, several nice restaurants with outdoor dining, and a casual café.

Inside the café, the walls were painted red and covered in Day of the Dead artwork. On the sign behind the register, it read: "Muertos Café." Nice. Someone had a dark sense of humor. A café for the dead was a first for me.

I ordered a cafecito. The espresso came in a small, heavy cup. At the bar, I added a splash of cream and a pinch of brown sugar—my reward for passing up the delicious-looking pastries in the glass case.

At the far end of the café, I found a seat next to a window overlooking a pretty courtyard filled with potted plants and hanging flower baskets. I was wondering if Ben Tomas was responsible for the landscaping here too when the sound of someone clearing their throat made me look up.

Stu Wells was staring down at me with the same infuriating, smug grin he had flashed the day we had met at the HOA offices. He was dressed in a black suit and white shirt. If it weren't for the sage-colored tie, he would have looked like a Secret Service agent, with his square jaw and sandy hair. My heart sped up in my chest. I set my coffee cup down. It rattled in its saucer.

"Congratulations," he said.

I cleared my throat. "Uh, yeah. Thank you." What did one say in such circumstances? *Gee, sorry I got the job and you didn't?*

"I have a few minutes. Can I sit down?" He nodded at the empty chair across from me.

"Why not?" I replied, pasting a polite smile on my face.

"I can't think of a single reason." He grinned. His eyes twinkled.

My pulse was racing like I had just seen a ghost. A nervous little laugh bubbled up. I really, really needed to calm down.

"So, yeah. Cora told me that you were interested in the security job too. Just to get it out there. Avoid any awkwardness."

One side of his mouth lifted in amusement. His eyebrows went up too. "Do I look awkward, Maddy?" The way he said my name made my belly go warm.

Whoa. Reel it in. Get a grip.

"Not really, no." I threw my hands in the air. "Come on. Give me a break. You've got to admit, it's just a little weird."

"Is it?" His eyebrows lowered.

"It is if you make it weird," I heard myself say. What the hell was *that* supposed to mean?

He leaned forward, resting his elbows on the table. "I'm not going to make it weird. No reason to. In fact, I only showed up as a courtesy to Eileen. She was my real estate agent and helped me beat out a dozen other offers for my house, so I owed her." Stu shrugged. "But I'm glad you got it. Really." He paused.

"Besides, you're legacy. Even if I wanted the gig, it never, ever would have happened. Legacy is king around here."

Was I imagining the faintest hint of bitterness?

He continued. "And even if you weren't legacy, it would have been tough to top your Occult Affairs experience." Now he sounded…what? Rueful?

I stared at him. "You own the largest private security firm in Los Angeles. I'm pretty sure you check more boxes than I do."

There was that smile again. "Well, that's all water under the bridge. No worries. All good."

I didn't believe him. His smile didn't quite reach his eyes. He rose from his chair. A few other women in the café looked up and gave him the once-over, along with a well-dressed man sitting near the door.

"I need to get into town," Stu said. "But I just wanted to say congratulations, and if you ever need anything, just let me know." His chin lifted, giving him a superior expression. "As I told the board, I have a lot of resources at my disposal."

Then he turned on his heel and strode out of the café.

There might have been water flowing under the bridge, but Stu Wells still needed to remind me he was a big deal security guru and I was just a lowly former cop.

Asshole.

I clenched my fists all the way to the bathroom. When I looked in the mirror, I groaned so loudly, a lady in a stall asked if I was okay. My hair was a tangled mess from my trek up the gully. A dirt smudge ran across my nose and all the way across one cheek. A piece of blue tape hung from the lapel of my jacket.

He could have said something. Instead, he had pretended like I didn't look an absolute wreck.

Double asshole.

Chapter 13

Something moved against my leg. My eyes fluttered open.

It had to be the cat. As a reward for finding the creepy hex bag, I had allowed him to sleep on my bed, with a stern warning not to go prowling around in the middle of the night.

I don't know what made me think I could negotiate with a cat.

The rhythmic movement continued. What was he doing anyway?

"Can you please stop?"

He didn't. In fact, he doubled down.

He managed to keep bumping against my leg while making a disgusting, wet licking sound.

"What the hell are you doing down there?" I reached over to flick on the lamp.

The green numbers of the clock read 2:55 a.m. The cat glanced up and blinked. He was scrunched over, propped up against my leg, a paw hovering near his mouth.

"Well?" I demanded.

The cat resumed licking and nibbling at his nails. When I was a kid, I used to bite my nails too, mostly from the stress of hearing my father abuse my mother. That was before we escaped and my mother became "self-actualized." That was her term for promoting her psychic abilities, but I called it "finding a new revenue stream."

Was the cat grooming itself so industriously because it was anxious? Or was it just part of its routine? Did I need to get his nails trimmed ? How did people transport cats anyway?

I nudged him, none too gently. "Cut. It. Out."

After a few moments, he did but then jumped to his feet, his tail puffing out.

Oh please. Not another hex in my house.

He tipped his head back and howled. My pulse skipped into overdrive.

I glanced nervously at the clock one more time. The Devil's Hour.

My phone rang. I snatched it off the table. It was Becca Tey.

"There's a fucking naked man trying to get into my house!" she cried.

I leaped out of bed in search of my shoes. "Are you okay? Where is he?"

This time, Becca sounded perfectly sober.

"I'm fine. I heard someone on the front porch, so I peeked through a window to see who it was, and there was this really freaky hairy guy pacing back and forth on the porch. I think he must have seen me because he started pawing at the door, and I could hear him grunting."

"Where are you now, Becca?"

"Locked in my bathroom. The one in my bedroom. And I locked the bedroom door too."

"Stay there, Becca. I'll call the guard station for backup. Don't move."

"You don't have to ask me twice. You should see the guy's dick. It's disgusting."

That was one thing I definitely *didn't* need to see.

I set the phone on the dresser, switched on the speaker, and called the emergency number while I threw on some clothes.

The guard on duty sounded shocked. "You're kidding?"

"Wish I was." I grabbed a jacket. "I want everyone who's available."

"Is it an entity?" The guard sounded nervous.

"Maybe. Now hang up and get a move on."

His guard cat duty done, the cat stretched out on the bed, yawning.

"You're killing me."

I ran to my Jeep and sped to Becca's house. The streets were quiet, but all the lights were on at the Tey residence. There was no sign of Hairy on the porch, but that didn't mean he wasn't around. He could have gone to the back, looking for a way in.

I didn't carry a gun since that would have required a training course and paperwork to get a permit. My days as an Occult Affairs officer were over, and I was now just an ordinary citizen who needed to follow the same rules as everyone else. But that didn't mean I was completely defenseless.

I grabbed a flashlight and a baton made of polycarbonate and aluminum—it was light and nearly unbreakable. When Occult Affairs collected my uniform, badge, and other job-related gear, they hadn't asked for it back, and I hadn't offered either. Oops.

The smart thing to do was wait for the security guards, but the adrenaline was rushing through my veins, and I wanted to see this thing for myself. I ran toward the side of the house next to the gully, figuring it would provide him the most cover.

Nothing.

I went around the other side.

Nothing there either.

I peered over the top of the fence surrounding the patio and swung my flashlight beam around.

And there he was, pacing like a bull along the length of the sliding glass doors.

"Hairy" hadn't come close to describing him. Not exactly werewolf territory, but definitely hirsute—as in, shaggy hair on his head and bushy face, wooly chest and back. He was short, bow-legged, and powerfully built. With all that going on, it was still impossible to ignore that other bit of anatomy screaming for attention. The damn thing practically hung to his knobby knees. Even from a distance, I could smell him too. A sharp odor—musky, animalistic.

My stomach churned.

The beam of my light caught his attention. He lifted his head and turned toward me, his lips curling. Hairy sniffed. Then he touched himself.

"Oh, hell no." I was running toward my Jeep, listening to him scaling the fence.

His feet landed hard and pounded against the ground as he came after me.

My hands were shaking so badly, I could hardly open the door to the Jeep. I climbed in, slammed the door, and punched the lock. Seconds later, his face appeared in the window, and I shrieked. Meaty fingers pawed at the glass. He pressed his face against it, and a long tongue licked the window.

Where were those guards?

Hairy disappeared from view. *Oh Jesus.* I reached across the seats and slammed the lock down on the passenger side. When I remembered the rear hatch, my heart nearly exploded in my chest.

He was back there, hands on the glass.

I clambered over the seat, shoving stuff aside, and dove for the small lever on the inside of the door. It clicked into place. The freak grabbed the handle. The hatch failed to open, and he wailed in frustration.

From over my shoulder came a flood of lights. When I turned back to the creature, we locked eyes. The hunger in his filled me with terror. Hairy might look ridiculous, even comedic, but the threat he posed felt real.

He looked past me at the approaching guards, snarled, and then ran up the street.

The guards didn't need any instructions. Two of them shot past me, running at full speed into the darkness. The other returned to his patrol car and roared up the road.

I got out, legs trembling, and began walking toward Becca Tey's house. When I reached the porch, my phone rang. It was a guard, breathless. They had lost Hairy at the top of the hill. I clutched the baton a little tighter.

"You've got to find him," I said. "I don't know what he is, but it's like he's in heat or something."

"What the fuck?"

"That's exactly what we don't want." There was no time to explain. Sexualized entities were exceedingly rare but nothing to mess around with. "Be careful," I said before we hung up.

Like that ever helped anyone.

I called Becca and told her to meet me at the front door but not to open it until I gave the all-clear. She tapped on the glass panel on the side and gave me a little wave to show she was there. I stood on the porch, peering into the darkness and gripping the baton with both hands, ready to swing. My jaw ached because of how tense I was.

Nothing.

I inched backward toward the door—feet shoulder-width apart, knees slightly bent, the tip of the baton raised over my shoulder.

"Open the door very slowly, Becca," I called. "If you see anything moving out here, shut it fast."

Seconds later, I was standing inside the entryway, my muscles weak with relief.

"You look like you could use a drink," Becca said dryly, arms crossed in front of her kimono.

I refused but followed her to the kitchen, where I gulped down a glass of water, trying to steady my nerves. Becca appeared to be perfectly sober. The kitchen had been cleaned since I last saw it. Not a bottle of booze out anywhere. The actress looked better too. Her eyes brighter, more alert, peering through the bandages.

"What the hell is going on here?" she asked. "First ghosts, now this!"

Whatever *this* was.

I shouldn't have been there, in that warm, safe kitchen. My old position would have had me outside, looking for Hairy. But my job description had changed. I was in charge of security. Now, I didn't have to do it all myself. I had people to delegate to, and the most important thing for me to do right now was provide reassurance to a worried, frightened resident.

Wait, that wasn't the only important thing.

An electric charge coursed through my body. A dangerous creature was on the loose in Chavez Ravine, and there was something else I needed to do immediately.

"Excuse me for a second," I said, holding up my hand.

I dug out my tablet, logged-in, and tapped out a message. A moment later, Becca Tey's phone screeched to life in her hand, making her jump. She stared down at the screen, her bruised eyes widening.

"We've never got one of these before," she said.

There had been no time to warn the board. Safety first and all that. I glanced at my own phone and sighed. Of course, the first ever emergency notification in Chavez Ravine history had a typo in it. *Ugh.*

SECURITY ALERT: An investigation is under weigh. Remain in your home until further notice. Do not go outside. Lock your doors. If you see any suspicious individuals, please call the emergency number. This is an automated message. Please do not reply.

Under weigh. Damn autocorrect.

My phone rang. It was Cora Bernal.

"What's happening?" Her voice was high and sharp.

"An intruder tried to break into a house in La Loma. I'm there now. The resident is safe, and the guards are looking for the suspect."

"The naked man?"

"That's the one."

My phone beeped. Another incoming call. Eileen Simpson.

"Cora. Can you please call the other board members and let them know what's going on? I need to stay on top of the search."

"Of course, dear." Cora sounded shaky but in charge.

She hung up, and I sent Eileen's call to voicemail.

I looked over at Becca, who was leaning against a counter.

"I have several guards out looking for that guy now. He doesn't appear to be a ghost, so I don't think he'll just disappear. If I'm right, they should find him soon."

I sounded so confident, I almost convinced myself. Almost.

Usually, when entities first appeared, they were disoriented and easy to round up. Some became aggressive, but even then, it was more lashing-out behavior than any sort of malicious intent. Hairy was in a class of his own.

Then again, I had no idea if we were dealing with an entity or something else.

A commotion from the side of the house made me bolt up from my chair. I turned to Becca.

"Go upstairs and lock yourself in the bathroom again." Then I dashed into the downstairs bedroom for a better look.

I opened the shutters and peered outside.

A blur of bright colors and hairy flesh greeted me. It took a moment to sort out what was going on.

Naked Hairy Man was face down on the ground, attempting to crawl away. A tall woman wearing a bright pink caftan pounded him with a wooden rolling pin. I couldn't get a good look at her face. From her movements, she was young and, by the way she was clobbering Hairy, very physically fit.

I ran outside, clutching my baton. Hairy had reached the edge of the front porch and was trying to pull himself into a standing position, which only opened him to a side blow from the rolling pin. I didn't have any cuffs, but the guards did, so I called Ron and told him to get there immediately. The woman in the caftan continued her assault.

She was screaming in Spanish. I hadn't heard such a barrage of obscenities since my mother dumped my father.

Another furious swing sent Hairy toppling to the ground. He fell on his back, his face twisted, and his hands came up to protect his eyes. Bad move. The woman took aim much lower, and before I could stop her, the rolling pin had connected with his man parts. His unearthly shriek of pain filled the night air.

Hairy doubled over on his side and went still. His face took on a distinctly gray hue. His limbs began to contort, stretching in impossible ways. Bones cracked and popped. His skin began to split and peel, like he was made of paper mâché instead of flesh.

The woman and I were frozen in place, riveted by the scene unfolding before us.

Hairy continued to writhe, eyes rolling back in his head, mouth opened in a silent scream.

The air had become thick with his musky scent.

With our mouths agape, we watched Hairy crumble, his skin flaking away, until there was nothing left but a pile of dust.

Chapter 14

After scraping Hairy's crumbly remains into a plastic bag, I walked the woman in the pink caftan back to her house. Julia Suarez lived two blocks east of Becca, in a house even quirkier than mine: two cottages joined together by a fully enclosed breezeway.

I managed to learn a lot in our few minutes together. Julia was chatty. Whether she was nervous about beating Hairy senseless with her rolling pin or if she was just a talker, I couldn't tell. She used her hands when she spoke. Her long nails would accidentally graze the side of my face, followed by excessive apologies.

Julia was younger than I first thought, somewhere in her early thirties. When I followed her into the house, I got my first good look at her.

She was curvy, with lots of wavy auburn hair. Her ear was bleeding where Hairy had ripped out an earring during their tussle. She disappeared into a bathroom to deal with it, giving me a chance to observe the room.

The walls were painted cream, but the place was still a riot of color. Furniture in yellow, pink, green, purple, orange, red. Lots of patterns too. Pillows with stripes, checks, and diamonds.

Somehow, thanks to design skills that have always escaped me, it all worked. It was lively and comfortable. The easy chairs had ottomans. The walls had built-in bookshelves holding pottery and figurines. I immediately recognized them as coming from the pottery shop in Palo Verde Plaza.

When Julia came out of the bathroom, she had a bandage around the bottom of her right ear.

"Do you by chance own that studio in Palo Verde Plaza?" I asked.

She gave me a blank look that said it all. The adrenaline had worn off, and shock was beginning to set in. I still had a lot of questions, and if I wanted answers before she crashed, I had better start asking.

"Why don't you sit down?" I nodded toward the turquoise couch. "Let me get you a glass of water or something."

Julia shook her head and went into the kitchen. "My mother always said I had a temper." She opened a cupboard painted green. "It finally came in handy tonight. Because that asshole showed up next door and I just kind of lost it, you know?"

I cleared my throat and sat on a stool at the kitchen's island. "Actually, I don't. You're going to need to walk me through what happened, step-by-step."

Julia pulled out a glass bottle of milk and poured some in a pan, then set it on the stove. "They can't charge me with murder, right? I mean, I was just defending myself. And my neighbor. And you saw what happened. He disintegrated...or whatever. Humans don't do that. Animals don't either. He had to be an entity, right? So, murder's not a thing I need to worry about, right?"

She was correct. That had been determined by the courts the year after the first entity waves.

There was only one problem.

"It's too early to say he was entity," I said.

Julia added cinnamon and a squirt of honey to the warming milk. "Then what else could it be?"

I shook my head. "I don't know."

"Well, it wouldn't be the first time monsters showed up in Chavez Ravine. At least, according to the stories in my family. I tried asking the board about it once during a meeting, and they shut me down pretty fast. Eileen Simpson and Dan Berman said they'd never heard the stories, but I could tell the Latinos on the board knew exactly what I was talking about, and they couldn't shut me up fast enough."

That got my attention.

"Monsters in Chavez Ravine? What *kind* of monsters? When was this?"

Julia thought for a moment. "Some time after the eviction process started and before the city changed its mind. Maybe in the early 1950s, yeah? My grandfather called them monsters, but my grandmother said they were more like demons. My grandparents were young, so they didn't actually see them. But they said the monsters were part of a plot to scare the residents out of their homes."

Were the monsters of Julia's grandfather's era actually entities making an early appearance? Or had they been something else?

I also wondered why my mother had never mentioned them. My grandmother had sold her home and left, though she later came to regret it. But we had another family member who had held out until the city finally gave in to public pressure and canceled their plans to demolish the old neighborhoods.

That relative's name was Lencha Bantacorte, the community's most famous bruja. Liliana, my grandmother, had trained under Lencha but had never attained her status or reputation. Maybe Lencha had never told Liliana about monsters in Chavez Ravine, which would explain why I had never heard about it from my mother.

On the subject of Lencha and Liliana, a thought began to bubble up.

Cora Bernal had wanted me for the security job, which I always thought was a bit odd because Chavez Ravine didn't have an entity problem. But what if it had a *different* kind of problem? One it didn't want to admit to. Maybe something supernatural. Then, with all the brujas in my family history, Cora might assume I would be the best person for the job.

Interesting. And a little alarming.

"Julia, is there any chance I can talk to your parents?"

She poured the warm milk into two ceramic mugs the color of the night sky. Julia set one down in front of me. A comforting aroma rose from the cup, and I took a sip of the sweet, soothing liquid.

"Not really possible. My parents have both passed. That's how I ended up with two houses. The one on the other side belonged to my grandparents. I use this house as a living area, the middle part as a studio, and the other house for the bedrooms."

The hot milk was beginning to work its magic, and my bones started to soften. "Before one of us falls asleep, you need to tell me what happened, while it's still fresh in your mind."

Julia nodded, crossed to the sink, and splashed water on her face before rejoining me at the island.

"Sure. A new couple just moved in next door, yeah? I've only met them a few times, but the girl said her husband was finishing up a medical residency somewhere and he'd be joining her in a few weeks. She's pregnant, and I knew she was probably alone. And then I heard screaming coming from their house. I looked out, and I saw her leaning outside a second-story window. She said a naked man was banging on the front door and was trying to get in, but she'd left her phone downstairs.

She was terrified. I grabbed the rolling pin to see if I could scare him off."

I stared at her over the top of my mug. "You didn't think to call the emergency number?"

Julia gave me a sheepish look. "No. I should have, right? That was totally stupid of me, but I was really pissed off. How dare some idiot scare her like that, yeah? She's pregnant!"

"So, you went running over there with…a rolling pin?"

"Yeah, it's heavy. When I got there, he was on the porch, running back and forth, making horrible noises and trying to break down the door. I yelled at him. And then you don't want to hear what he did next because it was disgusting. And wow did that really piss me off because I don't even like it when guys give me the once-over. And this was…worse.

"He came charging at me, practically slobbering, and I was like, 'Hell no, you don't.' He lunged at me. I ducked, but he still managed to rip my earring off, and that just made me angrier. So I started swinging, yeah? That really surprised him. I just kept hitting him, and then he tried to run away, but I hit him again and knocked him down. We kept going like that down the street until we got to Becca's house."

"Did he say anything?"

"No. He just sort of…grunted."

"No words?"

Julia frowned. "Now that you mention it, no."

Most entities were incapable of speech, though many could understand if you spoke to them. There were a few notable exceptions. Some of the younger gnomes were verbal and notoriously profane. The water sprites could talk too, but listening to them was dangerous. Their chatter could make people do things that were against their best interests. It was standard protocol to muzzle water sprites as soon as possible.

Julia rubbed an eyebrow. "Do you think he was an entity?"

Now, that was a perfectly good question.

Entities did *not* crumble and disappear like Hairy had. They stuck around whatever displacement center they were sent to. One of these days, that might change. Maybe they would snap out of their funk and revolt. That's what most of us who worked with entities feared. Privately, of course.

"We'll be looking into that." I rose to my feet, exhausted and wanting nothing more than to crawl into bed. "If you think of anything else, please call me." I gave her my phone number.

At the front door, Julia yawned and said goodnight.

I drove away slowly. Alone, with my nerves calmed by the milk, I took in my surroundings.

Julia's property was on the north side of the gully, separated by a thin green space. The house belonging to her new neighbors was situated right next door. The gully was so close, anything could climb out of it and reach the houses in no time.

Just like the ghosts Becca Tey had seen.

I needed to take another look at that gully.

Chapter 15

When the landscaping crew arrived at eight o'clock, I had already hit snooze several times. I stared up at the ceiling, willing myself out of bed, when the cat began meowing in the kitchen. He wanted his breakfast.

I stared at the stack of canned food, trying to decide which would smell the least disgusting. After careful consideration, I chose chicken and scraped the goop into his bowl. How had it come to be that I was feeding a chubby cat before I had even had my coffee?

I took a quick shower while the coffee brewed, then dressed in clothes suitable for another inspection of the gully.

My phone chimed. I quickly checked the message, hit email, and said goodbye to the cat.

"If anyone breaks in to hide another hex bag, you have my permission to scratch the hell out of them."

The cat didn't reply, fortunately, but he did walk me to the door. He stood in the entryway and watched me go.

"Weirdo," I said, locking the door behind me.

Instead of heading straight to my office—or, for that matter, to the gully—I drove to the HOA board meeting room. I had been summoned. Cora had messaged me saying she wanted to hear what had happened in La Loma in person. I had plenty to do, but I had some questions of my own. And besides, Cora was my boss. Technically, I reported to the entire board, but she ran the show.

The entire board was waiting for me in the imposing meeting room.

Oh goody.

I took a seat next to Charlie, then looked around. The first thing I noticed was a scratch on Hernan Frias's cheek. A jagged red welt surrounded by swollen skin.

"Ouch," I said, by way of greeting. "Looks like you have a cat."

Hernan smiled at me, his eyes wrinkling. "I have a rose garden. Some varieties have especially large, sharp thorns."

I returned his stare. Was I imagining things, or did the retired professor seem a little defensive?

There wasn't much time to ponder that because Eileen Simpson began talking. Or shouting, more like.

"First, Katherine Morris, then poor Becca Tey, and now this horrific incident. It's…unprecedented! What the heck is going on?"

I cleared my throat, trying not to let her rile me up, even though she seemed to think I was to blame. Eileen and the rest of the board had every right to be concerned. Unfortunately, I didn't have any answers for them, so I used my angry-public-calming voice.

"Let me walk you through what happened last night." And I did.

Eyes bulged. Mouths opened. Eileen and Dan gasped when I got to the part about Hairy crumbling. Charlie Perez and Cora Bernal exchanged looks. Neither seemed particularly surprised by my story, which shocked me. Hernan Frias's reaction was just as interesting. His jaw went all tight. He stared past me, as if lost in thought, and made a *hmm* noise.

"I've preserved the remains and will be sending them to a lab for analysis, but there are a few things we know."

I scanned the faces around the table. Yes, I certainly had their attention.

"You've already seen my report regarding the footprints we collected from Katherine Morris's backyard. Not Neanderthal. While that's very good news, it's too early to say what exactly we're dealing with here. Entities don't just fall apart and vanish, but this thing did. And then there's the incident with the ghosts in La Loma. Their behavior also differs significantly from what we've come to expect from entities. I have an arrangement with Occult Affairs to access their heat map, so I'll be checking that as soon as possible to see what, if anything, they can tell us."

Eileen bristled. "An arrangement? That's going to cost us, isn't it?"

"Not at all," I replied smoothly. "I'm just taking advantage of the connections I have there and passing that benefit along to the association."

Cora, Charlie, and Dan looked pleased. Eileen was trying hard to disguise her irritation but not quite pulling it off.

"I should also tell you...I inspected the perimeter up along Elysian Park. The fence is too short and made of wood. It's a piece of cake to climb over it or break through it. I recommend installing something made of steel, with anti-climb features—"

Dan Berman winced. "That sounds hideous."

I nodded. "It works, but you're right. It's ugly. Concrete is another option. Stone is great and looks good too, but it's definitely the most expensive option."

Charlie grinned. "Maybe we can convince the developer to pay for it. A new, more secure fence would be a good selling point."

There were nods all around.

I cleared my throat. "I also found that four of the surveillance cameras along Elysian Park are no longer working.

It's possible they were disabled, though I can't imagine by whom or why. We need to get them back online as soon as possible."

Eileen interrupted. "Stu was our consultant on the security cameras. He bought the system for us and handled the installation." Her chin lifted. "He gave us a discount."

Well, well, well. Stu was certainly tight with the board. Or with Eileen, anyway.

Cora frowned. "Why would someone disable the cameras?"

I shrugged. "Because someone doesn't want something to be caught on camera."

"That's a bit dramatic," Eileen scoffed.

"What's been going on in Chavez Ravine *has* been a bit dramatic, wouldn't you say?" Somehow, I managed to sound nonchalant. *Go me.*

"It most certainly has!" Eileen said hotly. "And I, for one, would like to know what you plan to do about it."

That tone again.

Cora Bernal rapped her knuckles on the table. "May I remind you that Maddy has just joined us? She's hardly had any time to get her feet under her desk, let alone solve problems like these, literally overnight."

"She lives here too now," Charlie piped in. "Maddy has every incentive to deal with all of this, especially considering how close she lives to where those things were seen."

Dan leaned forward, crossing his arms on the table. "You know, the timing of all this is interesting. All these appearances began the day Maddy arrived."

Out of the corner of my eye, I caught Cora and Charlie exchanging a look. It only lasted a second.

Dan paused, shooting me an apologetic smile before continuing. "We all know about her mother, Malena Bantacorte. Is there any chance this isn't a coincidence? That all of this is somehow connected to Maddy being in Chavez Ravine?"

For once, I was speechless. That was quite an insinuation. I did not communicate with entities, I wasn't psychic, and I certainly couldn't summon supernatural beings.

And I'd hardly spoken to the woman in two years.

Dan's question was utterly and completely ridiculous. No one was saying anything. I needed to defend myself in a straightforward, non-defensive, respectful way.

But when I opened my mouth, the only words that wanted to come out were, "Screw you."

So, I closed it.

Cora shifted in her chair. "No," she said firmly. "This isn't because of Maddy."

I expected her to say more, but her lips pressed into a tight line. She glared at Dan, who held up his hands as if surrendering.

Charlie got all squirmy too. "This is why we wanted her," he said in a low voice.

Eileen started ranting something about the need for a community meeting to reassure the residents, so I assumed I was the only one who had heard Charlie.

But I wasn't.

Cora gave a strangled little laugh. In a hushed tone, she said, "Oh, Charlie. Let's not scare her off so soon."

Cora's face and neck were flushed. She grabbed her purse and began digging through it.

"Oh, my goodness, I really need to get going. I promised my daughter I'd watch the kids this morning. Where are my keys? Maddy, do go ahead and contact Stu about the cameras. And let us know how you get on with your investigation."

The board president gave me a nervous smile, then left, Charlie on her heels.

I stared after them.

This is why we wanted her.

We. Cora *and* Charlie.

What the hell was going on?

Chapter 16

I left Stu a message about the security cameras before driving to the guardhouse in Bishop to ask Ron Mendez to take Hairy's remains to the lab for analysis.

Ron squinted at the plastic bag filled with gray crumbly bits and shook his head. "Last night was insane. Even crazier than usual."

The words caught my attention, like a worm on a hook. I leaned out the window of my Jeep. "What do you mean? Crazier than usual?"

Ron's eyes flicked upward. He let out a low moan and shook his head. "Oh man. I shouldn't have said that."

I hopped out of my vehicle and stood in the guardhouse doorway, putting my hands on my hips. "Please explain."

Ron shifted from foot to foot, avoiding eye contact. "I'm not supposed to say. Cora would kill me."

"May I remind you, I'm your boss?" My voice was gentle but insistent.

"But Cora—" Ron bit his lower lip. His eyes darted around nervously, as if he expected the board president to jump out from behind the hedge.

I tapped him lightly on the arm. When he finally looked at me, my gaze bore into his.

"We're a team, Ron. You, me, and the other guards. If we're going to be successful, we need to be on the same page." I leaned in closer. "Now, please, talk and don't hold anything back."

Ron hung his head. "Fine. You'll find out soon enough anyway. We can't keep it a secret much longer."

By his agonized expression, whatever he had to say was going to be good.

"The time for secrecy is over, Ron," I said sternly. "We've got important stuff to do. A community to keep safe. Whatever you and Cora know, I need to know it too."

Ron hemmed and hawed some more, and then his shoulders slumped. "I can't believe I messed up."

I didn't have kids, but I could still manage a scary mom voice. "Come on, Ron. We don't have all day."

He snapped his head up and straightened his posture. His eyes still avoided mine. Instead, they focused intently on the ground.

"I've had some calls from Cora to check out some stuff. At night. So, I did. And let me tell you, it was some weird stuff…" His voice trailed off.

I didn't know what I was expecting, but it wasn't that. "You mean, Cora called the emergency number to report something?"

Ron shook his head. "No. She called me directly." He paused for a moment, then added, "She made it clear she wanted to keep it quiet. Just between us."

I nodded, pretending to understand. "But why would Cora do that?"

"She said she wasn't sure what we were dealing with and didn't want to cause a panic."

"You called it 'weird stuff.' When you went to investigate, what exactly did you see?"

Ron took a deep breath and exhaled loudly. "Once, it was a giant dog wearing a white dress, like a bridal gown. It was tall as me, standing on its hind legs. Another time, I saw some skinny things, like ghosts with small heads. Those really freaked me out. And once, there were these huge birds at the top of Bishop, but by the time I got there, they were already flying away."

I stared at him for a long time, thinking. If these had been entities, the heat map would have flagged them. So, what were they? And why hadn't Cora said anything about them?

"Did all this happen in Bishop?"

Ron nodded. "At the top of the ridge. Cora lives up there. So does Charlie Perez. A lot of the old-time legacy people live up there. Hernan Frias too."

"Did Hernan see them?" I asked.

"No. He said Cora must have taken too much medication or something and was imagining things."

I didn't know Hernan Frias that well, but that didn't sound like something a supportive neighbor would say. "How about Charlie?"

Ron cleared his throat and nodded. "He's the one who saw the dog bride in his backyard. When I got there, he was as white as a sheet."

"After you responded, what did you do? How did you deal with these...things?"

"I didn't need to, really." Ron rubbed his hands down the front of his pants. "I saw them for a few seconds, and they took off."

"Did you try to chase them down?"

"No, ma'am. Cora told me not to."

Odd. Cora had called for Ron's help and then asked him not to do anything. And why Ron? There were other guards she could have called, including an older one with more experience.

"Any chance you're legacy, Ron?" I asked.

"Yeah, I am."

"Any chance you're related to Cora Bernal?"

His eyes widened. "How did you know? She's my grandma's cousin. They're tight. I've known Tia Cora since I was a kid. We do a tamale Christmas and the whole thing."

So, Cora had called Ron because he was familia. She thought she could trust him more than the other guards, who were not Latino and not legacy. Hmmm.

"When did all this happen?"

Ron rubbed the side of his face. "The ghosts happened a few months ago…but just a few times, and they didn't come back. And then there was nothing for a long time. And then there was the dog bride, just once, and then the next week, the birds. But nothing else happened until you got here and Naked Hairy Man appeared."

It took a moment for my mind to catch up, but I started connecting dots.

"Do the ghosts that appeared at Becca Tey's house match the description of the ghosts you saw in Bishop?"

Ron blinked. "Yeah. Pretty sure."

"And you didn't think to tell me?"

"I wanted to, but Cora told me not to say anything."

"Any idea why that might be?"

He shrugged. "She said she really needed you to take this job, and she wanted you to get settled in first without getting overwhelmed."

So, Cora didn't want to scare me off, which meant whatever she was holding back was serious. Good Lord, I was a former Occult Affairs officer. I had seen and dealt with more than she could ever imagine. And *she* was worried about overwhelming *me*? Hardly.

Something was up, and the only way I was going to find out what was to ask Cora directly.

More dots started lining up.

Julia Suarez had said something about her grandparents telling stories of monsters...

"Ron. Have you ever heard stories of monsters in Chavez Ravine? A long, long time ago?"

Ron rolled his eyes. "I'm not supposed to know about it, but I've heard Cora and my grandmother talk about it all hush-hush at parties and stuff. My mom says don't believe it. They're just old stories. But after what I saw? I'm not so sure."

"Do you think the things you saw were entities?" I watched him closely for his reaction.

He frowned. "Maybe? I've seen entities down in the city, but the things I saw don't really act like that. You know?"

Not exactly the most eloquent way to describe a gut feeling, but I understood it perfectly well. That's how it seemed to me too.

A little research and a good night's sleep were necessary before tackling Cora.

I stopped by the Library and Historical Records room in Palo Verde. It wasn't staffed, but I found what I was looking for easily enough in the drawers at the far side of the room. I rolled up several maps, slid them into an empty tube, and signed them out with Caitlin. She was dressed entirely in hot pink.

"No one's ever checked out a map before," she said, then went back to whatever she had been doing on her computer.

Shopping for clothes, probably. Something I still needed to do. I was running out of stuff to wear.

Back in my office, I made some coffee and unrolled the topographical map of Chavez Ravine across my desk. It kept curling up, so I anchored it with my phone on one side and a tape dispenser on the other. Immediately, I noticed something interesting.

The gully running along Becca Tey's house meandered all the way through La Loma into Palo Verde. It stretched past Katherine Morris's house too. Anyone—any*thing*?—hoping to avoid detection could stick to the gully and hide among the trees and brush. Which would be even easier at night.

I stared at it for a while. Had the gully always been there? Or was it man-made, a way of diverting rainwater around all the new construction? I found the oldest map in the pile. It was faded and sepia-colored, with lines drawn in dark blue ink.

And there it was.

The gully had been around for a long time. Well before the developers arrived.

I squinted at the tiny print next to the top of the gully, and my skin went all tingly.

"Phantom's Pass."

How about that? Coincidence, or something more? Just how old was the map I was looking at anyway?

It was a bit of a treasure hunt, trying to find the date, but I eventually located it in tiny block letters at the bottom right-hand side of the map, just below the border.

1943. That was pretty damn old.

No one alive today could tell me why the area at the top of the gully had been named Phantom's Pass. Had it always been a corridor for supernatural beings? If so, that would help explain what we were dealing with.

The library might have books or letters that mentioned the old stories. It would take time to go through them, but at least I would know more about what had happened all those years ago.

The question was, should I try to find out as much as possible before I confronted Cora Bernal, or could I trust her to tell me the truth?

Chapter 17

omething was beginning to bug me. I had witnessed three incidents in my short time as head of security for Chavez Ravine, and then I found out there had been at least three others. It was too early to say whether these were entities or not, but there was a decent chance at least some of them were.

So, I decided to go see Jo.

I wasn't above a little bribery. Knowing Jo loved sweets, I stopped at a bakery on the way to the station and bought some lemon drizzle cake and two fancy coffee drinks, ignoring the calorie count on the little placards behind the glass. I tried not to think about food that way, but it's hard to ignore all those warnings about the Great Midlife Metabolism Slow Down.

While I drove through the streets of Los Angeles, I viewed it with fresh eyes, having spent the last several days spoiled by the pristine neighborhoods of Chavez Ravine. LA was even dirtier, grittier, and more congested than I remembered.

I was already looking forward to going back up the hill to Chavez Ravine as soon as possible. Back to my house, my beautiful landscaping, my fancy grocery store. Talk about living in a bubble.

The station was grungy. The linoleum permanently scuffed and yellowed with age, walls a sickly shade of green. The desks were relics from the last century. I thought of my new office with freshly painted walls, the dark wood paneling, and my very own shiny coffee machine, which made espresso on demand.

A few former fellow officers stopped in the hall to say hello and give me a hard time about my cushy new job. Then, quietly, they asked me to keep them in mind if I ever decided to start a force up there.

I found Jo where she always was, glued to her desk in the command center, doing what she always did, monitoring the heat map and dispatching officers to deal with outbreaks.

A few brown hairs had escaped her low ponytail. Silver strands framed her face. It looked nice, like nature's highlights, but Jo was always threatening to bleach her hair to blend them in.

Her red glasses sat low on her nose. She glanced up, and her eyes widened in surprise.

When she noticed the coffees and the paper sack from the bakery, she grinned. "Are you on a mission of mercy?"

"I was in the area so thought I'd stop by, say hello, and bring you some treats."

Sometimes, I was shocked by how easily I could lie.

I held the tray just out of her reach. "You do deserve them, right?"

Jo tipped her head back and groaned. "You have *no* idea what I've been through today. A hound from hell—I think *literally* from hell—popped out on a movie set in Burbank. But get this. They're making a horror flick, so people thought the director—who's a bit of a joker—was just trying to scare them. Until the pooch wrecked the set and went after a camera guy. The only thing that saved them was a bad case of entity disorientation. But by the time we got there, it remembered it had wings and could fly. It took freakin' forever to capture it."

A shiver ran up my spine just thinking about that. Not long ago, I would have been one of the first responders. Sounded like a nightmare.

I set the coffee in front of her, then slid the lemon cake out of the bag and placed it on a napkin.

"You've definitely earned this, then."

A thought occurred to me.

"Question for you. Did that Hell Hound happen to be dressed like a bride?"

The cake stopped inches from Jo's red-lipsticked mouth. "Uh, no. But there's a reason you're asking, so you might as well tell me what it is."

I scanned the room. We were alone in the command center. I lowered myself into the chair next to her.

"Well, it's been an interesting couple of nights in Chavez Ravine, let's just say that." I gave Jo a quick summary of my first few days in the new job.

She frowned. "Since we talked, I've been keeping a close eye on Chavez Ravine. I mean, *really* close. As in, going over data. Historical data too. There hasn't been a single blip. No indication of entities up there. I've gone back months."

"Well, something's going on." I sipped my coffee and stared at the heat map display on the wall. Burbank still showed a trace of red. That wasn't unusual. Hot spots sometimes lingered for hours or even days. "Maybe they're new? Entities 2.0 that evade detection?"

Jo sighed. "That's what we've always feared, right? But we're in our sixth year with this heat map, and it hasn't happened yet. So why now? And why just up in Chavez Ravine?" She broke off a piece of cake, popped it into her mouth, and chewed thoughtfully. "Did all of this happen *after* you started your job up there?"

Aw, come on. Not Jo too.

"No," I said, a little too loudly. "Some of the incidents predate me, but apparently, the lady who hired me didn't want to scare me off, so she kept them a secret. Or something like that."

It felt good to talk about it. I didn't have many friends who would understand crazy work stuff.

Correction. I didn't have many friends *at all*. Sad, really.

"Why would she hide that from you?" Jo asked.

"No idea. But I plan on finding out." I stared at the lid of my coffee cup. "You know, these things don't really act like entities. They don't pop up all disoriented and confused. In fact, they seem quite, I don't know, purposeful."

Jo pressed her lips together and studied me for a few moments. I shifted in my chair, wondering what was coming, because I knew that look.

"Mads," she began slowly. "Have you talked to your mom about any of this?"

The hand holding my coffee jerked upward, and liquid jumped out of the sip hole. "Why would you ask *that*, of all things?"

Jo fixed me with a level stare, the one she reserved for officers who dared question her judgment. "Because she's a resource, Madeline. I know you two have a complicated relationship, but your mom's probably the most famous psychic in the world. There are documentaries about her. She founded the New College of Psychic Studies, didn't she? She knows all about magic and curses and psychic attacks. What if someone is invoking spirits or demons to attack Chavez Ravine?"

I sat back in my chair, stunned. That was serious Jo. No-nonsense, practical Jo.

"You've got to be kidding me!" My voice was shrill.

Jo sniffed. Her expression had turned to stone.

"Mads, may I remind you that you were employed by the Occult Affairs Division, whose sole mission is to deal with entities of supernatural origin? We've had ghosts, fairies, gnomes, trolls, giants, and creatures straight out of myths, and you're telling me I'm wrong to think a psychic can help?

"Come on, Mads. Think. Think past whatever grudge you're holding against your mother." She waved her hand in the direction of the heat map. "That thing up there is just a tool. One of the few we have. But it's not perfect, and it's not going to help you with whatever it is you're facing. If you want to get in front of what's going on in Chavez Ravine, you need to find some new tools."

Jo might as well have slapped me upside the head. As much as I didn't want to admit it, she wasn't wrong. And I hadn't told her about the hex bags. Someone with knowledge of magic—*black* magic!—was determined to get to me, and I didn't know what sort of harm they meant to inflict or why.

The truth was, I was putting off talking to my mother.

As soon as I mentioned those hex bags or the things wandering around Chavez Ravine, she would start going on about Lencha Bantacorte, my great aunt, and the magical destiny I had been resisting all my life.

Chapter 18

I had just returned to my office when I realized Stu Wells hadn't called me back about the cameras, so I texted him.

Call you in fifteen, he replied.

As restless as I was, I had trouble thinking straight about what I should do next. I started making a list. The first thing on it: try to find some record of monsters appearing in the old days of Chavez Ravine.

Many of the Mexican Americans who had lived there were barely scraping by. Most were uneducated. They didn't sound like the kind of people who wrote journals, but they might have left some records. After all, barely literate pioneers had chronicled their journeys across America. Their letters and diaries were riddled with grammatical errors and misspellings, but they still provided rich histories of the times.

The stories I had heard growing up about my grandmother, Liliana Bantacorte, and her aunt, the famous bruja Lencha Bantacorte, were part of my family's oral tradition. But as far as I knew, nobody had ever written about either of them.

But maybe some of the other families from Chavez Ravine had saved diaries or letters. Maybe, by some miracle, these writings were in the archives. I decided to hit the library later that day.

My phone rang. It was Stu.

"Maddy!" he said, like we were old buddies.

Not so fast, Slick. I cleared my throat. "Hello, Stu. Thank you for returning my call. I have a few questions about the camera surveillance system. I'm told that you—"

He interrupted. "Is there a problem?"

Dude, it's my turn to speak. "As I was saying, four of the cameras appear to have been disabled. I know you don't have anything to do with monitoring, but those cameras have been out for a while now, and I was wondering if that should have triggered some sort of alarm in our system."

A sharp intake of breath. A long silence. "Disabled? Are you sure? They've been intentionally taken offline?"

I bristled. "Yes, I'm sure they were disabled. They were online but not capturing any video. I may not be an expert on cameras, but yeah, it was pretty obvious."

"I didn't mean to imply..." Stu's voice drifted off. "Look, I'm just a little surprised, that's all." He paused. When he continued, he sounded as sure of himself as ever. "Which cameras?"

"The ones along the fence near Elysian Park."

Another long silence followed. "Do those cameras have a view of the construction going on at the new development?"

I sat up straighter in my chair. "Maybe, if they were pointed that direction."

"Look, Maddy, do me a favor and keep this to yourself, all right? But I've been hearing some things about the developer that have me concerned. Rumors mostly, at this point. No-bid contracts, supplier kickbacks, padded project costs...Maybe someone doesn't want a record of what they're doing up there."

Stu suddenly went up a notch in my estimation. He might have been smug, but he was my kind of smart.

"It's a possibility," I said, like it was something I had already considered.

"How about I take a look at those cameras myself?"

The offer came as a surprise.

And presented a dilemma.

If Stu Wells was responsible for disabling the cameras, he would be looking for a way to cover it up.

Why he would do something like that was beyond me. He lived in Chavez Ravine and had a vested interest in the community. But I just couldn't afford to trust anyone yet, even Cora Bernal and especially Stu Wells.

Unfortunately, I had no knowledge about camera forensics. But I *did* know someone who could help.

I was about to put Stu Wells to the test, but I needed to buy some time. "It's kind of crazy here today. Can I get the cameras to you tomorrow?"

"Tomorrow's fine. I can pick them up at your office in the morning, if you'd like."

We arranged to meet at 8:30 and said goodbye. I immediately called Jo's wife, Holly, who worked for the company that had developed the heat map and other entity-detection technologies, including surveillance cameras.

After carefully disconnecting the malfunctioning cameras and putting them in a cardboard box, I drove to Holly and Jo's Los Feliz neighborhood near Griffith Park. Their house sat at the end of a cul-de-sac, the same eye-popping lime green it had been seven years ago when they bought it.

Los Feliz used to be swanky, a tree-lined neighborhood with trendy restaurants and shops popular with celebrities. But a year after Jo and Holly moved in, entities started popping up all over Griffith Park.

Animal entities emerged in the zoo, a collection of historic trains attracted ghosts in Western wear, and a half-dozen celestial species floated around the observatory. Not to mention, the numerous creatures that loved the secluded hiking trails.

And they all drifted down into Los Feliz. Which, of course, tanked the neighborhood's property values.

Jo and Holly had depleted their savings to make the hefty down payment and didn't see any point in spending more to paint the house. They hated the lime green color, but they had become superstitious: for some reason, entities never appeared on their property, even though their lush backyard was just the type which usually attracted gnomes. They started to believe the awful green was the reason.

"That color is even too hideous for entities," Jo liked to joke.

Holly answered the door wearing a white tank top and denim overalls ripped at the knees. She had a platinum pixie cut with wispy bangs.

Holly was about ten years older than Jo but somehow managed to look younger. Probably because she was built like a wiry teenager and her face was lean and unlined, except for a few crinkles around her eyes.

Holly had moved to the states from Manchester, England, in her mid-twenties and still talked with a pronounced accent. When we first met, it had taken me a while to understand what she was saying because her voice was low and quiet but also rich and warm. When Holly spoke, people would lean in to listen.

Compared to her, I felt like an obnoxious American.

She gave me a quick hug. "What did you bring me?" Holly sounded excited, like I was about to hand her a gift instead of a box of defunct cameras.

But that was Holly. Jo always said she got wrapped up in her work, which was funny coming from Jo. They were perfect for each.

I handed her the box. "Just these dead cameras."

Holly peered inside. Her eyebrows—much darker than her hair—arched. "Your HOA did not spare any expense."

I followed Holly across the living room. It was bright and airy, with a vaulted, beamed ceiling. The house exuded rustic 1930s charm. In fact, it was so delightful, it took a while to notice the sloping floors and crooked doors. Colorful rugs covered sections of scuffed wood.

The living room was a mess. There were three empty cardboard boxes and two nylon tunnels, one rainbow-colored, with what appeared to be peepholes. There was also a scattering of small toys, including one shaped like a banana.

Holly saw me staring because she laughed, a nice low, rumbly sound. "We got a cat. Or, I should say, the cat got us. Because look at the place!" She suddenly stopped. "Fletcher, sweetheart, come and say hello to mum's friend."

A gray cat came bounding out from the hallway. It stopped several feet away and stared up at me with solemn yellow eyes.

"Isn't she lovely?" Holly said.

This was very un-Holly-like. She was not an effusive person.

I studied Fletcher. She *was* a nice-looking little cat. "Yeah, she's cute. Is she a kitten?"

Fletcher began swiping at the toy banana. It landed on top of Holly's sneaker, and she kicked it back with a delighted laugh. "She's a champion footballer, this one. But no, Fletcher's full-grown. She's a year old now. That's how long it's been since you were last here, Maddy."

"I know, I'm sorry." And I was. I liked Holly and Jo, I really did, but I hadn't been feeling very sociable, and the idea of attending one of their parties had just seemed too much.

Fletcher flopped on her back and waved her paws around.

"She's really small. Is she…a small breed or something?"

Holly frowned. "No. She's actually a British Shorthair and quite stocky."

Fletcher jumped to her feet and disappeared into a tunnel. A moment later, her round head popped out of a hole.

Holly turned to me and said, "Are you thinking about getting a cat? If you are, black cats are quite charming. My friend has an American Shorthair. We almost got one, but we fell in love with Fletcher here the moment we saw her."

I forced a laugh. "No, I'm definitely not getting a cat. But one did sort of make himself at home when I moved in, and I can't figure out who he belongs to."

Fletcher was now tearing through one of the nylon tunnels.

"If you're telling me Fletcher is a regular-sized cat, then mine must be Catzilla. He's at least twice her size."

Holly jerked her head back. "Bloody hell! What kind is it?"

"I have no idea."

"Do you have a picture on your phone?"

Of course, any proud cat owner would, but not me. "No, but it's red with stripes, with some spots on his stomach. He actually looks like a leopard."

And then I heard it. The unmistakable sound of pride in my voice, as if I were responsible for his striking looks. Which, if I were being honest, put Fletcher's to shame. Fletcher was attractive enough but also quite ordinary.

What was happening to me? Was I becoming a competitive cat lady?

Holly gave a little squeal, which brought me back to reality. "That sounds like a Bengal! Those are rare and expensive. Smart, too, and quite active."

Smart didn't even come close to describing that cat. He was also odd in a way I couldn't quite put my finger on. But the name of the breed got my full attention. "Bengal? As in, Bengal tiger?"

"I believe so. But I'm not sure there's any actual connection between the two. Are you going to keep him? What's his name?"

I sighed. "Two questions I can't answer."

We'd done nothing but talk about cats since I walked in the door, and I still had a lot of work to do in Chavez Ravine.

Holly must have sensed my impatience. "Let's take a look at what we've got, shall we?" She led me outside, across the well-tended garden, to a converted garage where Holly worked from home.

The space suited Holly perfectly. Small and spare with clean lines. A wall lined with monitors, switched off at the moment. An elaborate computer setup. A rust-colored leather chair on rollers and a rust-colored divan. Fancy but also comfortable.

Holly motioned to the divan. I sat down, leaned back, and stretched out my legs while she took out the cameras one by one and lined them up on the desk. My body felt heavy, and I realized how tired I was. Those nights chasing entities—or whatever they were—had caught up with me.

Holly picked up a camera and turned it around in her hands, examining it from all angles. She took a cable from a small drawer and plugged one end into the camera and the other into her computer. She tapped a few keys, and her screen filled with graphs and numbers.

"Electronically, everything's okay. Sensor's working just fine; image processing is all good."

She folded her arms across her chest and scowled at the camera for a few moments. Holly picked it up and turned it over a couple of times.

"Hmm." Holly twisted the lens, which slid out of the camera body. She held it to the light and squinted through it. She grinned. "Ah! Here we are."

I swung my legs off the divan. "What is it?"

Holly didn't answer. Instead, she tugged at something at the back of the lens.

"Black tape!" She held up her thumb. A small square of tape stuck to it.

With a soft cloth, she wiped the back of the lens, screwed it into the camera, and pointed it at a framed wedding photo. The picture appeared on the computer screen.

"You're kidding me," was all I could say.

Holly shook her head. "I kid you not." She repeated the process with the other three cameras, pulling strips of black tape from each.

"Low tech but effective."

What an idiot I am. "I feel like I should have been able to figure that out."

Holly shook her head slowly. "How would you even know the lens was removable? They're not in most security cameras. Interchangeable lenses are a premium option."

"Weird question, but would you mind putting the tape back on those lenses? I want to conduct a little experiment."

Holly gave me a suspicious look. "I will, but only on the condition that you let me in on the secret someday."

I nodded. Less than two minutes later, the cameras were back in the box.

"Thanks, Hol. I owe you and Jo a dinner."

Holly smiled. "Invite us over to your place when you're settled. I've always wanted to see what it's like up there on the other side of the gates."

"You're on."

At the front door, we exchanged hugs and said goodbye, Fletcher pushing her nose into my ankles. I crouched to pet her. Her bones seemed so fragile under my fingers compared with the giant thing back home—the Bengal.

What the hell kind of beast had I let into my house?

Chapter 19

Back at the office, I made a cappuccino and put the cameras on the credenza, ready for Stu the next morning.

Thinking about him again made my stomach flutter, but I didn't know why.

Maybe it was because I was afraid he would try to cover up the sabotaged cameras, which would mean he was involved somehow. Or maybe I feared he would be honest, in which case I would have one less thing to object to about the man.

Or maybe it was simply because I was about to see him again. Stu was smug and a little too slick for my taste, but he was also good-looking and interesting. If I had a type, he was probably it.

And, most importantly, he was single. So it was probably worth getting to know him.

A thought popped into my head, unbidden. If Stu Wells ever visited, how would the cat react to him? The cat strutted around the house like he owned it. Would Stu feel competitive? In fact, there was something a little feline about Stu.

I had to stop myself. Did I really just think that? Cat lady status confirmed. I was spending way too much time thinking about both of them. Time to get back to work.

I locked my office door, hopped in the Jeep, and drove up into the hills, wanting to see where Cora, Charlie, and Hernan lived. Their addresses were programmed into my handheld, so I knew exactly where I was going.

The homes up there were older. Not as big and fancy as some of the others, but there was something about their proportions that gave them a special sort of appeal.

The only exception was the home belonging to British pop star and part-time Chavez Ravine resident Bad Pete. He had built a large compound surrounded by high hedges, but the rest were like Goldilocks houses: not too big, not too small. Just right.

Ben Tomas had really knocked himself out up there. A tree-lined median separated the street. The landscaping had more of a Southwestern flare than other parts of Chavez Ravine. Many of the yards contained native plants and cacti.

I drove past Cora's place. Even if I hadn't known it was hers, I might have guessed from the color—the stucco a pale peach, the wood trim a sage green. It seemed very Cora.

Charlie's house was very Charlie too, somehow—gray with bright orange doors and window frames, palm trees lining the walkway leading to the front door.

The house belonging to Hernan Frias was the biggest surprise. It was Craftsman style and painted entirely black, except for the front door, which was a shiny red. Had he had to use his position on the board to get that color scheme approved? It wasn't bad, but it was unusual and didn't really fit with the rest of the community.

Hernan hadn't been kidding when he said he had roses. His garden was full of them—mostly red and white, some blooms as large as plates. Tiny yellow roses covered a trellis stretching from the sidewalk to the porch steps.

If he really tended them himself, he had quite the green thumb.

The guard, Ron Mendez, lived with his parents and grandmother across the street from Cora. The house was set far back from the curb. Or rather, the hous*es*. It looked like a compound. There were three separate buildings on the property, and I guessed a couple of generations of Mendezes called it home.

Good for them. Some families enjoyed being close together like that. No one could have paid me to live in the same *county* as my mother, let alone on the same lot.

My little home tour was interesting but told me little.

I hung a U-turn and headed back down the hill, when I realized the gully ran under the street midway down the block. The same gully that began in La Loma threaded between two houses south of Cora, dipped below a bridge, then narrowed and flattened out at the base of the hill. I had seen this area on the old map.

Cora, Charlie, Hernan, and Ron lived in Phantom's Pass.

The things Cora had seen must have traveled down the gully. *Mmm.*

A little freaked out, I drove back to my office in Palo Verde Plaza, checked under my chair for a hex bag—nothing—locked the door behind me, and headed to the library. As before, I had the place to myself.

I started at the walls lined with photos. There was an entire section devoted to Don Normark's work, which beautifully captured daily life in the villages before the city started kicking people out and bulldozing their homes. Some photos I had seen before—the black-and-white pictures showing residents at a packed city hall meeting, holding signs protesting the evictions—but others were new to me.

The protests had worked. The city backed away from its plan to build a housing project in Chavez Ravine. There were pictures of victory parties in the old neighborhoods, then more images of city council meetings where residents demanded compensation.

Still more captured construction projects: road paving, streetlight installation, a playground being built outside a brand-new school.

But by the time all that happened, many residents had taken the city's low-ball buyout offers and had left. My grandmother, Liliana Bantacorte, had been one of them.

Most of the thousands who had gone heard city officials had a change of heart and returned, with all sorts of compensation to make up for the upheaval they had been through.

But not my grandmother. She had protested along with the others but decided it was a lost cause and married a man from Salinas. Liliana moved with him to make a new life there and never knew the city had reversed course.

It was amazing to think, after all that time, I was living in her home. And rightfully so. The people of Chavez Ravine had fought hard to preserve their family wealth, and it was passed down through the generations. That wealth had grown and eventually built the beautiful neighborhoods filling Chavez Ravine.

I even felt a little sorry for my mother, who had never stepped foot in the place she had spoken of with such longing.

A small section of wall was dedicated to culture and folk history. There were pictures of festivals, with women cooking over open fires and rolling out masa for tortillas. Several pictures showed older women sitting at workbenches, mixing herbs and peering into children's mouths. These must have been the curanderas—the healers who dispensed centuries-old cures and sometimes came up with magical solutions to modern problems.

Like Liliana's aunt, Lencha Bantacorte.

My mother always said Liliana had been a curandera with extra skills, but Lencha was a real bruja, a woman who had learned the art of witchcraft while growing up on a ranch in Mexico. Did the library have any information about her, maybe letters or public records? Because if anything supernatural had happened in Chavez Ravine, Lencha would probably have been mixed up in it.

I went over to a computer sitting on a counter and wiggled the mouse. The screen came to life. It was a basic catalog system, nothing fancy, but it had a search function.

I typed in "Lencha Bantacorte." It felt funny to type in the surname. Bantacorte was rightfully my name too. The one I had changed to Madrigal—a name from my mother's side of the family.

Because my mother had made the Bantacorte name world famous and impossible to live with.

Oh my god, are you related to Malena Bantacorte?

Yes.

What's she like?

How much time do you have?

Can she really talk with entities? Do they really follow her around?

Yes.

It was not easy having a mother who was larger than life.

A long list of results popped up on the screen. The first one linked to a short biography, which I read through quickly. It had a bit of information about Lencha's life but not her death. Just that she had died at the age of fifty-five under "mysterious circumstances" at the home of a close friend named Bertita, who lived in Palo Verde.

Lencha had been single with no children. She had joined a group of women activists protesting the evictions. The city was using strong-arm tactics to push the residents out. It had razed the vacant houses in Lencha's neighborhood and "accidentally" bulldozed her small home. No mention of whether Lencha had been there at the time.

I typed in Bertita's name. A widow much older than Lencha. A real character, by all accounts, known for wearing a brimmed hat and smoking cigars. She had protested too and eventually died at the age of ninety-one.

I could only assume Lencha had moved in with the widow. But there was no mention of anything mysterious happening at Bertita's house that would explain how Lencha had died.

I looked around at the shelves of boxes. None were marked with catalog numbers or family names. These were probably filled with photos and letters that hadn't made it into the computer system yet.

It was time to hit the stacks.

I spent the next couple of hours going through boxes. There were lots of family albums and letters tied up with twine, but none labeled "Bantacorte." Not surprising. Lencha had never married and didn't have kids, as far as I knew. Who would have been around to take her picture?

It was like the woman had never existed, and yet she had, for fifty-five years. I swallowed. This was the sort of thing my mother loved to warn me about: waiting too long, missing out on marriage and kids, and dying alone.

Though, I wouldn't have been completely alone. At least, I would have a cat.

Chapter 20

Finding nothing about my great aunt, I moved quickly through the boxes, looking for letters, articles, or anything about monsters in Chavez Ravine. But after a couple of hours, I still had no insight into the monsters that had supposedly stalked Bishop, La Loma, and Palo Verde back in what I had begun to think of as "the old days."

I did find lots of binders with old census records and books chronicling the history of Chavez Ravine—stories of resilience while the three neighborhoods fought to keep their close-knit communities from being torn apart.

No luck verifying the old stories about monsters.

I paced back and forth. My next move was to confront Cora and go from there.

I put lids back on boxes and straightened up, when my legs started to tingle. The warning signs of a muscle cramp. I bent down and massaged my calves.

It was then I noticed two cardboard boxes sitting far back on the bottom shelf, which I hadn't noticed before. They were unmarked. I picked one up and turned to set it on a nearby desk.

The tingling sensation grew more intense. It wasn't sharp or sudden, like an electric shock, but more like a peculiar type of energy flowing through the muscles in the backs of my legs. I shook my feet to get it to stop, but it only spread upward to my chest and down my arms. My hands began to twitch. I held the box tightly, afraid I would drop it, losing control of my muscles.

Even though I had no idea what was going on, I didn't want to mess around. After quickly putting the box down, I reached for my phone to call the emergency number and request medical assistance.

But as soon as I released the box, the tingling stopped.

Warily, I reached out and removed the lid. The scent of old, musty papers made me sneeze. I peered inside. The box contained a stack of composition books, the kind with the classic marbled black-and-white design. There were at least ten of them.

I picked one up. In the white space on the cover, someone had scrawled in block letters: "PROPERTY OF TRINI DURAN: Do not read." Each notebook had a number.

Whoever this Trini was, she had been organized.

I settled down at the desk and opened notebook Number One.

My pulse began to race as I read. Trini wasted no time telling her story.

When the eviction notices came, she had moved out of Chavez Ravine to Boyle Heights. Trini was young, in her early twenties. She was content enough with her new life until Lencha and Bertita showed up at her door with news her father was in poor health, that she needed to come home and help him.

Trini refused at first, thinking the women were overreacting to her father's dramatic nature, but then he was attacked by a mysterious assailant and suffered a minor heart attack. She had no choice. Trini had to return home to care for him and tend to the family business, Duran Market & Liquor in Palo Verde.

I flipped ahead. Trini sounded like a young woman trying to break free from a suffocating family life, and the pages reflected her reluctance to return to the place she had tried so hard to escape.

About halfway through the first notebook, while I was quickly scanning the neat handwriting, a phrase caught my eye: "dog face bride."

I stopped scanning and went back a few paragraphs.

Trini carefully described a towering figure skulking in the darkness. It had the face of a dog and the body of a woman, with paws instead of hands and feet. The creature had been wearing a tattered wedding dress.

I marked the page with a piece of scrap paper. My heart raced, and I read on. That wasn't the only occasion Trini had seen Dog Face Bride, as she called her. She would appear after nightfall and linger outside on the porch.

Things just got more interesting from there.

Trini described strange beings appearing at night and frightening the residents. Many believed the city was behind it all, sending in goons dressed in costumes to pressure people into selling their properties. Trini called them *jumpers* and described them as ghostly pale, thin men who could leap higher than a house.

A few pages later, my heart froze.

A stocky, hairy, naked man—built "like a bull"—had broken into a young woman's home at night and tried to attack her. He might have succeeded if it hadn't been for her dog, which chased him away.

I sat back in my chair, stunned. It was true. I couldn't believe it.

Chavez Ravine *had* experienced supernatural creatures before, and it was all captured in the writings of a young woman who had seen it all herself.

Trini seemed like a no-nonsense young woman ahead of her time. A girl who ditched skirts and blouses in favor of dungarees and flannel shirts to chase monsters in the middle of the night. She described leading a band of locals armed with pistols and slingshots to fight the creatures haunting Chavez Ravine. Her partner, a young community organizer named Bobby, helped fight the monsters by night and put together protests by day.

What a remarkable pair they must have been. Why were there no photos of *them* on the walls?

What would the rest of the notebooks tell me? A lot, I suspected. But I was too restless to continue reading.

I was ready to visit Cora and demand an explanation.

After putting the notebook back in the box, I replaced the lid and slid it back onto the bottom shelf. But a faint tingling in my hands made me stop.

I couldn't leave the notebooks behind. They were important. Critical, even. It was possible I was the first person to ever read them.

Then my suspicious nature took over.

What if I left the notebooks behind and someone found them and took them? Someone who didn't want those old stories getting out. Not good for property values, and all that.

I was probably being ridiculous, but I didn't care. Those notebooks were coming home with me.

But how? I couldn't exactly walk out, carrying a box. That would look suspicious. Even Caitlin, who wasn't the most observant person in the world, might notice that.

I had an empty duffel bag in the back of my Jeep. That still might have been a bit much. But there was also a tote bag—one small enough to be overlooked but large enough for my purposes. I rushed out into the blinding sunlight, blinking, and retrieved the tote. In the lobby, I held it tightly against my side, facing away from Caitlin while I walked by. She was so engrossed in whatever she was doing on her computer, she barely looked up. So far, so good.

I quickly opened the box, took out the notebooks, and shoved them into my tote, then put the box back on the bottom shelf and pushed it as far as it would go.

For good measure, I grabbed some random books and stacked them in front of the box, completely obscuring it ffrom view.

I picked up my tote and was about to leave.

The library door flew open, and I jumped.

Hernan Frias barreled in, his black hair sticking up, damp like he had just come from the shower and hadn't had time to comb it. He wore black leather shoes but no socks. Hernan was breathless, and his cheeks were red.

I surreptitiously slid the tote bag to the floor by my feet. "Señor Frias!"

I'd not always been proud of how I handled surprises. For example, I had no idea why I said "señor." Or why my voice got all high and shrill. It wasn't exactly the coolest way to handle unexpected situations.

Hernan frantically scanned the library's tables, a hand pressed against his chest. Was he about to have a heart attack? His gaze darted around the room, seeming to miss nothing.

There was something in his manner, something desperate, that was setting off my alarm bells. My skin prickled.

What was he doing there? Why had he suddenly shown up? And why was he *so* anxious?

When he didn't say anything, I asked, "Are you having some sort of library emergency, Señor Frias?"

His wild dark eyes regarded me coolly. "I'm just surprised to see you here. I'd have thought you'd have more pressing matters than visiting the library."

Had I been imagining things, or had a faint hint of hostility crept into his tone? "Just doing a little research on the neighborhoods I'm sworn to protect." *Back atcha, señor.*

Hernan tilted his head and studied me. "Would this have anything to do with Lencha Bantacorte, by any chance?"

My mouth opened, then closed. Mostly out of surprise. Why would the retired professor have been worried about me researching my great aunt?

I gave a little nonchalant shrug. "She's a relative. Just one of several things I'm looking up when I have a few minutes."

I hesitated, choosing my next words carefully because I couldn't afford to make him more of a foe than he already was.

"My mother said Lencha was a powerful bruja back in her day. Cora mentioned you taught mystical studies, so you must know a thing or two about her."

Hernan took a deep breath. "The Bantacortes have always loved the limelight." He managed a thin smile. "Still do, by all accounts."

My eyebrows shot up. In just one go, Hernan had managed to hit me with a double whammy, taking digs at both my mother and my ancestors. *Well played, señor.*

He cleared his throat and continued. "I'm the volunteer manager here, and I know this place better than anyone. Is there something…*specific*…that you were looking for? I'll be happy to point you in the right direction."

Yes, there was something, and it was safely in my tote bag, which I needed to get past him. I picked up my tote and began inching toward the door.

Like heat-seeking missiles, his eyes locked on it immediately. "You do know we don't allow materials to leave the premises."

"Oh! Of course." I patted the tote bag. "This is just some stuff from my office."

I hoped he wasn't about to ask to inspect my bag. If he did, I would refuse, and things would get weird. But he didn't. Instead, he continued to stare at me.

I scurried past him. As I did, the hairs on the back of my neck stood up. I scooted out the door and turned around. He was still staring at me, his expression a mix of suspicion and something else I couldn't quite place.

Something darker.

Chapter 21

When I got back to my office, I was still thinking about my strange library encounter with Hernan Frias. I wished there was someone I could talk to about all this. Someone I could trust. I had Jo, but there was no way she could pick up the phone and listen to me gab while she was at work. The heat map kept her on her toes the entire shift.

I checked my email and read through the reports from the guard stations.

Nothing. Fortunately.

There was a note from one of the board members, Dan Berman, asking residents to keep an eye out for a husky named Benedict who had escaped his backyard. No mention of a cat.

Which reminded me, I really needed to stop at the pet store and pick up some cat toys.

My computer chimed. A new message had landed in my inbox.

It was from the lab. The analysis of Naked Hairy Man's remains had come back. I couldn't open it fast enough.

The report included a long list of materials: kaolinite, illite, smectite, iron oxide, silica, feldspar, calcium carbonate, sand, crushed shells, etc. The conclusion? Red earthenware clay, the kind used to make pottery. Oh, and field corn.

Well, *that* got my attention. Field corn and calcium hydroxide, also known as masa harina—the stuff used in tamales.

What. The. Hell?

I called the lab and talked with my contact there.

"It's crazy, right?" David said. That from the guy who had seen it all.

"That doesn't begin to describe it. Are you sure there isn't a mistake?"

"Unless the sample you sent in was contaminated with clay or masa…or both." He paused. "Any chance of that?"

I thought back to Julia Suarez, the woman who had taken out Hairy with a rolling pin. She made pottery. It was possible there was some clay residue on the bottom of her shoes, but she hadn't stomped over the remains.

And there was no evidence she had made tamales that night. I certainly hadn't.

"I'm pretty sure the sample was clean." I sighed.

"Could be our first golem," David said, followed by a crunching noise. Probably potato chips.

"What?"

"Oh, come on. You've never heard of a golem? It's from Jewish folklore. A creature made from clay or mud. They're supposed to serve whoever created them, but sometimes, they get out of control. My grandmother used to read me this story about a golem when I was a kid, and my mom used to get really mad because it gave me nightmares."

I pressed a finger between my eyes, wishing this weird day would end. "What explains the masa harina, then?"

"No idea. On days like these, I'm glad I do what I do and not what you do." He paused. "But seriously, what if it *is* a golem?"

"The heat map says otherwise."

What I didn't say was, the heat map hadn't picked up any entities in Chavez Ravine, *ever*. But thanks to David's analysis, maybe I could find another explanation for the trouble we had been having.

Weirdness took a toll, and I was tired. Physically and mentally. It was starting to affect my thinking.

There had to be clues in Trini Duran's notebooks. Maybe whatever had brought those things into Chavez Ravine back then had returned to torture us anew.

Reading those journals had just become my top priority.

My phone went off, and the shot of adrenaline woke me back up. It was Ben Tomas saying my backyard was ready. He asked me to meet him so he could explain a few things. It was just the excuse I needed.

I could spend the evening reading Trini's diaries, preferably with some Chinese take-out and a glass of red wine. Things were looking up.

Minutes later, I was in my kitchen, the cat swirling around my legs and complaining loudly about how hungry he was. I set the tote bag down on the counter and opened a can of Salmon Delite. The kitchen immediately reeked of fish. I quickly opened a window above the sink, hoping by the time I was done meeting with Ben, the odor would be gone.

When I stepped into the backyard, Ben was fiddling with a pot of flowers. He greeted me with a shy smile. "What do you think?"

I had been so busy I hadn't even noticed the progress he and his crew had made. The transformation was astounding. What had been a barren patch of dirt was transformed into a lush garden paradise.

A gravel circle, bordered by ornamental grasses and wispy flowers in shades of red and purple, provided enough room for a cozy outdoor seating arrangement. Pavestones formed a pathway through a small garden filled with succulents. There was even an olive tree.

Ben pointed at the base of the hill. "We planted some Algerian ivy. It's very hardy and will help prevent erosion once it's grown in."

I spun around, trying to take it all in. Under my bedroom window was a row of fuchsia plants in a delicate shade of pink.

"It's amazing, Ben!" I said when I finally found my voice. "But I don't understand. I know you do people's front yards, but you can't do everyone's backyards too! That's...crazy!"

He shrugged, but he was pleased. "There's a special fund the board can use at its discretion. For legacy stakeholders. I'm not sure what happened with your family—Charlie didn't say— but it sounds like the board voted to fix up the front *and* back. They even agreed to paint your house too, inside and out."

Charlie hadn't said a word, and I was touched by his thoughtfulness. I was also surprised the board had agreed to spend the money. On *me*. Or maybe it was part of a scheme Charlie and Cora had hatched to soften me up before spilling whatever secrets they were keeping.

Ben tossed some gardening tools into a tin bucket. "You've got a state-of-the-art drip irrigation system that operates on a timer. Let me show you where the control box is and how it works."

The cat sat on the other side of the sliding glass door in the sunroom and watched us. He almost appeared to be frowning.

When Ben had gone, I went into the kitchen and poured myself a glass of wine. The overpowering smell of salmon still lingered in the air, so I reached for the jasmine candle on the kitchen table and lit it. Then, I stacked Trini Duran's notebooks on the table.

With the cool breeze drifting in from the open window and the soft light, it felt like too much effort to move into the living room. I decided to continue reading where I was, sitting in a straight-backed chair that would prevent me from dozing off.

I grabbed the first notebook and picked up where I had left off.

A few moments later, the cat strolled in and hopped inside the tote bag. His head popped up just above the canvas, and he stared at me.

"Weirdo," I muttered.

The cat was unfazed. He ducked his head, disappearing. Apparently, he planned to keep me company from inside the tote.

While I read through Trini's diary, it became clear she had faced more than just supernatural incidents in Chavez Ravine. She had a morale problem on her hands. More and more residents were accepting buyouts from the city and moving away. The bustling neighborhoods were thinning out.

Those who had remained struggled with their decision to stay and fight the evictions. Tensions were high, and hope dwindled. Arguments and conflicts erupted among neighbors grappling with their uncertain futures. Many of the people who had lived in Chavez Ravine rented their homes, so they had no recourse but to leave when their landlords sold their properties to the city.

Salvio Duran, Trini's father, was still too sick to work, so Trini ran the store during the day and helped protect the community at night, sometimes going out on patrol.

Lencha was always in the background of Trini's accounts. People seemed to have thought she could do something about the monster invasion, and at one point, she *was* able to protect her own house. Maybe she did ultimately figure out how to banish the things.

I had a lot of reading to do.

In the pages of the second notebook, Trini faced some awful-sounding creatures on her nighttime patrols, including a hairy beast and the long, thin creatures that jumped and shrieked. But she discovered some of them were pretty easy to beat under the right circumstances.

A clicking sound broke my concentration.

Before I could investigate, a furry head emerged from the tote, green eyes wide and dilated, ears flattened against his head. The cat hopped out of the bag and crouched low, tail flicking back and forth.

His nemesis, the large hummingbird, was back, hovering above the fuchsia plants outside the window.

There was plenty of space for the cat to crawl out of the open window and leap at the bird. The bird seemed to be focused on me, oblivious to the angry furball just a few feet away. But the cat did not attack. Instead, he rose on his hind legs, fur bristling, and let out a chattering sound.

"*Ek ek ek.*" At that moment, he really looked like a leopard. A very angry one.

If I were that hummingbird, I would have flown away. But it didn't.

The two were locked in a stalemate—the cat reluctant to attack, the bird determined to watch my every move.

A chill ran through me while I watched the interaction between cat and bird. Their behavior was not normal. *Should I do something to break up their weird stalemate?*

With a loud *pop*, the candle on the table exploded, its flame crackling and dancing upward. The heat emanating from it was surprisingly intense.

I jumped to my feet.

The cat moved closer to the open window, his fur standing on end. He hissed. The hummingbird shot higher into the air, eyes fixed on the flame as if mesmerized.

I needed to do something, like find a fire extinguisher. Vaguely, I remembered packing one. Was it still in a box somewhere? Why wasn't the smoke alarm going off?

The candle melted in its holder. Blobs of flaming wax began dropping to the table. Panic set in.

The notebooks were right under the flames.

I reached out to grab them, but the intense heat made me recoil. It was as if the blaze had a mind of its own, growing hotter with each passing second. If I didn't do something fast, Trini Duran's notebooks would go up in ash. I dashed to the cupboard, grabbed a pitcher, and filled it with water.

The water might ruin the notebooks. But wet pages could dry. Maybe.

I had to take the risk.

Water arced through the air, landing on the candle and the notebooks, but had little effect.

A commotion at the window made me turn. The cat was hanging out, attempting to swipe at the hummingbird.

Behind me, the fire snapped and popped. The notebooks were engulfed. And then, the flames disappeared.

A guttural scream erupted from my throat.

My body trembled, and I collapsed against the counter, unable to tear my eyes away from the blackened mess on the table. In the blink of an eye, I had lost Trini's diaries and all the secrets they contained.

Behind me, the cat hissed angrily. I looked out the window. The hummingbird was gone.

Chapter 22

I spent a few minutes staring at the mess on my kitchen table, then grabbed a dish rag and a bucket to start cleaning up.

A face appeared at the kitchen window.

I let out a small shriek.

"Sorry! So sorry! Didn't meant to scare you. I knocked on the front door, but no one answered. And then I smelled smoke, so I came to check on you. Are you okay?" The face belonged to my neighbor who ran the pottery shop, Julia Suarez.

I glanced at the burnt notebooks on the table. My heart sank even lower. "I'm fine. I guess. I'll meet you at the door."

When I opened the front door, the cat brushed against my legs. He looked up at Julia with big, questioning eyes.

"What happened?" Julia stepped over the cat. "Tell me!"

She was wearing faded blue jeans, gold loafers, and a long cotton tunic in red, purple, and gold stripes. A headband held back her auburn hair.

Julia pushed past me into the living room, looking around wildly, then strode into the kitchen and gasped. "Oh no! What happened in here?"

The cat sat on his haunches and gazed up at me, seemingly caught off guard by the bold intrusion.

I leaned down and whispered, "She's okay."

Two things about that struck me. First, I didn't know why I thought Julia was okay. I just had a gut feeling. She might have been nosy, but she had good intentions.

Second, why did I feel the need to explain that to a cat?

He trailed behind me while I followed Julia into the kitchen. Her gaze was fixed on the charred disaster on the table.

"What did that?" she asked, her voice a mix of curiosity and wariness.

I cleared my throat. "A candle." I struggled to find the right words to describe the unexplainable. "It just sort of…exploded."

"A candle!" She gasped. "A candle did this?"

I nodded.

"Wow. Good thing you were able to put it out, yeah?"

She turned and handed me a small package wrapped in brown paper and tied with a purple ribbon. "I wanted to give you this. As a thank you for helping me the other night. And as a little housewarming present—one legacy stakeholder to another."

I gave a little laugh when I accepted the bundle. "I don't think I helped you all that much, Julia. You and your rolling pin took care of business pretty well."

"I guess, but I'm really grateful you were there for me, and you were so kind afterwards. You didn't have to be, and I really appreciate it."

I turned the package in my hands. It was heavy for its size. "What's in here?"

Julia shook her head and smiled. "Go on. Please. Open it."

I wasn't really in a gift-opening mood. But Julia wasn't the sort one could easily refuse, so I carefully peeled back the paper.

I recognized the figurine immediately—it was the same one I had admired at Julia's shop in Palo Verde Plaza. It was a woman with strong, striking features and long hair cascading down her back, holding a molcajete against her hip. Her face was tilted to one side, as if someone had just called her name. A secretive smile played around her lips. Her dress was exquisitely crafted, giving the illusion of movement.

I studied the figurine from different angles. The expression seemed to shift ever so slightly. I wondered how Julia had captured such subtleties.

"She's…magical," I said.

Julia's face lit up with a beaming smile. "Yeah, I think she's really quite special too. I've had a few people make me offers, but they didn't have the right vibe. I just can't stand the idea of the wrong person owning her. And then I met you, and I knew right away that you had to have her because she was meant for you. I know that makes me sound crazy, but it's the truth. It was just a feeling I had to honor, yeah?"

I nodded, but I didn't know, not really. Still, I was happy to be holding the figurine in my hands. It might have been my imagination, but it almost began to tingle.

"Was there a model for this? Is she inspired by someone you know?"

The cat jumped on the counter and began batting around the purple ribbon.

Julia snatched up the ribbon and held it above the cat's head. He stared at it for a moment before meowing loudly and jumping off the counter.

I watched him strut out of the room with his tail held high, as if Julia had insulted him.

"He's a big boy," she said. "What's his name?"

"Not sure yet."

"He looks like he'd be named Goliath or Hercules or something."

I sighed. "I haven't gotten around to naming him. He just kind of…wandered in one day."

"Oh! He must belong to someone, then. Have you tried asking the neighbors?"

My fingers spasmed around the figurine. I hadn't tried very hard to find the cat's owner, and I didn't want to think about why.

"Yes, but nothing so far. So, did you? Have a model for the figurine?"

"Yeah, but not in the way you think. I was inspired by a photo I saw at an exhibit downtown. It was a picture of someone you know. Lencha Bantacorte."

Julia must have noticed my stricken expression.

"That's the thing about living here, Maddy. Everyone knows everything about everybody. Well, maybe not literally *everything*, but people talk. And if you're legacy, like we are, it's a very small world. Besides, you're related to Lencha Bantacorte! How cool is that?"

I absently stroked the figurine. It was slightly warm to the touch. "Who told you?"

Julia wrinkled her nose. "Can't remember, honestly. It could have been Ben Tomas. He's been working on the house next door to me, and I'm always trying to get his attention, if you know what I mean. But God, he's clueless, or he has a girlfriend, or he's not interested in girls. Hard to say. Or it could have been Stu Wells. I see him at the gym sometimes. You've met him, right? You being in security and all."

I was about to ask why Stu Wells would talk about me, but Julia was already answering the question.

"He asked me if I knew you." Julia gave an exaggerated wink.

My heart thumped. "He did?"

"Yeah, he did!" Julia replied in a sing-song voice. "He wanted to know"—she paused for dramatic effect—"if you were single. How about that?"

"I'm not sure if he's my type," I replied stiffly.

Julia tossed her hair and snorted. "You don't like hot rich guys? Even nice ones like Stu? At least, he *seems* nice, yeah? Friendly without hitting on every woman he meets. I actually think he's kind of shy and a little awkward. It's cute."

I coughed. "Shy? Are we talking about the same man? He comes off as overly confident to me. Even kinda smug."

Julia grimaced. "Oh no! Not at all! Maybe he's just trying to compensate because he has a crush on you or something."

"He's a millionaire, Julia," I pointed out. "He's the CEO of a company. A *major* company. It's highly unlikely that he would have a crush on someone like me. And besides, we're both too old for crushes."

"Well, that's ridiculous! No one's ever too old for a crush, and you're gorgeous! Hey, not to change the subject or anything, but can you give me a little tour? I've always been curious about this place, yeah?"

Maybe Julia didn't want to change the subject, but I sure did.

"C'mon!" I steered her through the kitchen and living room, ending in my bedroom.

Julia looked at the bare walls, the crappy dresser, and the discount store nightstand. Her forehead wrinkled. "Is this it? Is this all your stuff?"

"This is everything. I really need to go shopping, but I *hate* shopping. And to be honest, I have no idea where to go or what to get. I've never had to furnish a place this big before."

Julia's expression brightened. "Would you like some help? I do some interior decorating on the side. Mostly for friends of friends. And I get discounts at certain stores. So, what do you say?"

She was looking at me hopefully, like she was asking me to do her a big favor.

"I'd love that!" And I meant it.

With Julia, shopping might even be fun, especially knowing that, at the end, my place would actually have some personality.

I still had the figurine in my hand, and I studied it for a moment. "Now, where should I put this beauty?"

The little statue started to tingle again, and an idea popped into my head.

The sunroom.

Julia followed me to the back of the house and watched while I put the figurine on the workbench. When the little clay feet touched the wood, it vibrated in my hand. I wondered if Julia noticed, but she was too busy admiring the garden and gushing about Ben Tomas's skills.

The cat sauntered in and jumped up on the counter. For a moment, I worried he would bat the figurine with a paw and send her crashing to the floor. Instead, he simply padded past, giving her a wide berth, then curled into a ball in a corner where the bench met the wall, as if to keep watch over Julia's gift.

"This is where my grandmother did her curandera work. Lencha Bantacorte trained her, so it's fitting that Little Lencha stays here."

With a critical eye, Julia surveyed the room. The terracotta tile floor glowed in the late afternoon sun.

"Then let's make this room top priority, yeah? The way it opens out onto the garden, we can make it a great place to hang out and relax." Julia strode toward the rattan screens separating the sunroom from the living room. She forcefully yanked at the nearest one, sending it crashing onto the tiled floor. "Say goodbye to these things. They're hideous."

The second screen clattered to the floor.

The cat briefly looked up but then quickly closed his eyes, as if he couldn't care less about home decor.

Julia and I agreed to get together Saturday morning and hit the shops.

"This is going to be so much fun!" She shimmied out the front door toward her old Volvo station wagon on the curb.

I returned to the kitchen, my heart heavy. The gravity of losing Trini Duran's notebooks sank in while I swept the charred mess into a trash bag. Whatever secrets her journals had held were gone forever.

Ashes in hand, I went through the sunroom on my way out to the trash can. When I passed the workbench and Little Lencha, I could have sworn I saw a flicker of motion.

As if the little figure winked at me.

I put the bag down on the bench, picked up the figurine, and examined her strong face and long hair.

She had the same enigmatic smile, her head cocked to one side, but there was no motion, no winking.

Of course, there wasn't. Clay figurines didn't wink.

I put Lencha down and went back to the kitchen. More than anything, I needed that Chinese take-out and glass of red wine.

Chapter 23

I made it through the night without my phone buzzing, so I woke feeling rested and refreshed. Until I remembered what was on my agenda: a meeting with Stu Wells about the security cameras and a confrontation with the board president. The woman who had hired me. Who had stuck up for me when other board members objected. Who had made my new home a reality.

It had to be done, despite all that.

I spent a little extra time fussing over my hair and makeup, pretending it had nothing to do with Stu Wells allegedly having a crush on me. How the hell was I supposed to act like a normal adult woman around him, after what Julia mentioned?

It was like being in seventh grade all over again.

With my primping done, I pulled on black pants and a white shirt—professional and sensible attire, just to prove I wasn't trying to impress anyone.

At exactly 8:30, Stu Wells tapped on the door and strolled into my office with two steaming cups of coffee and a brown paper bag.

My office suddenly seemed smaller with him in it. The scent of pine filled the room, probably from whatever soap or shampoo he had used that morning.

"And how are you this morning?" he asked. He put the bag and a coffee on my desk, grabbed one of the security cameras from the box, took a screwdriver from his shirt pocket, and settled into a chair across from me.

I took a sip of my coffee, enjoying the bold dark roast with a splash of cream. Just how I liked it. Nice.

"I got us a treat." He nodded toward the bag and began unscrewing a panel on the side of the camera.

I used a napkin to pull out a round pastry from the bag and gasped. It was a concha, one of my favorite Mexican sweet breads. But these were unlike any I had seen before. Instead of the usual vanilla or chocolate toppings, they were decorated with marigold-colored crumbles and a sugar skull at the center. They were exquisite.

"Where did you get these?" I asked.

"Muertos Café. It's one of their specialties, but if you don't get there early, they run out. I got there when they opened."

I gave an appreciative sniff. Cinnamon. A hint of nutmeg. My stomach rumbled. I had skipped breakfast. There was enough decoration on the concha to guarantee a sugar high, but I broke off a piece and popped it into my mouth.

I tipped my head back and chewed. "Thank you," I said between bites. "These are…heavenly."

Stu glanced up and smiled, his eyes crinkling in the corners. "I'm glad you like them. I thought you would."

Then he was all business. He focused intently on the inner workings of the camera, his expression serious.

I had been distracted by the unexpected treat of coffee and pastries. Now, I admired Stu's appearance: his sharp blue suit, rolled up shirt sleeves, and strong, tanned arms. His hands were nice, with trimmed nails and no rough edges. Either he knew how to use a nail file, or he treated himself to manicures, something I could never afford.

When I finally tore my thoughts away from Stu's grooming habits, he had crossed his legs and removed the lens, resting the camera on one knee and frowning.

"Do you by any chance have tweezers?"

I had never recovered from the time I discovered a rogue hair sprouting from my neck, so yeah, I had tweezers. *Always* had tweezers. I dug them out of my work tote and handed them over.

Stu pinched something between the tweezer's tips and tugged. I knew what that something was because Holly had put it back the day before.

It was a strip of black tape.

He held it up in front of me with a triumphant smile. "Here's what's causing our problem, Maddy."

I did my best look of fake surprise, but I was really focused on something else.

Stu had just said "our" instead of "your." Plus, he had pronounced my name in a strangely intimate way, causing butterflies in my stomach. His forearms peeking out from those rolled-up shirt sleeves were strangely sexy.

"Tape. How about that."

Stu began checking the other lenses. "I think we can safely assume this is what we'll find on the other cameras too."

"Shouldn't that have triggered some sort of alert? That the cameras weren't working properly?"

Stu shook his head. "Good question, but no. The cameras were technically functioning, and they were still recording. If someone had cut any wires, then yes, it would have sent an alert. But the cameras themselves are working. The video they're recording is just black."

My face was on fire. I should have known that. Instead, Mister Expert had to explain it to little old me.

"Ah, of course," I said, as if that were something I had just temporarily forgotten.

Stu demolished his concha in several bites. He wiped his mouth and regarded me with serious eyes. "Well, they're fixed now. I wonder who did this and why."

He gently put the cameras back in the box.

"If I may ask, when you report back to the board, please don't mention my concerns about the developer. He's in tight with Charlie and Eileen, and there's a lot of work for us to do before we say anything publicly, if we ever do. Are you okay with that?"

"Sure," I said automatically.

But he had done it again. *Us.*

I was lightheaded, partly because he was saying he expected to work together and also because he had passed my test: he hadn't disabled the cameras. So who had?

Stu rose to his feet and grinned. "Well, that was easier than I expected. See you around?"

He didn't wait for an answer. In a flash, he was out the door, leaving me gripping the arms of my chair as though it would take off like a rocket.

Chapter 24

Walking into Cora Bernal's house was like stepping into a French impressionist painting. All the colors were bright and carefree, the pillows floral, floors covered in spongy cream carpeting. It was airy and spotless. Dappled light poured in through an open window overlooking a patio with potted palms. The whole place smelled good too, like vanilla-scented candles. I felt like I was going to float away.

The house seemed to be having a similar effect on Cora's cherubic grandson. The six-month-old gazed up at me through half-closed eyelids from his bouncy chair.

"It's his nap time, but I think I'll just leave him there." Cora tucked a blanket around his lap. "Let sleeping babies lie and all that."

The child gave a little snort, turned his head, and fell asleep.

At least he wouldn't be a distraction. Luck was on my side, so far.

Cora wore a pink sweater and magenta lipstick, and we faced each other in easy chairs covered in pale rose plush. I sat at the front edge of mine so I didn't sink in or get too comfortable.

"You look serious," Cora said. "I hope it's not bad news. Is it?"

I sighed. There was no use beating around the bush. "Not really, but I do have some questions for you, Cora. Serious questions. I think you didn't tell me the entire truth about what's been going on here. I think you knew, even before you contacted me about the job, that Chavez Ravine did not have an entity problem, but rather a…historical supernatural problem. Am I right about that?"

Cora looked down at her hands folded on her lap. "Charlie warned me. He said you'd figure it out, and when you did, you'd quit. And we'd be back where we started. Up a ravine without a paddle, as they say."

At least she hadn't tried to deny it. I could only hope she would be as forthcoming in the rest of our conversation. "Why try to hide it at all?"

Cora met my gaze and gave a grim laugh. "Because we're desperate, Maddy. The truth would make most people run. And I was worried that what we need is something you would be reluctant to provide."

Cora shifted in her chair.

"I understand how difficult it must be to have a mother like yours. But I fear her larger-than-life persona has discouraged you from embracing your family history and the…benefits…that come with that history."

That made me sit up straight. "What does my family history have to do with anything?"

Cora didn't hesitate. She leaned forward, hands pressed into her knees. "Everything, Madeline. That's why I wanted *you* for the job. You said we have a historical supernatural problem, and that's exactly right. Not just anyone can help us solve it. We need someone exceptional. We need a bruja with special skills. And Madeline, I know this is hard to hear, but I believe that's you. You're a Bantacorte, related to Lencha Bantacorte, who banished the original monsters of Chavez Ravine."

I was speechless.

"I'm sorry I wasn't entirely truthful with you, Madeline," Cora said in a quiet voice. "I just wanted to give you a little time to get settled in to your new job, to get to know our community a bit, to see how special it is, to feel your own connection to this place and these people, before we told you."

It was time to set the record straight. I just hoped it didn't mean losing my new job and jeopardizing my home in the process.

"I'm sorry, Cora," I said firmly. "I may be a descendant of Liliana, but Lencha is a distant relation. I'm no bruja. I'm the least magical person you'll ever meet. My mother may have special skills—that whole thing she has going on with entities is some weird psychic connection—but it's not magic."

Cora shook her head. "Now, that's where I disagree with you, Madeline. I know quite a bit about your mother. I know she feels the magic within her, but she's chosen to channel her energy into entities because that's what she's been called to do. And it's certainly been lucrative for her. But you're *not* her. Madeline, it's time for you to accept that you have Lencha's powers within you too."

Cora didn't seem to understand.

"Even if I did that, Cora, it's not like flipping a switch. It's not like I'm going to wake up tomorrow morning thinking, *Ooh, I'm feeling kind of magical today*, and then all our problems are solved. Lencha learned the old ways from her mother in Mexico. You know what I learned from my mother? How to order lunch at Mexican restaurants. And my mother loves talking about how we're special, but that's *all* she does. Talk. If she had something to teach me, she would have done it years ago, don't you think?"

Cora's eyes narrowed. "It sounds like there wasn't much opportunity for that. She was busy trying to escape an abusive relationship and protect her young daughter."

I deflated like a balloon. Cora wasn't wrong there.

My childhood had been chaotic. Things calmed down when we moved to the middle of nowhere in the desert, at least for a while. I escaped, went to college, and joined the Los Angeles Police Department.

When the entities started showing up and the city built the first entity refuge just down the road from my mother's place, she "activated," as she likes to call it. She walked straight into the center and asked if she could meet with one of the residents. I have no idea how she convinced the powers that be to let her inside, but it was the first "conversation" between a human and an entity.

"Cora, I didn't come here to talk about my mother, but I honestly don't think she'd be much help. She might make things worse." A thought bubbled up. "Wait a minute. Didn't you say Hernan Frias taught mystical studies or something? Maybe he knows something about brujeria."

Cora's head snapped back. A hand fluttered to her chest. "Hernan? I don't think so, Madeline. He's studied it, of course, but he's just an academic. He has no skills himself." She hesitated, then frowned. "He does go on about one of his ancestors who lived here in Bishop. Hernan says he was a brujo, but the records show he was a minor curandero. He sold some cures from the back of his liquor store, but they never worked. He never practiced brujeria.

The HOA president seemed to warm to her topic. Her eyes brightened while she talked about the old neighborhoods.

"There were very few true brujas in Chavez Ravine. In Palo Verde, a woman named Catalina Montez was quite powerful, but she died without children. And then there was Lencha, of course, and her niece Liliana. Hernan's ancestor was nowhere near that caliber. And speaking of Hernan, I'm not comfortable telling him about all this. Please trust me. Let's let this conversation stay between us."

That was the second time in twenty-four hours I had been asked to keep a secret from someone on the board. What was it with Chavez Ravine and its secrets?

I had no choice but to trust Cora if I wanted to keep my job and home. But I needed her to trust me too, enough to stop hiding things from me.

"Okay. Do you have any idea who was behind the original monsters that appeared in Chavez Ravine? There's got to be a connection between what was happening back then and what's going on now. If we figure that out, it will give me a starting point."

If I had left Trini Duran's notebooks in the library, where they belonged, I might have been able to find that out on my own.

The baby gave a little cry, then went quiet again. A delicious, savory aroma wafted in from the kitchen, and my stomach rumbled in response.

Cora got up, checked the baby, and rearranged his blanket. She began pacing in front of the door to the patio. "My mother said there was a man on the city council who was determined to go through with the city's eviction plans. I don't know if he had a financial interest or what, but he became very angry when the residents of Chavez Ravine had the nerve to resist. My mother believed he became so angry that he conjured the monsters to scare the residents out—"

"Are you saying he was some kind of witch?" I interrupted. "On the city council?"

Cora nodded. "That's *exactly* what I'm saying. He was originally from Scotland or Ireland or someplace." She sniffed. "He was very powerful and wasn't above using dark magic to get his way. Others on the city council shared his views, though they probably didn't know what he was doing. Lots of people in those days were prejudiced against Mexicans. They didn't care that the people who they were kicking out were Americans too. And taxpayers. To them, they were just a bunch of Mexicans."

It would have been easy enough to find out about the city councilman online or, failing that, at the library downtown. "He's got to be dead by now," I mused. "Unless he was…immortal?"

Cora's eyes snapped open. "That's impossible!"

I shrugged. "Not that long ago, the world thought trolls and ghosts in cowboy hats were impossible too, and yet, here we are."

"I would have heard something about it if he was still alive," Cora said faintly.

I wondered how she would know that unless he lived in Chavez Ravine. Cora was a big fish in a small, gated pond, and I didn't think she had much influence beyond the community's guardhouses.

"Let's hope we're not dealing with an immortal witch," I replied.

Cora sighed heavily. "Madeline, I've told you everything. So now it's your turn. Please tell me you'll start developing the powers you were born with. Please put yourself on the path to brujeria while you try to figure things out. Will you do that? We *need* you to do that."

She made it sound so easy. It was my turn to sigh.

"Cora, I wouldn't know where to start."

Cora sat back in her chair and stared at the ceiling. "I see. So, if you're not going to develop your skills, how are you going to keep this community safe? What's your plan?"

"I need to find out who's been conjuring the creatures and why. That should give me some ideas about how to stop them." I hesitated, but the rest had to be said too. "Cora, we've lost some valuable time here. I hope that from here on out, you'll tell me everything you know. Even things you just suspect."

Cora looked like a chastened schoolgirl. I didn't think I had been that harsh, but maybe she wasn't used to people being so straightforward.

"Of course, Madeline. Of course." She hurried over to her grandson and fussed over him, her back to me. When she turned around, she had regained her composure. "I'm heating up some tamales. Why don't you join me for a quick bite before you go."

I grinned. "You don't have to ask me twice. I love tamales."

We left the baby asleep in his bouncy chair and went into the kitchen. The tile floors and wood cabinets were beige, but the room had a festive red chili motif, from string lights to pepper garlands and wreaths. There was even a cow skull painted turquoise and decorated with red chilis. I wondered what the rest of the house looked like and whether Cora had stuffed all the personality in the kitchen.

Cora lifted the lid off a tall stainless pot, releasing a cloud of steam into the air. She grabbed a pair of tongs. "Pork or jalapeno and cheese?" When she noticed my expression, she laughed. "Or both?"

"Both, please!"

When Cora set the plate in front of me, my mouth watered. "Sauce? Cheese?"

I swallowed so I wouldn't drool all over her hand. "Yes, please."

The red sauce was smoky and creamy. Combined with the salty crumbles of cotija cheese, the first bite of pork tamale was savory heaven. I finished the rest like I was trying to set some kind of speed-eating record.

Cora returned to the stove and waved the tongs in the air. "There are more if you want them!" She flashed me a mischievous grin.

I rubbed my stomach and let out a groan. "As much as I'd love to, if I eat any more, I'll slip into a food coma."

Cora chuckled. "You definitely have to come over for dinner sometime so I can make you one of my famous margaritas. People say they're even better than my tamales."

I scanned the kitchen with fresh eyes. It wasn't just spacious; it was equipped in a way that hinted at the owner's expertise. Pots and pans of all shapes and sizes dangled from racks above the expansive island in the center. A bowl of salt was in easy reach of the stove, and glass jars filled with spices lined the shelves, each labeled with bold handwritten text.

But when she mentioned the margaritas, it hit me like a bolt of spicy, delicious lightning.

"Oh my god! You're *that* Cora!"

She let out a hearty laugh. "I thought you knew."

Cora Bernal wasn't just president of the Chavez Ravine Association; she was also the founder of the biggest tamale empire in Los Angeles. Her authentic, gourmet tamales were sold in restaurants, in stores, at the airports...everywhere hungry Angelinos might gather. Which explained—legacy status aside—how she could afford such a beautiful home in Bishop.

Everyone knew her story. She had started with a small restaurant specializing in tamales and margaritas and, over time, had built it into one of the most renowned family-owned restaurant chains in all of California.

I was seeing Cora in a whole new light. While I had always respected her, I had vastly underestimated the woman. I had assumed she had married into money, but she was the genius behind a wildly successful business, and I was embarrassed by my assumptions.

Cora must have noticed the shift in my expression because she raised an eyebrow.

She opened her mouth to say something, when a loud noise from the living room startled us both. I leapt up and raced toward the source, with Cora close behind.

We entered the living room, and I spotted the culprit.

A large hummingbird floated in the air, its iridescent feathers shimmering in the soft light. It appeared to be the same one that had showed up at my house the evening the candle fire destroyed Trini Duran's journals.

"Not that darn bird again!" Cora picked up her crying grandson.

A porcelain vase lay in pieces on the floor.

The hummingbird began moving frantically, staring at us with—and though it was impossible—an insolent gaze bordering on downright hostility. How a hummingbird could have such an expressive face, I had no idea.

And then, his wings a blur of movement, he darted out through the patio doors and disappeared.

I turned to Cora, who was staring outside, the baby pressed against her chest.

"Frequent visitor?"

Cora's gaze remained fixed on the patio doors, a furrow forming between her brows. She shook her head slightly before turning to me with a forced smile. "I know this is going to sound a bit crazy, but I don't like that bird. There's something off about him, the way he shows up when he does. It's almost like he's…watching me."

I knew the feeling.

Cora kissed the top of the baby's head. "I don't know about you, but I can use a cafecito."

"Definitely," I replied.

The hummingbird was one more piece of the mystery I needed to solve. And like all mysteries, it was going to take some serious coffee to figure it out.

Chapter 25

When my phone went off in the middle of the night, it startled me and the cat. He leapt into the air, landed on my stomach, jumped to the nightstand, and knocked over a glass of water. I cursed and quickly answered.

Ron Mendez was on duty at the Bishop gate and had received a call from Katherine Morris. He couldn't give me any details because she had been hysterical, but she had said something about creepy guys jumping in her backyard.

I promised to meet him there.

"Don't approach them alone," I warned.

"I won't. I've already called for backup."

That was going to be tough. We were short-staffed that night, down to two guards. I could have hired some temps but had decided against it. Didn't want to blow the budget on my first month into the job.

I threw on some clothes. When I went into the sunroom to fetch my sneakers, the cat was sitting by the sliding glass door, perfectly still, staring into the backyard. I followed his gaze.

A flash of white near the base of the hill...

My heart bumped in my chest.

The cat howled.

Something was standing behind a palm tree. A tall figure peering around the trunk. Glittering red eyes...

Ben Tomas, master landscaper, had ripped out the dingy backyard lights but hadn't installed the new fixtures yet, so I ran to the kitchen and grabbed a flashlight. When I returned, the cat was standing on his hind legs, hissing, fur puffed out.

I pointed the flashlight at the tree and flicked it on.

Reading about Dog Face Bride was one thing. Seeing it was a lot scarier.

I was accustomed to all sorts of entities, but this thing got to me. For one, it was menacing. Its teeth were long and sharp, and it seemed to be grinning, as if relishing the violence it was about to inflict. Despite the frilly, tattered dress it was wearing, it could rip my face off if given half a chance.

And yet, it didn't move. It stared at me, lips curling into a snarl. Nothing was audible through the glass, but I could imagine it growling.

I had to get to Katherine Morris's house, but leaving that creature in my backyard seemed wrong. It might try to attack me on my way to the Jeep, or it might try to get into my house and hurt the cat. The cat was tough, but he wouldn't stand a chance against a monster dog.

Ideally, I would call for backup, but everyone was needed at Katherine's house.

Which left me with limited options. I grabbed my baton and my entity smoke pouch and slipped out through the side door. Hoping to catch the creature off guard for a brief but crucial advantage, I crept around to the backyard.

But when I rounded the corner, the Dog Face Bride had moved to the middle of the yard and was lowered into a crouch—an attack position.

The cat frantically scratched at the window in warning.

"I see it," I shouted, flicking on my flashlight.

Whether it was the sudden flood of light or my loud voice, Dog Face seemed startled. It paused long enough for me to throw the pouch to the ground and stomp on it, releasing a burst of purple dust into the air.

Dog Face didn't fall in a heap like an entity would have, but it stumbled around and coughed, giving me enough time to run in and clobber it with my baton. It fell to the ground, but I wasn't taking any chances. I swung my baton once more.

That just made it mad.

It scrambled toward me on all fours, lunging at my ankles. Sharp teeth tore through my jeans but missed my flesh. With a rush of adrenaline, I kicked it in the face, the tip of my boot connecting with its forehead. The creature let out a yelp and fell to the ground. It rolled onto all fours and scurried away up the hill, whimpering as it went.

That was good enough for me.

I ran to my car and sped toward Katherine Morris's place in Palo Verde. There were a couple of guard vehicles parked outside. The house was mostly dark except for a single light glowing from a window in the back. Whatever was happening had not attracted the attention of the neighbors.

Yet.

I moved between the houses, using the dense vegetation for cover. My heart raced while I made my way to the Morris's backyard. The side gate was wide open, so I walked through and braced myself.

It was dark, but in the glow from the garden's path lights, I could see what was going on.

Tall, pale figures jumped straight into the air. There were five of them—all the same humanoid shape, with impossibly long limbs and small heads. They looked more substantial than ghosts and much stranger.

The figures soared high into the air, as if spring-loaded, each leap taking them closer to a large window where Katherine

Morris stood, hands cupping her face in a parody of horror. She gaped at the jumpers.

Crouched behind a stone wall near the deck were Ron and the other guard. I dashed toward them.

The creatures didn't seem to notice me. They kept up their silent jumping, making no noise, even when their feet touched the ground, which just added to their creepiness.

When I squeezed in next to Ron, his body gave a violent twitch.

"Hey, calm down. Didn't mean to startle you."

"What should we do?" he hissed.

That was a great question. I had left my purple entity pouch at home in the backyard. It wouldn't have done us any good anyway. It needed refilling, and I hadn't yet figured out how I was going to come by the purple stuff, now that I was no longer with the PD.

The eerie figures continued their unnatural, rhythmic jumping, slowly drawing closer to the window. Katherine Morris stood frozen in fear. My mind raced, trying to come up with a plan.

I remembered Trini Duran's journals and how she had found some of the monsters easy to beat.

"Katherine looks hypnotized…or something," Ron said in a low voice.

That was worrisome. I needed to do something quick.

"We need to distract them," I whispered to Ron. "Get them away from the house."

Ron blinked. "Like, yell at them or something? Have them chase *us*?"

He and the other guard huddled together, their faces pale. When they had landed their cushy security jobs in Chavez

Ravine, they probably never imagined they would have a night like this.

I scanned the backyard, looking for inspiration. My eyes landed on a garden hose neatly coiled on the ground. I hoped Trini was right and these things would be easy to take out.

"Ron, you're with me. We'll use that." I pointed at the hose, then turned to the other guard. "You get into the house and take Katherine out through the front door. Carry her if you have to. If you can't make it outside, there's a panic room off the kitchen. Lock yourselves inside."

He looked at me with a grateful expression, then ran to the front of the house.

I gathered some rocks bordering a pathway. Ron crossed himself before picking up the hose, then bent over the faucet sticking out of the stone wall.

"Ready?" he whispered.

"As I'll ever be. Go!"

My voice caught the attention of one of the jumpers. It stopped halfway up its trajectory, its small head swiveling on its skinny neck until it found the source—*me*. Frozen in the air, it tipped its head back and let out a piercing shriek, making my blood run cold.

Ron turned on the faucet full blast and aimed the hose at the leaping figures.

The spray of water had an immediate effect. The figures seemed to lose all coordination while they tried to evade the liquid assault.

I started throwing rocks, aiming for their little heads but happy to connect anywhere.

Next to me, Ron had adopted the wide stance of an action hero on a movie poster. I would have gotten the giggles under different circumstances.

The jumpers' eerie shrieks drowned out the rushing of water from the hose and Ron's triumphant cries. Behind the window on the second floor, the face of the guard momentarily appeared next to a startled Katherine Morris, and then both vanished from view.

The watery onslaught and my rocks took a toll on the ghostly figures. They began twisting wildly, shrinking and fading away. Their cries became distant. From nowhere, a mist appeared and surrounded them. After a few moments, they disappeared in a swirl of vapor.

The thin cloud rose high above the trees and drifted to the west.

Chapter 26

The midnight shenanigans at Katherine Morris's dragged into the wee hours because, as she came out of her terrified trance, she had questions.

She assumed she had experienced an encounter with entities, and I didn't try to correct her. It was better to let her believe it than to explain Chavez Ravine was plagued by a different breed of supernatural nuisances. Ones that confounded the new chief of security.

We took Katherine to my office to calm down. She refused to go back into her house and called a friend to ask if she could stay over until her husband returned from his business trip. That didn't bode well. The board wouldn't be happy about an owner being too frightened to stay in her expensive home, but it was beyond my control.

I was able to sneak a call to Cora while Katherine cried and drank hot chocolate. Cora, of course, was horrified by this latest turn of events but seemed pleased enough with how I had handled things.

Ron checked the logs and said some residents had called the non-emergency number to report white lights floating around Phantom's Pass.

"Near the gully?" I asked.

Ron nodded.

Katherine Morris's home was just two doors north of the gully. I was pretty sure those lights were the jumpers making their way toward her house. But why? What was so special about Katherine Morris that Hairy and the jumpers all targeted her?

It wasn't like the old days, when a witch on the city council tried to scare the Mexican American families into leaving. Katherine and her husband weren't Mexican. They weren't legacy stakeholders. The Morrises had paid for their house and had been approved by the Chavez Ravine Association.

And yet, the supernatural pests seemed to be similar to the ones Trini described in her journals all those years ago.

Cora had said Lencha Bantacorte used magic to send the creatures back to wherever they came from. So why were they back? Did Lencha's protective spell wear off?

There was no way of knowing, but that didn't stop me from mulling it over until I eventually fell asleep.

I awoke at nine o'clock. The cat slept in too. It took three cups of coffee to fortify me enough to open a can of food. I opted for the least pungent choice: chicken. The cat devoured it quickly, then guzzled down water like he had just been rescued from the desert. Sated, he strode to the sunroom and began meowing loudly. I followed.

Like a good guard cat, he was pacing in front of the sliding glass door. I scanned the backyard for any sign of Dog Face Bride. There was nothing. I could only hope I had done enough damage to make it disappear for good.

The cat rammed his head into my leg.

"Dude, you have a litter box." I sighed and slid open the door.

The cat dashed outside and disappeared behind the palm tree. I wasn't too happy with that. It was where Dog Face Bride had hidden. But all was fine. The cat raced back into the house, then jumped onto the workbench. He and Little Lencha gazed at me with unblinking eyes.

There was something unnerving about the statuette. No matter where I stood in the room, Lencha's eyes seemed to follow, almost like she was trying to catch my attention. From what little I had learned about her in Trini's notebooks, Lencha was probably dying to tell me what an idiot I was for letting the journals burn.

Getting ready for the day was a struggle. The shampoo refused to come out of the bottle, forcing me to use all my might to squeeze it out. The handle of my razor snapped off. I ran out of my favorite face cream, the one promising to fill my wrinkles, so I had to resort to my backup lotion, which left my face feeling oily.

After multiple tries, I managed to achieve a straight line with my eyeliner, but the result still didn't look quite right. The combination of dark circles under my eyes and even darker eyeliner made me look hard, like I was posing for a mugshot. I dabbed on some concealer, but it refused to blend in, leaving me looking like a raccoon, so I rubbed it off.

While I didn't consider myself particularly vain, I never went anywhere without makeup. It was like my armor, protecting me from the world. And I never forgot my earrings. Without them, I felt naked. This daily ritual was important to me.

When I got to the office, I checked under my chair for a hex bag. Then I glanced under my desk and a couple of other spots where one might be hiding. A thought occurred to me: maybe whoever had planted the hex bags was the same person who conjured the monsters. It was unlikely there were two people conjuring and hexing. One made more sense. And that simplified things—we would only need to find *one* suspect to solve *both* problems. But how were they related?

I made myself another cup of coffee and viewed the camera feeds to see if I could find the glowing lights people had reported witnessing. It took a while, but I eventually spotted them. They were definitely the Jumpers. From the second story of a house, their heads would look like blobs of light. Lanterns maybe.

I tried to find them emerging from the gully, curious whether they had headed straight for Katherine Morris's house or had wandered around a bit first. That would tell me something interesting. Were they targeting Katherine? Or was it all just a wild coincidence?

Entities didn't decide where they appeared. There wasn't a mastermind orchestrating their emergence into our world. Or at least, that's what my mother had determined after her interviews with them. Was it the same with these things?

My phone rang. It was Cora Bernal, breathless.

"Madeline, we have a meeting with the board at eleven. Things are moving faster than I'd like and in a direction that makes me uncomfortable, but it has to come to a vote. As president of the board, I only have one vote, but I want you to know in advance that I stand behind you."

My stomach dropped. What the hell was she talking about?

"What's happening, Cora?" My voice was faint, like it was coming from the far end of a tunnel.

"I apologize, Madeline," she said, her voice filled with regret. "This meeting won't be fun. But we'll get through it, I promise. Just be prepared."

And with that, she hung up.

Chapter 27

My head pounded, my stomach was unsettled, and I struggled to catch my breath while I walked into the HOA conference room. Maybe it was the lack of sleep, too much coffee, or anxiety over what was about to happen. Likely a mix of all three.

I glanced around at the five board members seated at the table. It took all my energy to appear calm.

Cora gave me a warm, reassuring smile, but she kept shifting in her chair. Charlie made do with a nod. His eyes were kind but worried. Both sat together on one side of the table.

A chill came from Eileen Simpson and Dan Berman on the other. Their faces were tense and pinched.

"Good morning, everyone," I said in my best cool, pleasant tone.

Eileen had gone extra heavy with the black eyeliner. Her knotted necklace looked like chainmail. She let out a dismissive laugh. "There's nothing good about it, thanks to you."

My toes curled. I folded my hands on the table. "Thanks to me how, exactly?" My voice was louder than I intended.

Eileen threw her hands into the air. "For failing to secure our community and allowing Katherine Morris's residence to be attacked! For a *second* time! You should have anticipated this and planned accordingly, but instead you took no—"

"Proactive measures," Dan Berman interrupted. A few strands of long gray hair escaped his ponytail and curled around his long face.

"Exactly!" Eileen's bejeweled hand slapped the table. "As far as we can tell from the meager reports you've provided us, you did nothing. And now Katherine Morris is all over social media, talking about those awful things that tried to get into her house and saying Chavez Ravine has an entity problem that we've been trying to cover up. And this morning, Katherine's husband called and asked me to list their house."

Charlie pinched the bridge of his nose. "It's not all bad then, Eileen. You'll make a fortune from that commission."

"That's not funny, Charlie," Eileen snapped. "If people start moving because they're afraid to live here, that's not good for any of us. It spells disaster for our community *and* our property values. Oh, and let's talk about disclosures. The Morris's will have to disclose that they've been plagued by entities, which means every real estate agent in Southern California will know."

"That's all we need," Dan said. "We'll end up like Los Feliz. No one wants to live there."

So that's what Cora had been trying to warn me about, in her not-very-specific way. I had been on the job for less than a week, and I was being attacked for not having accomplished a year's worth of work. While I had felt weird vibes from Eileen Simpson, I never thought she would be so unreasonable. Or so...unhinged.

I cleared my throat. "May I point out that I have personally responded to every emergency call, regardless of the hour, and that both times at the Morris home, we dispatched the threats? There was nothing to suggest, after the first incident, that Katherine Morris was at any particular risk for a second attack. As you well know, we're neither budgeted nor staffed for round-the-clock patrols at any one residence.

"These occurrences—or whatever they are—are brand new, and it will take time to understand them and contain them. It took years for Occult Affairs to develop a plan of action to deal with entities, and it's still far from foolproof. Their system is in no way preventative. It's reactive because there is no predicting what will emerge next or where. I think we can do better, but it will take time. And money."

Hernan appeared to have had even less sleep than I got the night before. His skin was gray, the dark circles under his eyes pronounced. His gaze bore into me. "I'm sorry, Maddy, but we need solutions. As I told Cora, these things are entities. We hired an entity expert, and the results are disappointing so far."

"Very disappointing!" Eileen said in a sing-song voice.

I resisted the urge to smack her, but man, it was hard. Cora gave my elbow a gentle squeeze, and I took a few deep breaths to calm myself before responding.

"I still don't understand what you expected, given the very short time I've been here." The next words were out of my mouth before I could stop them. "Nobody could have prevented what happened at the Morris house."

Well, that wasn't so smart. I knew what was coming next.

Eileen wagged a finger at me. "Oh, I don't think *that's* true. We wouldn't be here if some people on this board had listened to me and hired Stu Wells, like I'd wanted."

I had teed it up perfectly.

"Eileen!" Cora gasped. "That is not productive."

"It's downright mean," Charlie chimed in. "And inaccurate."

Eileen tapped her fingernails on the table. The bright red nail polish caught my attention. Was the color a coincidence or a hint she was out for blood?

"Stu Wells is neither here nor there, as we've already voted to go down this difficult path. Cora, as board president, please explain what this means for…" Eileen's voice trailed off.

Either she had forgotten my name or didn't want to say it out loud. Whichever, it didn't feel great.

All eyes were fixed on Cora, including mine. My stomach fluttered while I waited for her to say something. She simply stared down at a manila folder, her mouth set in a grim line.

"I will say, I would have preferred to avoid this." Cora let out a heavy sigh. "But it came to a vote and passed three to two." She pulled out a piece of paper and slid it toward me. "Madeline, this is a performance improvement plan. It outlines specific goals you must achieve. It allows you thirty days to achieve those goals. Failure to meet them will result in your termination."

I stared at the paper like it was a viper about to strike. A performance improvement plan. A PIP. Like I was some kind of screwup. It was insulting. Humiliating.

Would they actually fire me a few weeks after I started? I had never been put on a PIP, but I had seen them. This one was suspiciously short. I picked it up and gave it a quick scan.

It was short because it was laughable.

"Did you have a lawyer look at this?" I asked.

Eileen, Dan, and Hernan exchanged uneasy glances. Eileen lifted her chin.

"We didn't need to. We downloaded a template."

Well, they had gotten what they paid for. I snatched a pen from a decorative bowl on the table and scribbled my signature.

"There. I signed it. But I'll be honest, it feels like a setup."

Eileen's eyes narrowed. "What's that supposed to mean?"

"It means there's no mention of any training or resources or support to help me be successful," I said. "And just a reminder, I'm still in my probationary period. This...document...isn't even necessary."

Hernan's expression was dark. "We want you to understand the depth of our concern, Miss Bantacorte."

That made me sit up straight. "Madrigal," I corrected. "My name is Madrigal."

"Is it? My apologies, Miss...Madrigal," Hernan replied.

His gaze shifted toward Cora who, I have to say, looked pleased I was pushing back.

I crossed my arms in front of my chest. "Without the support of the board—and by that I mean considering any proposals I might have for beefing up the staff and investing in equipment—anyone in this position is doomed. Unless they're magic."

That sent Hernan into a coughing fit. Dan quickly refilled his water glass and patted his back.

"I'm sure Madeline will take all of this *very* seriously." Charlie's casual tone, combined with the smirk on his face, made it clear he didn't take it seriously at all.

His attitude seemed to infuriate Eileen.

"Charlie Perez, we would appreciate it if you wouldn't undermine our actions here this morning. In response to the alarming events in Palo Verde last night, we need to communicate to our membership that the board is taking these threats very seriously, and we need to have something in place that shows just how serious we are."

So that explained the PIP. It was pro-forma. Something the board could whip out and wave around during a meeting to show just how committed they were.

But maybe not only that. Maybe they also wanted someone to blame if things took a dark turn.

"I'm sure Madeline has a lot to do today," Cora said. "So why don't we let her get on with it?"

In the lobby, Caitlin stared intently at her computer screen while I walked by. So, she knew. Of course she did. She had probably printed out the form and filled in the blanks. I hurried past her, my face a mask.

Outside, the sun shone brightly, and the birds chirped loudly—a stark contrast to the gloomy tone of the meeting.

I was halfway to my office when Charlie Perez caught up with me.

"Hey, Maddy. Just between you and me? Back there, that was all board politics, and you just happened to get caught up in it. Keep your focus on the job, and everything will work out."

His kind words unleashed something inside me, and I felt like crying. It might have been board politics, but it seemed personal. An attack that questioned my skills and professionalism.

No. For me, it was more than that.

For normal people, a job was just something they did for money, a means to an end. Most people—*smarter* people—did not allow their jobs to become their lives. Not me. My job *was* my life. That stupid PIP hurt me all the way to my core.

I gave a strangled laugh. "That's all I've been doing since I got here, Charlie. Focusing on the job. And look where that's got me. A damn PIP."

"Don't let that get in your head, Maddy. We hired you for a reason. Just focus on that."

"If you're about to give me the embrace-your-magic talk, please spare me."

Charlie rubbed his hands together. "Oh man. If I had a lineage like yours, I'd be doing whatever I could to become the most powerful brujo in all of Chavez Ravine. Then nobody could mess with me."

"If I could transfer it to you, I would. Because I sure as heck don't know what to do with my so-called lineage."

Charlie lifted his eyebrows. "Seems to me that would be easy enough to find out. It's a simple call to your mother, the famous Malena Bantacorte."

Now that was a laugh. There was nothing simple about my mother.

"I'd better get back." Charlie patted my arm. "Hernan has added another item to the agenda, and it's going to be a doozy."

I rushed to my office, a flood of emotions threatening to overwhelm me. Once inside, I locked the door and burst into tears.

Chapter 28

After such a terrible morning, I decided to treat myself to lunch. I wanted something quick and casual, so I drove to Muertos Café. It was mostly known for its breakfasts and pastries, but it served lunch too. I got there at two thirty, just before closing time.

At the counter, I ordered tomato bisque and a grilled cheese sandwich, then found a small table in the shaded courtyard.

The next day was Saturday, my shopping day with Julia Suarez, which I had been looking forward to. But after the morning I had, I wondered if I should cancel. I had planned on loading up my credit cards, but if I lost my job, how would I pay the bills? Cora and Charlie were on my side, but it was two against three. If Eileen, Hernan, and Dan wanted me gone in a month, there wouldn't be much Cora and Charlie could do to save me.

If worse came to worst, I could always get my old job back at Occult Affairs. Maybe even try for a position in the command center with Jo. Working at Occult Affairs was not the best option, but it provided a steady income, and getting rehired was a sure bet, due to the unit's high turnover.

With my legacy stakeholder status, I was pretty sure I could make an argument for keeping the house.

Of course, some things would change. Almost certainly, I would have to pay HOA dues. Those were calculated by some formula having to do with the location of the property and the square footage of the house. Could I even afford it? Chavez Ravine was an exclusive community. The fees could be astronomical. And what about all the landscaping Ben Tomas had done? Would the board try to charge me for that?

I was so preoccupied I didn't even notice the server putting plates in front of me. One moment, the table was empty. The next, I was breathing in the delicious aroma of basil and toasted bread. I turned around in my seat and waved at the server while he went back into the restaurant. He smiled and gave me a thumbs-up.

Muertos elevated the basic lunch combo of soup and a sandwich to a whole new level. The tomato bisque was tangy, the grilled cheese filled with gooey gouda and brie. The bread was fresh and herby. It was enough to make me forget my fears of a meltdown in my personal economy, at least for a few moments.

The restaurant door opened. I glanced up, expecting the server and craving a cafecito to get me through the afternoon. But it was Stu Wells who greeted me. My heart sank. I needed my full faculties and a good night's sleep to get through a conversation with him, and at the moment, I had neither.

I looked him over despite myself. He was wearing shorts and a blue T-shirt. His hair was damp and stuck to his forehead. He had nice, muscular legs, and I tried not to stare when he sat down across from me.

"I stopped by your office to see how you're doing," he began. "But you weren't there, so I'm glad to have found you here."

"I'm fine," I lied.

Then his tone sank in. Or maybe it was the choice of words. Why would Stu feel the need to check on me? *Dammit.*

It had probably been Caitlin. The two seemed awfully cozy. She had probably messaged him the second I left the building.

Stu raised his eyebrows. "I'm glad to hear that. Personally, I think it was over the top. Hell, you discovered the broken cameras in your first couple of days. You're obviously on top of things. But hey, good for you for taking this morning's meeting so well."

I forced a laugh. "Wow. You must be really tight with Caitlin. Or maybe Eileen told you?"

Stu's mouth opened and closed. He stared at me for a long moment, his blue eyes suddenly solemn. "Uh, no. The board minutes went out. It's all in there, along with your report explaining last night's incident."

"The board minutes?" I echoed.

Dear God. My performance improvement plan was included in the board minutes for the entire community to read?

Stu recrossed his legs and cleared his throat. "Yes. They go out pretty fast. They have some new transcription service. All they need to do is check it for accuracy, and then boom, Dan blasts it out."

"Oh hell." That was all I could say. I felt like I had just been sucker punched.

"I'll be right back." Stu disappeared inside.

I grabbed my phone and checked my email. There it was. The Chavez Ravine Association Board Minutes.

In a closed executive session, the board placed an employee of CRA on a performance improvement plan to address concerns about a failure of security measures that resulted in the aforementioned incident on Reposa Street in Palo Verde. The disciplinary action was taken on a vote of three in favor, two opposed.

The week before, the HOA had announced me as the new chief of security. The minutes didn't actually name me, but who else would they place on a PIP? Anyone who was paying attention could figure it out.

My head seemed like it was filled with helium. This didn't actually change anything, but it did show that a majority of the board had lost confidence in me to carry out my duties. The residents hardly knew me. What would their reaction be when they read that? Would they demand my resignation? I could be out of a job even faster than I thought.

Stu returned holding two small glasses. He slid one in front of me. I stared blankly at the golden liquid.

"What's this?"

"Reposado tequila," Stu said. "It looks like you could use this."

"It's not even five o'clock," I protested.

"You were up all night," he said with a sigh. "Drink that, go home, drink some more, and get some rest. And for whatever it's worth, I plan on having a little chat with Eileen. I have a feeling she had something to do with this. She can be a little overzealous." He let out a bitter laugh. "Eileen's really something."

I sipped the reposado. Its heat slid down my throat. I preferred wine, but the smooth, mellow tequila, with hints of oak and honey, was nice too, so I sipped some more.

"What do you plan on saying to Eileen?"

"The obvious," he replied, recrossing his legs. "I will tell her that you are a highly skilled professional who deserves the respect and support of the board without an onerous power play looming over your head. I will strongly recommend that they revoke it." He drank his tequila down in one shot. "Unless you think it's none of my business or that I am being too…intrusive."

It certainly couldn't hurt, but I was puzzled why he would bother. We hardly knew each other.

Was this his way of saying I needed to be rescued? Big, powerful Stu Wells helping a floundering newbie, using his important connections to calm the troubled waters? It made my jaw go tight. Despite the soothing effects of the tequila, I couldn't help but bristle at the idea.

"No, no," I said coolly. "Do whatever you think is best."

"Well, I should get going." He stood, looking a bit awkward. "If you need anything, just let me know."

Stu nodded once and left Muertos café, leaving me on the patio. I had never felt more alone or isolated.

Chapter 29

I was soaking in the bathtub, drinking a glass of red wine, when Julia Suarez messaged to confirm our shopping trip the next morning.

Pick you up at 9, I replied.

The cat was perched on the counter, observing my every move. I flicked a little water his way, and with a quick swipe of his paw, he knocked a lipstick tube onto the floor.

"Hey!" I cried.

He glared back at me and held his paw above a very expensive contour stick.

"Don't you even think about it," I warned him.

His paw lowered. *Splash me again, human, and see what happens.*

I sipped my wine and sighed. "Okay, I promise. I won't do it again."

After a few moments, the cat made himself comfortable atop a new hand towel.

Half an hour later, Julia messaged again.

Just read board minutes. WTF! So stoooopid. Talk tomorrow.

Great. I had hoped to have a nice, drama-free day focused on furniture and clothes, but now, Julia was going to want a blow-by-blow of the humiliating meeting. Shopping trip ruined before it even started.

My peaceful bath was interrupted by a loud knock at the door. I gritted my teeth, hoping whoever it was would leave. But the knocking persisted, growing louder and more urgent. I quickly dried off and wrapped myself in a robe before going to answer it.

It was my neighbor, Leo, the lawyer with the black hair and striking silver streak, looking slick in a white button-down shirt and pinstriped trousers.

"Hiya! Sorry to drop in like this, but Toby called me about the board minutes, and I can't believe it! He's at the restaurant, and I just *had* to talk to somebody about it. It's…ludicrous! There's no way in hell we're going to tolerate this."

"That's nice of you," I said faintly, taken aback by his outrage on my behalf.

Leo gave me an odd look. "What do you think? You're new here. Is this something you would support?"

Now I was confused, and my face must have shown it.

"Oh, I'm sorry. With all you had to deal with last night, you probably haven't had a chance to read them. Am I right? I'm talking about Hernan Frias's proposal to change the stakeholder status rules."

"No, haven't read about that yet," I admitted, then motioned for him to step inside. "Why don't you go into the kitchen? Pour yourself a glass of wine. I'll change and be there in a second."

When I entered the kitchen sporting sweats, Leo was sitting at the table with two generous glasses of pinot noir. The cat was curled up on his lap, purring loudly and contentedly.

Leo looked up and grinned. "We've been getting acquainted!"

I plopped down on a chair and watched in amazement. The cat had never shown me any affection. To be fair, I hadn't tried to pet him, nor would I have dared to lift him up and place him on my lap without wearing armor.

"This big loaf just hopped up here, looking for a little love, didn't you?" Leo continued.

I shot the cat a disgusted look. "So, what's this about Hernan's proposal?"

Leo sipped his wine. He lifted his eyebrows in approval. "This is delicious! Well, Hernan thinks the rules regarding stakeholder status are too limited. Right now, the way it works, only direct descendants are considered legacy. But he wants to expand it to include other family relations, like nieces and nephews and even cousins. That means every time a house comes up for sale, there would be a lot more people eligible to apply for legacy. Hernan says that's only fair because the evictions would have affected many generations, but I think that's going way too far."

Leo stopped long enough to take another sip of wine.

"This whole stakeholder business was started to address the wrongs inflicted on the community, and it's done what it was supposed to do. I mean, if the evictions had gone through, sure, it would have impacted all future generations, but they didn't! The city reversed itself and made reparations. In all honesty, if this proposal were to go through, it would mean it would be nearly impossible for anyone without a family connection to Chavez Ravine to buy a house here."

I stared at Leo, trying to process it all. It took a moment, but all the pieces suddenly clicked into place.

"Hernan's trying to turn back time! He's trying to return Chavez Ravine to the way it was before the city tried to evict everyone—a Mexican American community!"

Leo snapped his fingers. "That's exactly what I think!"

"But that would be...exclusionary! Discriminatory! Is it even legal?"

"Hard to say," Leo replied glumly. "Chavez Ravine is private. It accepts no government money and is funded entirely by residents. That's what makes our HOA dues so high. The association can do pretty much whatever it wants. There have been several disputes that have gone to court, but the association has always prevailed. Of course, this could change that."

"Isn't this something the residents would need to vote on?" I asked.

Leo scratched the top of the cat's head. "Definitely. I can't imagine anyone who isn't legacy voting for it, though. Why would they? There are all sorts of implications and—"

Leo was interrupted by a deafening roar coming from above. The cat jumped off his lap and onto the kitchen counter, gazing out the window.

Leo and I stepped into the front yard to watch a helicopter flying overhead.

"What the hell?" Leo had to shout to be heard over the racket.

I squinted up at the helicopter, straining to make out the brightly painted logo on its side. My heart sank.

"It's a news chopper," I shouted back.

The media had arrived.

Chapter 30

Leo took my arm and steered me back to the kitchen, then closed the door behind us. A lock of silver hair fell over his forehead, and he brushed it away impatiently. The lawyer looked serious.

"This is going to get crazy. The girl in Palo Verde blew it up on social media today, and it's been all over my feeds. She was going on and on about monsters trying to get her last night, saying we have an entity problem and there's some kind of conspiracy to cover it up. That's the kind of thing the news stations are going to be all over."

Of course, he was right. Usually, entities weren't breaking news, and they hadn't been for a long time. The breathless enthusiasm of the early days was gone. For the most part, entity sightings were treated like any mundane crime report.

But Katherine Morris's posts had changed all that. If the Chavez Ravine Association had tried to cover up an entity problem, it made perfect fodder for the kind of sensational coverage some members of the media loved.

When I worked in Occult Affairs, we had a public relations person who dealt with the media. Did anyone on the board play that role?

I rubbed the back of my neck. The calm of the bath was gone, and a new wave of stress tightened my muscles. "I didn't really pay attention to social media today," I confessed. "Were her posts that bad?"

Leo grimaced. "Oh yeah. She was pretty…hysterical."

"*You* don't seem too concerned about any of the stuff we've been dealing with lately. Aren't you worried about the possibility of an entity problem? You're an owner too."

Leo shrugged. "I'm a defense lawyer, so no. Entities aren't fun, but they don't get drunk and drive around, killing people. And they don't beat their spouses and send them to the hospital. Plus, we lived in Studio City, south of the boulevard, and let me tell you, it was a nightmare after the banshees popped up in the canyon. They wandered around, wailing for weeks, before Occult Affairs rounded them up. But nobody got hurt. It was just annoying."

"I heard about those." I pointed the remote at the TV and turned it on.

It took me a while to find the right channel. My TV viewing was mostly limited to streaming British murder mysteries.

"Here we go!" Leo's voice perked up.

A man in his fifties, with bronze skin and pearly white teeth, sat behind a sleek blue news desk.
He was introducing a reporter standing in a familiar spot. *"And now we go live to Lonna Manning, joining us from just outside Chavez Ravine. Lonna?"*

A woman with smooth, jet-black hair and high cheekbones faced the camera. *"That's right, Andy. I'm at the La Loma gate—one of the two entrances to the exclusive gated community. We tried to get inside, but we were turned away by a security guard who told us only residents are allowed in at this time. The images you're seeing on your screen are coming to you from LiveCopter8. That's the prestigious Palo Verde neighborhood, where last night's incident occurred.*

"The homeowners association that governs this tight-knit neighborhood high above the hills of Los Angeles declined to speak to us on camera. We wanted to know…is Katherine Morris right? Were the ghostly creatures and the troll-like man that showed up at her house part of an

entity outbreak that the association refuses to acknowledge? The HOA didn't answer, but it did release a statement that reads: Security measures are in place to protect the residents of Chavez Ravine, and recent incidents are under investigation."

The anchor popped back up, with Lonna Manning squeezed into a square box over his shoulder. *"Lonna, what does Occult Affairs have to say about all this?"*

Lonna did a lot of nodding before replying. *"I checked with the spokesperson at Occult Affairs, and she told me their technology shows no entity appearances at Chavez Ravine. She refused to speculate on what social media influencer Katherine Morris allegedly experienced. I've also tried talking to several residents going in and out of the gates. None agreed to speak on camera, but privately, they said tensions are running high here due to incidents they describe as disturbing and mysterious. I'm Lonna Manning, live from Chavez Ravine. Andy, back to you."*

My phone rang. It was Jo at the command center.

"Why haven't I heard from you today?" she barked. "All the shit that went down last night…I really expected you to check in."

My heart went into overdrive. That's exactly what I should have done first thing in the morning. In fact, I hadn't thought of the heat map all day. The PIP had me too preoccupied.

Leo tapped my shoulder and mimicked walking with his fingers.

I'd better go, he silently mouthed. He gulped the last of his wine.

I nodded and walked him to the door. The helicopter had disappeared.

"Well?" Jo pressed.

"Well, what? You're the one with the heat map. You tell me. Did we or did we not have entities here last night?"

"Of course not! I would have let you know, just like I promised to. But if they're not entities, Maddy, what the hell is going on up there? What have you got yourself into?"

Now, that was the million-dollar question.

"I have no clue," I admitted with a heavy sigh. "Things are really weird."

I glanced out the front window. Some of the neighbors were gathering in my front yard.

"I wish I had time to explain, but now is a bad time." I was tired to the bone and just wanted to finish my wine and go to bed. But that wasn't going to happen.

I promised to call Jo back once things calmed down.

"Don't forget," she grumbled.

I peered through the front door, scanning the small but growing group. Many of them I had met when I was looking for the cat's owner.

Nobody had pitchforks or seemed agitated, but they appeared to be debating something. Maybe trying to decide who should knock on the door.

I didn't want to let things get that far. Then I would have to invite everyone inside. I wished I had time to change into something other than my sweats. *Oh well.* I opened the door and went outside.

"Is everything all right out here?" I asked in a cheerful tone.

Anxious looks rippled through the group. I plastered on a smile and stared at them expectantly.

That seemed to work.

The mother of two teenagers staring at me stepped forward. "I'm Danielle Conner. That's my husband, Josh, and that's Ella and Kyle. We're just worried about everything we've been hearing, and since you're the security boss, we thought you might be able to tell us something?"

Her voice went all high and squeaky at the end. Danielle had shoulder-length brown hair and wore oversized tortoiseshell glasses.

In the distance, the sun was beginning to set behind a row of palm trees. I pushed my shoulders back and cleared my throat.

"I'm afraid I can't tell you more than I already put in the report sent out by the HOA board today. But what I can say is that whatever those things were last night, they will not be returning. My team successfully dispatched them. The hairy intruder that bothered some other residents was also dispatched and—"

"Does that mean you killed them?" Kyle asked, eyes bulging. His heavily gelled bangs stuck out like the rim of a ball cap.

Trust a kid to go right to the heart of the issue. In Occult Affairs, we had a whole set of terms to camouflage reality, and we always got away with it. But we didn't usually brief teenagers.

"Did we kill them? Sort of. Technically, they're not living beings, at least not by our standards, so one can't actually kill them. I prefer to use the term 'dispatched' to avoid any confusion. But the outcome is still the same. You don't have to worry about them any longer."

Kyle frowned. "But what if there are more?"

"Then we'll deal with those and dispatch them too." I tried to project confidence.

"But we've never had this kind of problem before." Danielle sounded aggrieved. "That's why we moved here. So we wouldn't have to deal with this bullshit."

"Mom!" Ella cried. "Language!"

Kyle puffed out his chest. "Yeah. This is bullshit."

Josh, a thickset man with lots of dark facial hair, put a hand on his son's shoulder. "Okay, that's enough of that. There's no reason to disrespect our new neighbor. She's got to be just as concerned as we are about everything that's happening." He paused, his eyes sliding toward me. "Miss Madrigal, I won't sugarcoat it. I'm worried too. I promised my family we'd be safe from entities here. We're here because Chavez Ravine doesn't have entities, or so we were told."

A distinguished man with short silver hair and a small mustache stepped forward and introduced himself as Gerald. He turned to Josh. "I'm not sure if you read your disclosures, but if you had, you'd know there's no guarantee this is an entity-free zone. There's no such thing. All it says is that Chavez Ravine hasn't had an entity appearance, and if there was one, it would be noted in the disclosures."

Josh's face began to redden.

Gerald hurried to add, "Your real estate agent should have reviewed them with you. But some of them want to make a sale so bad, they'll tell you anything you want to hear. Either way, it seems to me the board made a smart move hiring Miss Madrigal, with all her experience in Occult Affairs. Now that we have a problem, we've got just the right person to handle it."

Danielle's eyes widened. She gazed at her husband, scowling. "Did you read the disclosures?"

Josh shook his head. "No. You're the paralegal. I thought you were going to read them."

The conversation had just taken an intriguing turn.

"Who was your real estate agent?" I asked.

"Eileen Simpson," Danielle and Josh said in unison.

So, Eileen Simpson had made it sound like Chavez Ravine was immune from entities. No wonder she was panicking and looking for someone to blame.

That knowledge wouldn't get me out of the PIP, but it did make me feel a little better.

Only later, when I crawled into bed, completely drained, did it dawn on me that not one of the visitors who came by my house brought up the performance improvement plan. Not a single person questioned my capabilities or competence.

The cat jumped on the bed and curled up on the backs of my knees. In moments, we were fast asleep.

Chapter 31

It wasn't even noon, and I had already racked up enough charges on my credit card to make me dizzy. But that was shopping with Julia. She swept through showrooms in jeans and a hot pink top, auburn hair piled high on her head, the heels of her mules slapping against the hardwood.

"That's perfect!" she squealed, pointing at a very expensive sofa covered in an unusual shade of silver-gray fabric.

I bought it, of course, because once I saw it, I had to have it. And the round teal velvet cushions too. And the teal ottoman, with orange and red stripes in a nubby material I was sure the cat would like.

My shopping guide didn't like things that matched, so every piece had to be chosen carefully. The coffee table and end tables took the longest because there were so many options.

Still, shopping for furniture wasn't nearly as bad as I had feared it would be. Julia was in her element, too preoccupied to ask about the performance improvement plan.

Until lunch.

We decided we had burned enough calories walking around showrooms to deserve a treat. Turned out, Julia loved Phillipe's Deli in downtown as much as I did. She ordered the beef French dip, and I ordered the lamb and Swiss. We added sides of macaroni salad and kosher pickles, then found a booth in a corner where we could talk.

Julia's eyes rolled back in her head when she bit into the sandwich. "However they make this bread, it's magical. I've been coming here since I was a kid. How about you?"

I added a thin layer of incredibly hot mustard to my sandwich and shook my head. "I didn't grow up in LA. I came here for the first time when I started working at Occult Affairs.

"Oh, that's right. I heard your mom is Malena Bantacorte. You grew up next to that first entity refuge out by Palm Springs, yeah?"

So, Julia had watched one of the documentaries about my mother. Luckily, the filmmakers had mostly left me out of it.

"Not exactly. They built it after I left home."

"So, what's going on with that PIP?" she asked between bites of her sandwich.

I sighed and took a sip of root beer before answering. "It's complicated, but I think it might have something to do with Eileen Simpson promising buyers that if they bought into Chavez Ravine, they would escape entities once and for all."

"Sounds like Eileen." Julia crossed her arms in front of her chest and mimicked posing for a photo. "She specializes in luxury properties and a luxury clientele. She prides herself in knowing every house in Chavez Ravine. Have you seen her posters? Gag. It sounds like she's just trying to cover her butt. From what I've seen, she's got Dan Berman in her pocket. I actually think he has the hots for her. But I don't get why Hernan Frias would go for putting you on a PIP because he's all about Latinos and stakeholder status. I'm surprised he didn't come to your defense."

"He's been a bit…off since we met. Even before I had the job."

"Oh! You said 'off' and that reminded me. I heard he had cancer a year or so ago. Leukemia. Maybe he's still going through treatments or something. That could be making him cranky."

"Maybe," I replied. "He doesn't look sick, but that's a possibility. Who knows? Maybe he just doesn't like me. It could also be my mother. He doesn't seem to approve of her much."

Julia gave a derisive laugh. "I think I can explain that. He's probably just jealous. Did you hear that he was some kind of professor of mystical studies? He's written a bunch of books and stuff. Every once in a while, he gives talks at the community center. About the mysteries and magic of Mexican sorcery and whatever. I went once, mostly for the wine. And okay, also because I was curious, yeah? He went on and on about learning his skills at his grandfather's knee and that he had a famous brujo relative in Bishop, but people couldn't care less. They kept asking if he knew anything about Liliana or Lencha Bantacorte. *Your* relatives." Her eyes widened in realization. "That's probably it. You've got three famous relatives, and he's got nada."

We finished our lunch and headed back to the Jeep to continue our shopping. I couldn't shake the feeling there was more to Hernan Frias than met the eye.

We ended up in Larchmont Village, a small, trendy neighborhood bordering Hollywood. Julia's choice, of course.

I checked the public Occult Affairs website to see if the area was experiencing any significant entity issues. We were in luck. Larchmont had recently been beset by a colony of Jackalopes, but they had all been rounded up.

After our heavy lunch, we needed perking up, so we sipped iced coffees at an outdoor café under a leafy canopy of trees. It was a beautiful day. The sun bathed the storefronts in a golden light.

A few minutes later, we were heading for an old, dingy warehouse.

"Okay, this is my absolute favorite clothing place in all of LA," Julia gushed, steering me toward a shop. "It's a hidden gem, I swear!"

I peered through the front door. Compared to the other stores, with their brightly lit windows decked out with mannequins, this place almost looked like a library. It had a dim interior lit by table lamps. Two whimsical floral displays provided the only indication there might be something interesting going on inside.

"They sell clothes?"

"Of course they do." Julia's eyes sparkled with excitement. "They're one-of-a-kind pieces, though. The women who run the shop are designers, and they sell their samples here, so they're a fraction of the cost of what you'd pay elsewhere."

Julia pushed open the door, and a bell tinkled overhead when we entered the shop.

The air was scented with lavender and sandalwood, and classical music played in the background. My eyes adjusted to the dim light. Racks of clothing in rich fabrics lined the walls.

A woman with wavy blond hair looked up from behind the counter and smiled warmly at us. "Hola, Julia! You brought a friend today?"

"Hola, Nina. This is Maddy. She needs a new wardrobe for work…and life."

Nina smiled. She was around my age and very petite. "Then Maddy is in very good hands. What kind of work do you do, Maddy? Maybe I can point you in the right direction. We have a lot of new pieces in, and I have some in the back I haven't put out yet."

Before I could answer, Julia said, "She's in security, and you should see her in action. She's just…wow."

I blushed. "I could say the same for you, Miss Rolling Pin," I muttered under my breath.

Nina's eyes lit up. "Well then, I might have just the thing. They're a little unusual. We were just having fun with ideas for a special show and came up with them. You don't mind bright colors, do you?"

"Yeah, bring on the bright colors! I want to see!" Julia followed Nina through a door.

That left me alone to look around. Julia hadn't been exaggerating when she said no two pieces were alike. But the styles were interesting, and the pieces were well-made— something a real woman might actually wear, not just a ninety-pound model. The shop was small but well organized. The inventory seemed to be sorted by color, with eveningwear toward the back. I quickly peeked at some tags. The prices were surprisingly affordable.

The two women returned shortly. Julia practically bounced over to me, holding a stack of brightly colored clothes.

"These are so cute!"

I smiled, but I was skeptical. Julia was a flamboyant dresser who seemed to look good in just about anything. I needed something more conservative.

"What are they?" I sounded slightly suspicious, even to my own ears.

Nina answered. "My partner wanted to see if we could update the trench coat. We made it softer, a little less structured. I think you're just going to have to try one on."

Julia handed me one, and I held it up. The fabric was a vibrant turquoise. It had pockets and a skinny belt, just like a regular trench coat, but it was unlike anything I had ever seen.

"Go on, Maddy. Try it on," Julia urged.

I tugged it over my shoulders and pulled it closed, loosely tying the belt. A mirror was sandwiched between two racks of blouses, and I chanced a look at myself. The lightweight coat draped nicely over my frame, and the color complemented my complexion in a surprising way.

Julia clapped her hands, eyes dancing with excitement. "It's perfect, Maddy!"

Nina nodded enthusiastically. "It suits you so well."

It was as comfortable as the lightest of sweaters. "But what would I wear it with?"

"If it's for work, I'd pair it with a column of color. Black top. Black pants. That pop of color in the coat will bring it all together. You could also go with gray, tan, or white. Anything neutral." Nina knew her stuff.

"Black is more my thing," I said.

Within minutes, Julia and Nina had filled a dressing room with pants and tops, all in black and gray. I hated trying on clothes, but there was no avoiding it. At least Nina's dressing room didn't have three-way mirrors.

I was also relieved to discover I had lost a bit of weight despite missing a worrisome number of weightlifting sessions at home. That's what happened when I spent my nights pursuing entities. Or whatever I was chasing around Chavez Ravine.

The turquoise trench coat worked with each top and pants combo.

Julia smiled with the satisfaction of an artist admiring her canvas. Then she met eyes with Nina, who left the changing room and returned with an entire rack of trench coats in an array of vibrant shades—deep purple, fiery red, emerald green, and gold.

Julia could barely contain herself. "Look at all the colors it comes in!"

While working in Occult Affairs, I had become accustomed to wearing a uniform. Just grab something from the closet and go. I could easily imagine myself wearing a soft, light trench coat over a different top and pants every day. It would be simple and comfortable, and it would look good too.

The bells on the front door jingled, and Nina hurried away to greet her new customer.

"I'm about to spend a lot of money, aren't I?"

Julia smiled. "She said she'd give you fifty percent off if you buy them all."

"Why would she do that?"

"Because they're perfect for you, but they're not for everybody, yeah?" Julia raised an eyebrow. "Maddy, do not—repeat, do *not*—pass up this deal."

I looked at the coats hanging on the rack. Buying so many of the same style might have been excessive. But it did seem like they were made just for me. If I didn't take them, I'd be sorry, and with the discount, they were very affordable. Cheaper than something boring from a discount store.

And then I remembered the PIP. If I wanted to keep my job, looking professional wouldn't hurt.

"All right. I'll take them all."

Julia clapped her hands. "That's the way to go! Wonderful!"

She grabbed the pile of coats and hauled them up to the counter at the front of the store. I took out my credit card once more, and in moments, we were back out in the bright sun.

While we were walking back to the Jeep, Julia turned to look at me.

"Now that all our shopping is done, I have a little surprise for you." Her eyes sparkled with mischief.

I sighed. Whatever she had in store, I hoped it didn't cost a lot of money. I had already spent more in one day than I usually spent in six months.

Chapter 32

We cruised through the streets of Los Angeles, but Julia insisted on keeping our destination a secret. All she would tell me was that it was in North Hollywood.

"Are you sure that's a good idea?" I asked.

It took her a few seconds to figure out what I was talking about. "Oh! I think that's all under control now. At least, that's what they said on the news."

"That" referred to an incident involving some idiot who had decided to enslave a couple of tall, gorgeous elves. They had appeared on stage at the El Portal Theater in the middle of *A Midsummer Night's Dream*. He caused quite a stir when he grabbed them and hauled them into his van.

It was the first time someone had captured an entity intending to force it into prostitution.

And it would probably be the last.

When they found themselves in the back of his van, the elves bonked him on the head and left him "elf twisted." That's the term we used in Occult Affairs for someone—usually a civilian—who tangled with elves and ended up disoriented, with a headache and numbness in the limbs. They eventually recovered, but it took an unpleasant few weeks.

All of this had happened shortly before I left Occult Affairs, and I was grateful Jo hadn't sent me out. From what I had heard, it had been a nightmare trying to catch the elves and neutralize them.

"I heard there might be a few elves still hiding out," I said. We drove past the Television Academy.

"There were, but the news said your mother came in and talked them into giving themselves up," Julia replied.

She made it sound like the elves were some sort of criminals, but I let it go. Somehow, I had missed the news my mother was involved. It was no surprise, but it did make me wonder how much longer she could keep it up. My mother took care of herself and was always full of energy, but she wasn't getting any younger.

"Besides," Julia said, "they've never had entities where we're going. And we're almost there. Make a right at the end of the block."

I drove into the parking lot of what used to be a warehouse. The façade had been transformed to look like a log cabin, and I finally understood Julia's plan. We were at the NoHo Axe Bar. I couldn't believe it.

"You're kidding?"

Julia's face lit up with a smile. "I'm not! You've never been before? It's such a blast! You're going to love it, I promise."

I had heard about places like that, of course. But while I was with the LAPD, my job had been filled with plenty of thrills and adventure, especially those involving deadly weapons, so I never went.

Julia must have noticed the hesitation on my face "Oh, come on. This is the perfect way to release all that toxic stress. Especially after dealing with that ridiculous PIP situation. Plus, the drinks are amazing."

I followed Julia into the bar and was surprised at how many people were inside. The axe-throwing lanes were full, and the lounge area was packed. A line had formed at the bar. It was like stepping into a hunting lodge: paddle-shaped ceiling fans, deer heads mounted on the walls, plaid-patterned couches, and tables made from tree stumps. A chalkboard above the bar listed the day's only special: bison burgers.

I took in the spectacle. "Axe-throwing and booze. What can go wrong?"

Julia laughed and tugged me toward two empty bar stools at a high-top. "Calm down. No one here is missing any limbs."

The bartender, who could have easily passed for a rugged mountain man in a Western movie, noticed Julia and immediately made his way over to us, ignoring other customers in the process.

"Hello. My name is Zack, and I have the pleasure of serving you this afternoon. What can I get for you two lovely ladies?" He casually leaned against the table. Zack was certainly laying it on thick.

It was hard to tell, but I suspected he might be quite handsome under all that facial hair. His biceps were definitely impressive.

Although he addressed both of us, it was clear all his attention was on Julia. And I couldn't blame him. Her tanned skin was radiant, and her auburn hair was pulled up into a bun, with strands escaping to frame her face and cascade down her shoulders.

"What do you recommend?" she inquired with a playful smile.

"May I suggest the Hatchet Highball?"

Julia swiveled on her stool and turned toward me. "Does that sound good to you?"

"As long as there's alcohol in it, I'm all for it."

Zack smirked. "I'll make 'em doubles."

I glanced toward the reception area, where a burly man in a muscle T-shirt and overalls stood behind a desk made of reclaimed barnwood and rusty metal brackets. A line was beginning to form.

"Should we put our name in or something?" I asked Julia.

She shook her head. "Nope! I already made reservations." She glanced at her phone. "We have thirty minutes until our scheduled slot. Just enough time for a couple of rounds. And don't worry. You're not driving home. A friend of mine is swinging by to pick us up on his way back to Chavez Ravine."

My eyebrows rose with curiosity. "Who's the friend?"

"Ben Tomas." Julia winked. "I'm hoping that one day my persistence will pay off, yeah? I swear, he doesn't seem to get the hint. And no, he's not gay because I asked him."

I chuckled. "That was…direct of you."

"It's the best way to be sometimes." Julia shrugged. "Other times, it can be a disaster." Her oval face twisted into a grimace. "And Ben's bringing one of his guys to drive your car back."

I studied her for a moment. She had spent the entire day helping me shop for furniture and clothing. Then she had organized this outing, making reservations and arranging transportation so we could arrive home safely. And all of this on top of giving me Little Lencha. I was suddenly touched by her generosity and friendship.

Julia took her Hatchet Highball from Zack, a flirtatious gleam in her eye. She had swept into my life like a whirlwind, and I took a moment to appreciate all she had done for me. I had always been reluctant to show my feelings, but it was time I made more of an effort.

"Julia," I began. "I just…I want to thank you. For everything. Today has been…fun. *Really* fun. And because of you, I'm going to have a nice place to live and nice stuff to wear. I mean, you really went above and beyond today, and I truly appreciate it."

Julia's eyes widened. "Hey! That's what friends are for, right? And God knows you deserve a break and some fun. Besides, I can't think of anyone but you who would go axe-throwing with me. Because you're a badass."

I laughed. "Hardly. Let's just see how well I do once I've got an axe in my hand."

As it turned out, even after two Hatchet Highballs, I didn't do too badly. A second burly man in overalls—this one bald—handed each of us a small hatchet. He showed us the proper technique for throwing it at the wooden target painted with a bullseye. Our first throws went wild, but we cheered anyway. It felt good to heave the axe and have it stick, even if it was way off target.

After a few tries, I remembered to follow through and let my arms continue the throwing motion after releasing the hatchet. It embedded itself in the outer ring of the target. We both did a little victory dance.

When it was her turn again, Julia pretended to be Eileen Simpson mincing up to the throwing line, and that set us off. We were laughing hysterically when our session ended.

We made our way toward the front, passing an area enclosed with netting. Two men wearing camouflage baseball caps were arguing loudly.

"You're pinching it the wrong way, Chad," the taller of the two said.

Both had dark hair and sharp features.

"Fuck you, Tanner," Chad snapped. "I'm pinching it fine. Worry about your stance. It's totally fucked."

The men gripped bright orange slingshots, each equipped with a thick yellow rubber band. Their target was a stack of beer cans, which they were trying to hit with small steel balls. Despite their complaints, both were excellent marksmen. They made it look easy, but I suspected it was anything but.

I immediately thought of Trini Duran and her trusty slingshot. If she had been able to take out monsters with it, maybe I could too.

The thought of having a slingshot on hand to deal with the things appearing in Chavez Ravine seemed like a very good idea. Slingshots were quiet and lighter than handguns and, based on Julia's rolling pin experience with Hairy, would probably be very effective.

Chad noticed me staring and held out his slingshot. "Want a go?"

"I've never used one before," I admitted.

Tanner leaned toward him and muttered, "She's out of your league, asshole."

The offer was tempting, but dealing with those two guys was not, so I shook my head. "We're out the door, but thank you."

Off in the distance, Julia was chatting with Zack.

"We've got a bunch of how-to videos online," Tanner said eagerly. "Slingshot Academy. Just look us up. We've got links to buy the slingshots and advice about what to buy. Whatever you do, please do *not* get skinny bands. They break, and they're a total waste of time."

"I can give you my number if you think you might need some in-person tutoring," Chad offered.

Tanner nudged him in the ribs. "Moron."

I hurried away. When I was about to turn a corner, I heard, "I would so do her."

A part of me wanted to turn around and smack whichever idiot had said it, but it wasn't worth my time or energy.

Outside, the sun was just beginning to dip below the horizon, painting the sky with shades of pink and orange. While we waited for Ben Tomas, unease settled into my stomach. I had made it through the day without being fired or getting an emergency work call. But who knew what the night held. Or the next day, or the day after that?

Chapter 33

When I entered the kitchen, I was greeted by the cat pacing back and forth. He let out a string of angry meows, scolding me for staying out so long.

"You have a litter box, you know," I said, letting him outside.

Darkness descended, and the crisp spring breeze carried the scent of jasmine and orange blossoms from a neighboring yard.

After the cat finished his business, I treated him to a can of Salmon Delite, then opened the windows so the fresh air would chase away the smell. The cat devoured his food in record time, then gazed at me expectantly with large green eyes. The poor guy had been left alone all day, so I took pity on him and sprinkled some kibble into his bowl. He ate that up too, then sauntered into the living room, jumped onto the couch, and promptly fell asleep.

Was it possible to train a cat to keep off the couch? Probably not. At least, not this cat. So far, he hadn't shown any interest in scratching up my stuff, but it was a risk bringing in expensive new furniture.

Had I even made up my mind to keep him? That simple question made me realize I was conflicted. I liked the idea of having him around. And he had earned his keep with the hex bags. But was I ready to be a cat owner, with all the responsibilities that came with it? The vet and grooming bills?

After a full day of shopping and axe-throwing, my feet were aching. I could have easily called it quits and gone to bed. Instead, I went into my home office, logged onto my computer, and watched the first video on The Slingshot Academy site. I watched another and another, then checked out the hardware they recommended.

After browsing all the options, I settled on a model recommended for hunting small game. It had a front-end stabilizer and promised reduced vibration, better balance, and a high degree of accuracy. I added a pack of sturdy bands, a wrist brace, and a large box of metal ammo to my cart. When it was time to check out, I selected express shipping, swallowing hard at the extra fee. My monster-killing slingshot would arrive the next day.

I couldn't help but smile. A feeling of lightness spread through me. I already felt better prepared and empowered—a nice change from the gloom that had enveloped me after I got saddled with the PIP.

After I closed my laptop, I took a quick shower and climbed into bed. Next to the cat.

———·≻·→·⫟⫟⫟⫟·∢·≺·———

The buzzing jolted us both awake. It was my phone, of course. When I noticed the time, I wanted to scream. Three o'clock. What was it with this place and three a.m.?

With my heart pounding in my chest, I answered.

Ron. He was pulling another overnight shift. The cat, disturbed from his slumber, rose to all fours, fur bristling.

"It's Palo Verde this time," Ron shouted into the phone. "There's a party at the Smith house on Davis Street, and there's some wild dogs or something."

"A party?" I echoed. "At three in the morning?"

"The girl who called it in said her parents are away. Can you meet me?"

"Be right there. But Ron, did the girl say where the dogs were?"

"In the backyard. They've surrounded the guests."

I wished there was a way to send an alert only to those in the immediate area of an incident, but our technology wasn't advanced enough. Though I was planning to recommend we change that, for now, alerts went to everyone or no one. I decided to hold off until I got there and assessed the situation firsthand.

After pushing aside the covers, I pulled on jeans, a sweatshirt, and sturdy boots. Once again, I was going to the scene of an incident without a proper weapon. I had my baton, but using it against something with sharp teeth meant getting closer than I liked.

Until my slingshot arrived, I had no real protection. But I knew who probably did.

It nearly killed me to do it, but I owed it to the people I had sworn to protect to swallow my pride and ask for Stu Wells's help. After three rings, he picked up.

"Maddy. Hi. Everything okay?" His voice was thick with sleep.

"Actually, I could use your help."

There was a long pause. "Oh yeah? What did you have in mind?"

My legs felt like jelly. This was really too much. It was a bit late for a booty call.

"Stu, this is an emergency. There's a bunch of dogs from hell ready to attack people in Palo Verde. Do you have a gun?"

That woke him up. "Of course I do. Where are you?"

I texted him the address. "If you've got any silver bullets, those might be helpful," I added, but he had already hung up.

There was no mistaking the house—a three-story Craftsman large enough to be a small hotel. According to my tablet, it belonged to a Thomas and Wendy Smith, parents of two college-aged kids.

The house was all lit up but strangely quiet. I crept toward the backyard. People on a second-floor deck hung over the railing, shouting warnings to someone below.

I gritted my teeth and clutched my baton, then pushed through the gate leading to the backyard.

My blood ran cold.

A pack of giant dogs, six of them, loosely surrounded a group of partygoers, trapping them in a hot tub. The dogs weren't just big. They were ugly: skinny bodies; thick, wrinkled skin; patchy fur. I could see them clearly, thanks to all the string lights across the pool and patio area.

Ron and a guard named Brandon were on the patio, backs pressed against the wall of the house. They yelled at everyone to stay calm and remain in the water. I counted six people, an equal mix of girls and boys, who appeared to be in their late teens. They were huddled in the middle of the in-ground hot tub connected to the pool.

The dogs snarled menacingly, their eyes glowing red in the moonlight. Charming.

I was on the other side of the pool, but if they noticed me, they could reach me in seconds. Even with a baton, I was no match against six of them. I backed out of the gate.

"Do something, for God's sake," a woman yelled from one of the houses next door.

I ignored her but made no attempt to shut her up. All that yelling was providing me with cover.

I messaged Ron.

Is there a hose?

A moment later, he replied.

Yeah. We'll do it. We're closer.

I watched while Ron and Brandon—a thickset young man with a golden cap of hair—grabbed the garden hose coiled nearby, then stealthily approached the monster dogs. Water sprayed from the nozzle in a forceful jet.

The stream hit their thick, wrinkled skin but had no effect. Unlike their glowing, jumping buddies, these things weren't bothered by the wet blast.

The hot tubbers were starting to panic, their cries mixing with the menacing growls of the creatures.

If the water didn't hurt them, what was keeping the dogs from jumping into the hot tub?

A young man with spiky blond hair saw me and shouted, "Would you fucking kill them already?"

The dogs began closing in on the hot tub, undeterred by the water streaming over them.

The people in the tub started screaming. "Help us! Do something!"

"Get into the pool!" I yelled.

They all jumped over the low wall into the pool, but the dogs simply turned to follow them, sniffing at the water's edge. The teens began screaming and brandishing purple pool noodles like swords. The whole scene would have been funny if the creatures hadn't been so terrifying.

Where the hell had they come from?

"Screw the hose," I called to Ron and Brandon. "Let's try throwing things. Hard, heavy things."

Ron plucked a canned drink from the outdoor fridge and hurled it at one of the dogs. The beast yipped but kept its uncanny focus on its prey in the pool.

A yelp was more of a reaction than we had received because of the water, so I moved across the patio toward Ron and Brandon.

When I reached into the fridge to hand them more beverage cans, something prodded me in the back. I let out a gasp. It was Stu, dressed in a black sweatshirt, his hair mussed. He handed over a large caliber gun—a .44 from the looks of it—while staring at the dogs with his mouth agape.

Stu kept the rifle for himself, which was fine by me. I was better with handguns anyway.

"Thank god," Ron muttered, setting a beer can on the pavement.

One of the beasts had lowered itself at the edge of the pool, both paws slipping into the water.

Without hesitation, Stu stepped away from me, aimed at the beast, and fired. The blast was deafening. The enormous hound toppled into the water with a splash. Its companions turned and trained their fierce growls in our direction.

I expected them to rush us, but instead, they approached slowly, heads low, red eyes glittering.

The devil dogs were fierce, but they weren't too bright. Clustering together like that made them easy targets. One by one, we took down the hellish creatures. Stu downed four more of them, but I managed to get one, and it felt good. My firearms training at the LAPD had paid off.

The backyard fell silent.

Then a cheer erupted from the pool.

The partygoers, still clutching their pool noodles, were laughing and crying with relief. Ron and Brandon hurried over to help them out. Stu kept his rifle trained on the dead monsters.

The guy with the spiky blond hair slipped on the wet pavement and fell on his butt. I reached out a hand, hauled him to his feet, and handed him a towel.

"Took you fucking long enough to save us," he snapped before stumbling toward the house.

Even though I had never met him before, there was something familiar about the angles of his face.

I hadn't expected a thank you, but I didn't expect that either.

"Manners," Stu warned in a low voice.

The young man paused long enough to turn and stare at Stu. His eyes widened. "Oh, hey, Stu. Wow, man. I'm really traumatized or something. Didn't recognize you."

Stoned was more like it, judging by his dilated pupils.

A smile played around Stu's lips, but he didn't reply.

"What a jerk. You know that kid?" I asked when everyone was inside.

Stu let out a deep sigh and ran a hand through his hair. "Yeah, that was Mason. Mason Simpson."

My heart sank. "Oh, no. You mean…Eileen's son?" Panic was bubbling up in my chest.

"Her one and only," Stu replied. "He's her pride and joy."

Chapter 34

Another day, another humiliating experience in front of the Chavez Ravine Association board. Although this time, Cora and Charlie were a lot more vocal defending me against Eileen Simpson, who was on a tirade.

"My son almost lost his life last night," Eileen said. "From what he told me, your big containment plan was spraying those things with water and throwing a few beer cans! That's how you respond to situations? It's beyond ridiculous! The only reason he and his friends weren't ripped to pieces by those...abominations...was Stu Wells arrived just in time and blew them to pieces. You're on a performance improvement plan. Do you call your response an *improvement?*"

"Water worked the last time," Cora replied hotly. "There was no reason to think it wouldn't work again. If Maddy *hadn't* tried the water before resorting to firearms, you'd be complaining about *that.*"

Before Eileen could reply, Charlie said, "You've got a short memory, Eileen. You voted *against* allowing our security team to carry guns. You said that would send the wrong message to the homeowners, remember that? Maddy couldn't have used one anyway. And if Stu had become an employee, he wouldn't have either."

Charlie made an excellent point, but Eileen was too angry to listen. She shook her head and gave me an intense stare. "Do you have anything to say for yourself after what happened last night?"

I certainly did. "Listen, you stupid cow. Your son was drunk and stoned last night. I wouldn't trust a word that came out of his entitled little pie hole."

Okay, I didn't say that, but I really, really wanted to. Instead, I swallowed hard and forced myself to speak in the same calm tone I used on agitated entities. "There are several ways to deal with entities and—"

Eileen interrupted, practically shouting, "We do *not* have a problem with entities!"

"It doesn't really matter what you call them, does it? They're disruptive, potentially dangerous things that appear out of nowhere. Don't call them entities if you don't want to, but it doesn't change the fact that we have to figure out where they're coming from and how to get rid of them. And that is going to take time."

I cleared my throat.

"And while we're on this topic, my neighbors, the Connors, mentioned that you promised Chavez Ravine was immune from entities when you sold them their house. As someone who has experience in Occult Affairs, I can say, with absolute certainty, no place is immune from entities. If residents are shocked by what's happening because they were led to believe it was impossible, that's not *my* doing. I strongly suggest we work together to give our owners accurate information and help calm their nerves while we solve this problem."

Eileen's face lost all its color. Dan Berman moved around in his seat and stared directly at the real estate agent through his rimless glasses.

Charlie tugged at his earlobe. "Oh man, tell me that's not true, Eileen."

"It's none of your business what I tell my clients." Eileen's response was sharp, but she refused to make eye contact.

"It's *absolutely* our business," Cora said angrily. "This isn't just something between you and your real estate clients. You're on the board. If you made false claims, the association can be sued."

"I sold the Connors their house before I joined the board," Eileen replied stiffly.

Charlie shook his head. "That's not going to stop anyone from dragging the association into court with you. You should never have said that, Eileen."

Dan held up his hands. "I think we're getting away from the issue at hand, and that's Madeline's performance—or lack thereof—last night. She was clearly unable to handle the situation on her own, and I have to say, I'm very, very concerned about that."

My chin lifted, and my blood began to boil. "I'm the one who called Stu Wells for help. I'd say I acted decisively and appropriately."

Charlie clapped his hands together once, then gestured toward me. "That's correct." He turned back to face Eileen. "Look, I understand you're upset about your son, but I have to wonder what he and those other kids were doing in the early hours of the morning while the parents weren't home? Knowing what's happened lately, they put themselves in a risky situation, if you ask me, and then Madeline and her team had to be called out to rescue them."

"No one *asked* you," Eileen thundered.

"I think we should consider setting a curfew for outdoor parties," Cora suggested briskly. "Violations would result in a penalty."

"That's ridiculous," Eileen retorted.

Dan shrugged. "It sounds reasonable to me. I'd vote for it."

Eileen gasped at the unexpected act of betrayal. She let out an irritated sigh before speaking. "It's a shame Hernan couldn't be here this morning. He would definitely have something to say about Madeline's failure to perform her duties last night."

I hadn't noticed Hernan's usual chair was empty.

Cora leaned over and whispered, "He called in sick today."

I nodded before standing up from my chair. "Well, if that's all, I should really get back to work."

Eileen merely shrugged and began scrolling through her phone.

As I left the conference room, I heard Charlie say, "Now, Eileen, I want to hear more about what you've been telling your clients about entities…"

I drove back to party central to follow up on the previous evening's events and collect samples of the creatures' remains.

When the Hell Hound tumbled into the water, it dissolved, which was weird because the hoses seemed to have no effect. Regardless, that one left no remains to collect. The other five had disintegrated into the same crumbly, powdery substance as Hairy.

We gathered as much as we could to send to the lab, but I didn't expect any groundbreaking discoveries. Just clay and masa again, most likely. The one person who might be able to tell me something about the creatures was my mother. It was worth taking the chance. The worst she could do was say she had no idea. Also, it was about time I started defrosting the relationship I had put in the deep freeze.

I boxed up a sample for my mother, dropped it off at a package delivery service in Bishop, then messaged her to let it know it was coming. She replied immediately.

Thrilled to help!

Back in my office, I reviewed the footage from the security cameras. Sure enough, at 2:45 a.m., the dogs had trotted along Paducah Street, eyes glowing, and then disappeared down a steep embankment leading to the gully.

Phantom's Pass was really living up to its name. Time for another walk through the gully.

After changing out of my new purple trench coat, I slipped on an old flannel jacket I didn't mind getting dirty. I had spent good money on my new wardrobe, and I had every intention of protecting my investment.

Halfway to Bishop, my head began to pound, and my muscles started to ache. My face also felt strangely numb. Stress could have strange effects on the body, and after the chaotic events of last night, combined with my lack of sleep and the added pressure of the PIP, I wasn't surprised to feel a bit off. Hopefully, it wasn't anything more serious.

I pulled into the market for a bottle of sparkling water and some aspirin. When I reached for my wallet in the center console, something caught my eye: a small cloth bag wedged between boxes on the passenger seat.

Another hex bag.

Not daring to touch the thing with my bare hands, I grabbed two plastic bags from the back and used them as protective gloves. I carried the brown paper bag to the lawn near the road. After a bit of a struggle, I untied the string and looked inside. Once again, it was a mixture of salt, ground glass, and who knew what else, but this time, it had the faint odor of urine.

How long had that thing been in the Jeep? My drive to work was so short, it could have been there all night, and I might not have noticed.

Since moving to Chavez Ravine, I had become sloppy about keeping the Jeep locked at night. I had even made the mistake of leaving the passenger side window open a few inches. That must have been enough for someone to flick the hex bag inside.

Whoever was planting those things was no quitter.

I called the guard on duty and asked him to bring a sturdy plastic bag, then told him to dispose of it in a trash bin somewhere across town, far from Chavez Ravine. He seemed mystified but was happy enough to oblige.

In just a few minutes, I felt better.

In Bishop, I parked on Paducah Street and retraced the steps of the monster dogs. I had no idea what I was looking for, but it felt good being outside in the fresh air, with the sun on my face. My feet carried me along the winding gully and up the hill. The earth beneath my boots was hard from lack of rain, and the distant chirping of birds served as a peaceful soundtrack to my journey, calming my nerves. A nature walk was the perfect antidote to my encounter with Eileen Simpson.

I walked all the way to Palo Verde. After scouring the area and discovering nothing, I turned around and headed back down the hill. My feet were tired, but my mind was clear. For a long time, I sat in my Jeep, staring off into the distance.

I had a problem. One with no clear solution in sight.

On the verge of tears, I thought about calling Julia, but as much as I wanted the company, the thought of explaining everything sounded exhausting. What I really wanted was a cocktail. The clock on the dashboard read four o'clock, but I had been working since three in the morning, so I felt justified.

I made a U-turn to go home.

A white medical transport van slowly passed by, headed up the hill. In the passenger seat, face in hands, was Hernan Frias.

Cora had said he called in sick from the board meeting that morning. Julia had mentioned he had battled leukemia. Seeing him in the van suggested two things: he wasn't well enough to drive himself, and he didn't have anyone else to turn to for help.

It occurred to me I knew very little about his personal life. Was he married? Did he have children? If so, did they live in Chavez Ravine or somewhere else entirely?

I trailed the van at a safe distance while it drove up the street, then pulled over when it turned into Hernan's driveway. The door slid open, and he emerged cautiously, as if afraid of falling. He waved to the driver before slowly hobbling toward his house, his head hanging low, a cane in one hand. This was quite a contrast to the man who had come barreling into the library, no assistance required.

But Hernan Frias was a mystery for another day.

I drove to Olga's Cantina & Grill a few blocks from Palo Verde Plaza. The bar area was already bustling with people despite the early hour. Most of the crowd seemed to be on the younger side. The atmosphere was laid-back and casual, the interior filled with dark wood and colorful prints of Mexican folk art. I glanced at the chalkboard menu and noted that Olga's served both Tex-Mex and Baja-Mex. Couldn't go wrong there.

Several people were gathered around someone at the bar. Everyone spoke in loud, excited voices.

"Devil dogs? Where did those come from?"

"What the hell is happening around here?"

"Oh man, that was awesome, the way you killed those things."

I froze. There was only one person they could be talking to, and it was the one person I wasn't prepared to see.

For one thing, I looked a mess. For another, my hands had gone all sweaty, and my tongue was like a lead weight in my mouth—a sure sign of impending incoherence. And yet, I couldn't resist the urge to confirm it was indeed Stu Wells at the center of that crowd.

I edged along the wall, stopping just before reaching the end of the bar.

It was Stu, all right, sitting on a barstool. He was dressed in a crisp blue suit, with his white shirt collar unbuttoned at the neck. The man seemed unusually lively for someone who had been blasted out of bed at three in the morning. Or maybe that had more to do with the attractive woman with short red hair next to him. Her gaze was fixed on the man like he was a yummy dessert.

Was that…?

Yup. My stomach lurched at the sight of Caitlin, the receptionist.

When Caitlin spoke, Stu leaned toward her with a charming smile that made his eyes crinkle. When Stu spoke, Caitlin threw her head back and let out a hearty laugh.

I watched them together, unable to deny how much I had wanted to believe Julia when she said Stu Wells had feelings for me. But now, it was clear my friend had been wrong.

I felt like a fool for ever believing her in the first place. How pathetic was that?

Very.

Before he could spot me, I slinked out the door.

At home, I fed the cat, ordered Thai food, and opened a bottle of the fanciest pinot noir in the cupboard. I was halfway through it when my phone chimed.

A delivery.

I went to the front porch and plucked a box off the welcome mat. My slingshot had arrived.

I placed it on the floor. From my usual spot on the ratty old couch, I stared at it while I sipped my wine.

I should send it back. What was the point of even opening it? I had never used a slingshot in my life. What had made me think I could learn how to use one well enough to take out a supernatural creature? And was there even a point to learning new skills? My future as head of security for Chavez Ravine was iffy at best.

At least I had my house. It was my only consolation.

Maybe I should get out in front of the whole thing. Call it quits. Make leaving my choice and not the board's. In the morning, I would hop on the phone with HR and get serious about rejoining Occult Affairs.

The mere thought made my body hurt.

The cat seemed to sense my dark mood. He rubbed against my legs, but when I reached down to pet him, he darted away.

"I should call you Stu, you shifty little beast." My voice was laced with bitterness, turning into laughter that bounced off the walls.

From the hall, the cat peered at me suspiciously. And I didn't blame him. I sounded a little unhinged.

Chapter 35

The lab results were waiting in my inbox when I checked my phone the next morning. The devil dogs' remains were, as expected, made up of red clay and masa. I stared at the screen. A wave of frustration washed over me. How could these supernatural creatures have such mundane origins? In his email, David took the opportunity to express his theory again.

Now will you believe me about a golem?

Somehow, that didn't sound so crazy anymore. It certainly wasn't any worse than a witch sitting on the city council, conjuring monsters to scare off the residents of Chavez Ravine.

It was seven o'clock, and the sun had yet to break through the overcast skies. The gray clouds mirrored my somber mood. I was feeling just as gloomy as I had when my eyes finally closed the night before.

After I gave the cat his breakfast—I *always* seemed to be feeding the cat—and let him outside—he *still* refused to use the litter box—I made my bed and put away my new clothes. When I was done, my closet was transformed into a wonderland of trench coats in a rainbow of colors.

I reached out to touch one made from a soft, teal fabric. It was a beautiful shade, like a far-off sea in a fairy tale. I had never owned such colorful clothes before. The coats seemed to shimmer under the single bulb in the closet. The one closest to me, a vibrant shade of crimson, had a neat row of decorative buttons on the lapels. Upon closer inspection, I found they were in the shape of little skulls and crossbones. An intriguing choice—one that suited my mood. I pulled it off the hanger and tossed it on the bed.

As I got dressed, thinking about what I would say to Occult Affairs HR, a frantic scratching noise from the living room brought me to my feet.

I rounded the corner to the living room, and I couldn't believe my eyes.

The cat had not only managed to open the slingshot box, but he had also torn off the bubble wrap. The slingshot lay gleaming—a silent invitation for me to pick it up. The cat meowed loudly, his paw hanging in midair above a box of steel ammo.

"I get it."

Though I didn't know much about cats, this certainly couldn't have been normal behavior. Nor was the way he stared at me, with an intensity that creeped me out.

I took the hint and reached for the slingshot. Carefully, I opened the small box of ammunition and dropped a handful of pellets into the pocket of my sweatpants.

The morning clouds were thinning, and a soft light filled the garden outside. I stepped out onto the grass. The chill of the morning dew seeped into my bare feet. The cat padded along behind me.

I loaded a steel pellet into the crook of the band and pulled back, aiming for the trunk of the palm tree. Ben Tomas would have had a fit if he saw what I was about to do. I pulled the rubber strap back and, with a flick of my wrist, let it go. The projectile zoomed through the air and slammed into the dirt hill behind my intended target. My aim was a mile off.

I sighed and tried again. Each attempt was a little closer but still far from the target.

The tension in the band was strangely unpredictable. A few times, it snapped back against my fingers with a sharp sting, causing me to cry out in both pain and surprise. I gritted my teeth and tried to relax, but I tensed up instead, which made my aim even worse.

My fingers began to throb. In her journals, Trini hadn't mentioned how long it had taken her to learn how to use her slingshot or whether she'd had expert help. For a moment, I considered calling the guys from The Slingshot Academy, but the idea was so repellent, I decided to push forward on my own.

It couldn't be that hard, could it? Yes, it could. Even after watching a few how-to videos and following them step-by-step, it was harder than it looked. *Much* harder.

I really needed better targets. The recycling bin was full of empty wine bottles, but I didn't want glass all over my lovely backyard.

The bag of plastic water bottles I had stored in the sunroom for recycling...

From her perch on the counter, Little Lencha seemed to be watching my every move. Her clay eyes followed me around the room, and the hint of a mischievous smile played around her lips. I shook my head, trying to push away the irrational suspicion she was alive.

The sun broke through the clouds and bathed the room in a beautiful, golden light. When I turned to gather up the water bottles, Little Lencha almost appeared to be glowing, illuminating the dark corners of the sunroom.

My heart skipped a beat. With trembling hands, I reached out to touch her, half expecting the clay folds of her dress to soften into real fabric. That didn't happen, but the figurine was warm in my hands, as if pulsing with a strange energy.

Whatever dark thoughts had consumed me were gone. Little Lencha's radiance seeped into my blood, pumping me with hope and optimism. And a moment later, something more.

Defiance.

I sat on the floor, soaking up the sun streaming through the windows, then closed my eyes.

My ancestors had lived in Chavez Ravine. I was a legacy stakeholder. My grandmother, Liliana Bantacorte, had practiced the healing art of curanderia within the walls of the very house I had inherited. Lencha Bantacorte had dispensed cures and magic just blocks from where I stood. I had every right to live here, as much right as Eileen Simpson, Hernan Frias, and Dan Berman. It was time I took that more seriously.

And what's more, I had a responsibility to protect the community. Not just because I was the head of security, but because the community was relying on me. The *entire* community, not only the board.

Long ago, the residents had fought back against the city's evictions and won. That never would have happened without grit and determination.

Where were mine? Was I really going to let Eileen Simpson bully me into quitting?

I had survived a chaotic, abusive childhood. My mother had escaped my father's control. Lencha Bantacorte was a rebel and a bruja. I came from a line of women who refused to be sidelined.

And I wasn't some kid trying to figure out her life. I was forty years old, knew who I was, and was confident in what I wanted.

It was time to embrace my heritage and my legacy and call upon the spirits of my ancestors.

With newfound purpose burning in my heart, I rose to my feet and marched into the backyard, leaving behind the soft glow surrounding Little Lencha. I put the water bottles on the retaining wall separating the garden from the hill behind it and picked up the slingshot.

The cat sat off to the side, watching me intently. A strange triangle of connection formed between the three of us: me, the cat, and Little Lencha. I measured the weight of the slingshot, took a deep breath, and focused on the bottle on the far right.

With a steady hand, I loaded a steel pellet into the slingshot, pulled back the elastic band, and took aim. My pulse quickened, and I released the band with a satisfying twang. The steel ball shot through the air, hitting the bottle and knocking it off the wall.

I gave a whoop of victory and quickly reloaded. One by one, I sent the plastic targets tumbling to the ground. When I turned around, I could swear Little Lencha winked.

Chapter 36

The next day got off to an unexpected start.

Just as I was putting on my red trench coat and heading for the Jeep, the furniture movers pulled up. An entire day early. I locked the cat in the bathroom and went outside to greet the crew.

A bearded man with tattoos running down his arms walked toward me.

"Madeline Madrigal?" he asked gruffly.

"That would be me." I giggled for no good reason.

He gave me an odd look and handed over a clipboard. "Initial beside each item after we unload it. Check to make sure there's no damage before you initial, though. If you miss something, it's on you."

Wow. Even the delivery guys sounded like they were putting me on a PIP.

They wasted no time getting to work. I told them where to put each piece, though I suspected Julia would want to come over and rearrange everything. While they carried a wicker couch into the sunroom, the cat's muffled meows came from inside the bathroom.

When the movers left, I let him out, and he shot into the living room like a rocket, strutting around the new furniture, sniffing each piece suspiciously.

Finally, he settled on the ottoman with the nubby fabric and jumped on top. He turned a few circles before curling into a ball. I felt a ridiculous sense of satisfaction: I had predicted he'd like that ottoman.

The house suddenly looked inviting with all the new furniture. I couldn't wait for Julia to see it. But that would have to wait. I had work to do.

After I settled into my office, I immediately called Jo to see if she knew anything about golems.

"Are you telling me that's what you're dealing with up there?" She cleared her throat. "I thought that was a Judaism kind of thing. Aren't Mexican Americans mostly Catholic?"

"They are, but the guy at the lab keeps talking about golems." I explained the lab analysis showing the creatures' remains to be a mix of red clay and masa harina.

Jo gave a loud snort. "Maybe someone was trying to conjure up killer tamales and things got out of hand.

Killer tamales. I immediately thought of Cora, then pressed a finger between my eyes.

Cora? Could she have been behind the creatures? She *did* have her secrets, but I just didn't picture her as a closet bruja.

"So, do you know anything about them?" I pressed. "Golems, not tamales."

Jo had gone through intensive training to help her in the identification of emerging entities. To hear her tell it, we had been lucky. So far, we had managed to escape fire-breathing dragons, minotaurs, and ogres, with their unsatiable appetite for human flesh. The trolls we had seen were small and not too violent. They were mostly peaceful, though they did eat palm fronds and cactus fruit, along with the occasional small animal when the opportunity presented itself.

But I couldn't remember her ever saying anything about golems.

Jo sighed. "You know the basics, right? Someone with big ideas decides to create an artificial human being from mud, but because it's artificial, it doesn't have a soul. The story goes that some rabbis forever ago created golems to do stuff for them, but sometimes, they got out of control. We haven't had any here, although we do have a rabbi on standby in case one shows up."

"You said human beings created them. I guess the hairy guy could technically have been a golem—he looked like a person...mostly—but the devil dogs don't fit that description."

"From what you sent me, they don't sound like golems to me. Actually, none of them do."

There was a long pause.

"I could send one of our experts out to you. On the downlow. You know, to have a look around. Help you out a little."

That was something Occult Affairs had always wanted to do—send someone in to figure out why Chavez Ravine had never had an entity problem—but the community was notoriously private and had refused every request. There wasn't a darn thing the city could do about it. With me on the inside, Jo was hoping to sneak someone in.

"That's not a good idea," I said.

In fact, it was a terrible idea, and not just because I would lose my job if the board found out. I had met the division's *experts*. They were mostly annoying know-it-all academics who had suddenly found themselves in high demand when the first big earthquake struck and unleashed the entities. I didn't like the idea of some expert making my job even more difficult than it already was.

Jo groaned. "I knew you were going to say that. The least you can do is invite me and Holly for drinks."

"That might actually happen now that I have new furniture," I said, smiling.

"Wow. Did you get a coffee table, or do we still have to put our glasses on your weight bench?"

"I'm not sure you'll be able to handle it, but I even got coasters. I'll have you two over as soon as I can."

We hung up.

A thought had been nagging at me for a couple of days, so I went through the security camera footage from the previous night. Even though we hadn't had an incident, creatures might still have been out there, roaming around.

I didn't find anything, but it was only one random night. So I went back a couple of days on either side of each reported incident and scanned the footage.

Bingo.

On the night before Hairy first appeared at Katherine Morris's house, he had darted across Garabaldi Street in Bishop, not far from Phantom's Pass. The video was forty-five seconds long and grainy, but there was no doubt it was him. I would have loved to know where he had come from, but none of the other cameras picked him up.

Then I checked for Dog Face Bride, the Jumpers, and the Hell Hounds. Each time, I was able to find them somewhere in Bishop but only fleetingly. Unlike the entities I was used to, these creatures did not act confused. They moved with purpose, almost like they were on a mission. And like Hairy, they were only caught on camera once. Where they came from was still a mystery.

I messaged Cora, asking if she had the exact dates when she had first seen creatures in Chavez Ravine, but she couldn't recall. Neither could Charlie or Ron Mendez. I assigned Ron to review all the footage recorded at night in Bishop, starting three months back.

"Can I use your office?" he asked hopefully.

"No! You've got plenty of time at the gatehouse."

He gave a long, suffering sigh. "All right. I'll see what I can find." There was a long pause. "After that shitshow with the dogs, do you think they'll let us carry guns?"

"That's a good question," I replied. "I'm not sure."

Honestly, I wasn't convinced that was such a good idea. Firearms might be helpful when we dealt with increasingly dangerous creatures. But I didn't know if I would want to entrust guns to the rank-and-file guards. Things were becoming scary and unpredictable, and I didn't need a guard freaking out and shooting at shadows.

I spent the rest of the afternoon on mundane tasks: going through the security budget line by line and researching fencing options to shore up the border between Chavez Ravine and Elysian Park. Time flew by, and when I glanced at the clock, it was nearly five thirty. I was out of food at home, for me *and* the cat, so I locked up and headed to the supermarket.

While waiting in line at the butcher counter, a familiar voice came up the aisle behind me.

"No, I swear, Mom. We were in the pool forever before she finally showed up, and when she did, she did absolutely nothing. Worse than useless. You've got to get rid of her, Mom. Get Stu."

Another voice I knew. "It's complicated. She's legacy."

"That's bullshit. What's that got to do with anything? Either she can do the job or she can't, and she can't. Legacy doesn't mean she's qualified. That's not fair. You can't let them get away this, Mom. You've got to do something."

"Can you please lower your voice?" Eileen Simpson hissed, loud enough for me to make out what she said one aisle away. "We're in public."

It sounded like Junior was used to getting his way.

"Mom! You're not listening to me. Those dog things almost killed us, and she almost let it happen."

Maybe my new red trench coat was giving me newfound confidence. Perhaps it was the memory of hitting all the targets with my new slingshot. Or I just wanted to show Eileen I wasn't afraid of her *or* her bratty son.

Whatever the reason, I got out of line, swept around the corner, and acted surprised when I saw them.

"Well, hello!" I said cheerily.

Eileen eyed my outfit through narrowed eyes. "You shop here? Isn't there a store closer to you in La Loma?"

A subtle poke at my neighborhood—downscale compared to the ritzy part of Palo Verde, where she lived.

I ignored this and turned toward her son. "How's the hangover?"

"That was two nights ago," he said.

I nodded solemnly. "Mmm. And what a night it was." I lowered my voice. "I understand you and your friends were all underage. This is a private community, so you may think you can get away with it, but just a word of advice: consider being more discreet in the future. Neighbors complain, and there could be consequences for openly flouting the rules."

Eileen gave me a tight and icy smile. "We'll keep that in mind, thank you."

I nodded, then turned on my heel. Two sets of eyes definitely bored into the back of my head while I made my way back to the butcher counter.

Chapter 37

The next several days and nights were quiet and uneventful, but my anxiety increased while I braced for another attack.

Every morning before heading to work, I practiced with my slingshot in the backyard. From the counter in the sunroom, Little Lencha would watch me while I knocked down plastic water bottles one by one. It was getting easier to hit the targets, but they didn't have sharp teeth, and they weren't rushing toward me. The prospect of more encounters with dangerous creatures lingered at the edge of my thoughts like a shadow.

As promised, the Morris's listed their Palo Verde house with Eileen Simpson. Charlie confided it wasn't generating much interest, so Eileen was freaking out. And, of course, blaming me.

Julia came over and helped me arrange the furniture. When she was done, my house was transformed from bland to colorful, cozy, and inviting.

One thing still bothered me. The cat.

Julia reminded me to contact Dan Berman so he could send a message to all the residents, but I couldn't bring myself to do it. Finders keepers. Whoever had owned him should have taken care not to let him outside. He could have been run over by a car or eaten by a coyote. Or attacked by a golem, the way things were going.

The cat had claimed the striped ottoman in the living room as his own. I didn't dare put my feet on it, but for some reason, that didn't bother me.

Thursday, I met Julia for happy hour and tacos at Olga's Cantina. I half expected Stu to be there with Caitlin, but he didn't show up. In fact, I hadn't heard from him since the night of the Hell Hounds.

At home, I took a hot bath and went to bed early.

At exactly two forty-five in the morning, my eyes snapped open. My heart pounded so hard, the blood whooshed in my ears. I got up, went to the bedroom window, and peered through the curtains. A beautiful full moon lit the backyard. There was nothing there.

I peered out into the front yard, but it was clear too. All the doors were locked.

I chalked it up to nerves and climbed back in bed, pulling the covers up to my chin and staring up at the ceiling. After taking deep, calming breaths, I was drifting off to sleep when my phone screeched.

It was five minutes after three. Of course.

It was Brandon calling with an emergency. Naturally.

"Ron's off tonight." Brandon sounded panicked. "There's some giant birds at the top of Bishop. Bad Pete was just getting home, and they went after him, so he called. I'm here, but you've got to come fast."

Bad Pete, real name Pete Drury, was a world-famous pop star who lived most of the time in the U.K. It had been big news when he bought a place in Chavez Ravine as a homebase for his U.S. tours.

"Where's Pete now?" I flicked on the lamp on the nightstand.

The cat leapt off the bed and stared at me with his green eyes.

"He's trapped in his SUV. Those birds are crazy big. You better call Stu and tell him to bring his rifle."

Wow. Even my own staff doubted I could handle my job. "Stay in your vehicle," I barked, then hung up.

I threw on some clothes, grabbed my slingshot and ammo, and raced out the door. As I sped toward Bishop, my mind raced, trying to recall if we had ever responded to avian entities in Occult Affairs. I couldn't remember any, but that didn't mean none had ever appeared. There were just too many to keep track of.

I was having second thoughts about not calling Stu, but I decided not to out of sheer stubbornness. My whole career, men had explained things I already knew and tried to give me orders. I didn't need a man to take care of some stupid birds. Not now that I had my slingshot.

When I arrived at the top of Bishop, the flashing lights of Brandon's car, still parked in the street, were visible. There was a sleek black SUV in the driveway, surrounded by a small flock of massive blackbirds. The whole scene was illuminated by the full moon.

I counted three of the giant birds swooping and diving in a frenzied attack on the SUV. It had tinted windows, so I couldn't see inside, but I could hear it loud and clear. Pete Drury was laying on the horn.

I wasn't sure of the layout of the property beyond the tall gate leading to the house, but if the garage wasn't attached, it would be nearly impossible for Pete to get inside without being attacked.

He was truly stuck.

I pulled up next to Brandon's car and quietly got out. There was no way to protect myself if the birds came after me, but I had to do something. At least this time, I wasn't unarmed.

I reached through the window and grabbed my binoculars from the glove box. When I focused them on the heads of the huge birds, I let out a breath of relief. They didn't have human faces. *Thank goodness*. That meant they weren't harpies. Once, a pair of harpies had shown up at the docks in Long Beach. They were real trouble, causing chaos and destroying equipment, until Occult Affairs was able to intervene.

Still, the sight sent shivers down my spine. These things were ugly, with pointed heads and sunken eyes. They had large, clunky beaks filled with sharp teeth. Their only redeeming feature was their shimmering plumage.

Brandon had ventured outside his car and was cowering behind the door, looking at the birds in horror.

It was time to make my move. I dashed toward the closest palm tree, hoping the birds wouldn't notice, raised my slingshot, and let a pellet fly. The first shot struck a bird in the chest. It shrieked in pain and dropped like a stone, hitting the pavement with a sickening thud.

I felt surprised and a tiny bit proud. But there was no time to gloat.

The other two birds turned their attention toward me, their white eyes locking onto mine.

Inside the SUV, Pete kept hitting the horn.

Brandon shouted a warning.

The birds swooped down toward me with terrifying speed. I threw myself to the ground just in time. A whoosh of air fanned my back as they passed overhead. After scrambling to my feet, I loaded another steel pellet into the slingshot and let it fly, nailing one of the birds in the head.

Brandon cheered when it toppled to the ground.

The remaining bird let out a deafening cry and veered away from me and the SUV. It circled above the trees of a small park near the end of the road.

The SUV door opened a few inches.

"Hang in there, Pete," I shouted. "Stay inside your vehicle, please."

At the sound of my voice, the bird whirled around and soared toward me. I held my ground. After all, I had taken out two of them. I could do it again.

With its massive wingspan, the giant beast reached me in seconds. It dove, talons extended, beak open wide. In the moonlight, rows of needle-like fangs shined.

My hands were strangely steady. I took aim once more, releasing the pellet in one smooth motion. Everything happened so fast. I couldn't say exactly where it hit, but the pellet did its job. The monster bird plummeted from the sky with a bloodcurdling screech, still headed straight for me. I had to jump to the side to avoid being struck.

My chest heaved. I got up and stood over the shimmering heap. All three birds were dead.

Thanks to me. *Only* me. Not me and Stu or me and Brandon.

I had done it myself. With a slingshot—a weapon I had known nothing about the week prior. A weapon I had discovered quite by accident but would never be without again.

In my head, I thanked Trini Duran.

I gradually became aware of my surroundings. On one side was a stunned-looking Brandon. And on the other, a tall, lanky man of around thirty, with dark skin and a shaved head. "Bad" Pete Drury was even more handsome in person than he was in the tabloids.

"That was some David and Goliath shit right there! Where'd you learn to use that thing? That was wicked!"

Honestly, didn't some things just sound charming when said with a British accent?

"Just glad it worked," I said faintly. The adrenaline was draining out of my body, leaving me weak-kneed and fuzzy-headed.

In the moonlight, we watched the bird in front of us begin to transform. Its once shiny feathers were now dull and stiffening. I looked to the other two bodies near the SUV. The same thing was happening to them.

Brandon knew what to expect, but it was all new to Pete Drury, who took a step back and clutched my arm. "What's going on?"

I was too tired to properly explain. "Well, there's dead. And then there's deader. These things are on their way to being deader. But the important thing is, you're safe, and they won't be bothering you again."

"Brilliant!" Pete Drury turned and walked back toward his SUV, holding his phone in the air and saying something I couldn't quite make out.

Chapter 38

The next morning, I woke up to a message from Stu.

Way to go, Maddy!

I had no idea what he was talking about—the birds, maybe?—but it felt nice anyway. A flush of warmth spread across my chest, but I needed coffee before I replied.

I was just about to step into the shower when there was a loud, persistent knocking on my front door.

Julia and Leo stood on the porch, grinning.

"Did you see it?" Julia exclaimed, pushing past me into the entryway.

Leo followed her inside, giving me a quick hug and a peck on the cheek. In the living room, he paused and scanned his surroundings before placing his hands on his hips. "Oh my god, your place looks amazing! The colors! Where did you find that couch?"

"Never mind that!" Julia said. "Maddy, did you see it?"

The shower and coffee seemed like a faraway memory.

"See what?" My mind was foggy from lack of caffeine, and I was still preoccupied by the close call with the giant birds.

Leo, already dressed for work in a charcoal suit, held out his phone. "Pete Drury posted a video. A video of *you*, Maddy, taking down those pterodactyls with a slingshot! He's calling you his hero!"

"Yeah…and…" Julia pumped her hands in the air like she was dancing at a club. "It's gone viral."

Bad Pete, international music pop star, had *recorded* me? He was telling his legion of fans I was his hero? Impossible.

"Check it out!" Leo played the video on his phone.

The video showed me in action, feet wide apart, hand pulling the elastic band to my cheek, then releasing the ammunition just as a bird swooped down to attack. Pete captured each shot, along with the targets falling to the ground. In the background, he narrated, talking about bravery and marksmanship.

Julia and Leo cheered along with the video. I watched, stunned. At first proud, then embarrassed at being thrust into the spotlight.

Julia insisted on watching the video over and over while the number of views climbed. Tens of thousands of them. Comments began flooding in.

"You're such a badass!" Julia enveloped me in a sandalwood-scented hug.

Leo nodded, his expression turning solemn. "That's true, but Maddy...after this, the board can't keep you on that PIP. They just can't."

The morning unfolded, and my house became a revolving door of well-wishers. Becca Tey, bandages gone, brought a bottle of wine. The Connors and their two teenagers stopped by before the kids headed off to school. They wouldn't leave until I promised I would show them how to use a slingshot.

The older gentleman who lived down the block, Gerald, said, "I have no idea how much money they're paying you, young lady, but you should ask for a raise."

"I wouldn't have figured you for a Bad Pete fan." I laughed.

"Oh, I'm not, but my granddaughter is. She sent me the video."

This was getting out of control.

Then my phone started blowing up. Reporters somehow got my number and wanted to interview me. I refused. The last thing I needed to do was bring more attention to the community, though it was hard to imagine more recognition than the video was getting.

Then came an enormous flower arrangement from Pete Drury, with a note thanking me for rescuing him and VIP tickets to his next show. He included his mobile number in case I ever needed anything.

Cora called, apologizing for taking so long to reach out to me. "I'm afraid I'm not on social media. Ron came over to tell me."

She paused.

"Now listen, Maddy. Considering everything that's happened, I've called a special session of the board. I'm proposing that we terminate the PIP immediately. Charlie's all for it, of course, and I'm sure Dan will agree. He's friends with Pete Drury, and I'm sure he's seen everything."

If Dan voted with Cora and Charlie, that was three against two, and I could kiss the PIP goodbye.

"Thank you, Cora. I really appreciate that."

After I was able to shoo everyone out and get ready for my day, my phone buzzed with another message from Stu. In all the excitement, I had never responded to his first text. And yet, here he was, trying again. Nice.

How about a celebratory drink at Olga's? Six o'clock?

A smile tugged at the corners of my mouth, and I typed out a one-word reply.

Sure!

Celebrating with Stu at Olga's sounded like the perfect way to cap off the surreal events of the last few hours.

At my office, the madness started anew. A steady stream of people—some I barely knew and many I had never met—stopped by to congratulate me for killing the creatures and saving Bad Pete. Several of them took the opportunity to grill me about what I thought was going on at Chavez Ravine and how I planned to solve the problem.

It was all overwhelming because I didn't have any good answers. Maybe I wouldn't have to worry about the performance improvement plan much longer, but I was still no closer to figuring out who—or what—was behind the supernatural attacks plaguing the community.

My phone rang. At first, I ignored it. But then I saw the number. It was my mother.

Here we go.

I answered reluctantly. "Hi, Mom."

"Mija," she said, which was how I knew she had bad news. She wasn't the type of mother to use endearments except in extreme circumstances.

"Yes. How are you doing?" Our conversation hadn't even started, and I already sounded beaten down.

"I saw the video," she said in an offhand way. "I had no idea you could do stuff like that. Good for you. But that's not what I was calling about…" Her voice drifted off, and a kettle whistled in the background. My mother was always drinking tea.

I braced myself for what would come next, and she continued.

"That sample you sent me. The remains of those awful dogs. It took some doing, but I'm getting an idea of what's going on, and I don't like it, Maddy. You need to be careful. *Very* careful. You're dealing with something dangerous. I won't sugarcoat it. It's black magic."

My mouth went dry. "How do you know?"

"I just do," my mother said briskly, as if I had challenged her.

"Okay. So, it's black magic. But someone's got to be behind it, right? That kind of stuff just doesn't happen for no reason."

"Of course not. But there's something about it that's hard to explain. Like it's masked. I can't tell where it's coming from or who's responsible."

I thought for a moment. "Mom. Have you ever heard about the witch on the city council who conjured up monsters to get people to leave Chavez Ravine? You know, a long time ago?"

"No. But that doesn't mean anything. I probably don't know half of what actually happened back then."

"Do you think that witch could still be alive?"

My mother gave a thin, brittle laugh. "Oh, Maddy. After everything we've been through, don't you think anything's possible?"

"I guess so." I sounded like a sullen teenager. "I guess I'm just at my wit's end."

My mother sniffed. "Well, get over it. Considering what you're dealing with, Maddy, you'll need all your wits about you. Promise me you'll be careful."

"I promise." But it was an empty vow. How could I keep my guard up all the time, especially since I didn't know what to watch out for?

"Maddy, do you think we could catch up soon? I wish you had told me about living in my mother's house. I don't know how that happened, but I'm happy for you, of course."

My mother's voice shifted from aggrieved to wistful.

"I just wish I could see it for myself."

Me too, but there was no way she would ever make it past the guard's gate. The woman was an entity magnet. Wherever she went, they followed.

I was silent for a little too long because she added, "Why don't you come to see me? I have a pool."

"Are you still in Palm Springs?"

"Yes, but I just bought a place in Beverly Hills. You can really get a deal there these days, and I made an agreement with the gnomes."

I laughed. "I'm sure you did. You'll have the best garden in the neighborhood."

Chapter 39

Celebrity had its downside. With the constant interruptions, as satisfying as they were, I was totally unproductive in my office, so I decided to head home.

But once there, I began to fret about the board meeting, during which, if Cora got her way, my PIP would be rescinded. I still couldn't get any work done.

So, I unpacked the last of the moving boxes. That took a couple of hours. All the while, I eyed the clock, wanting to leave plenty of time to get ready to meet Stu. An epic shower session to shave was needed. I'd been neglecting my usual routine and had nearly reached werewolf territory.

Which got me wondering how much attention I should pay to my bikini line.

I needed to rein in the crazy. It was way too early to be having those kinds of thoughts.

I carried the empty boxes to the sunroom and stacked them in a corner next to the old workbench. Julia thought the wooden planks gave the room "texture" and provided a nice "architectural feature." She suggested I have it refinished and stained. Maybe, I thought. I kind of liked the rough wood and well-worn surface. Still, I added refinishing the workbench to the long list of improvements I would someday make.

The bench, along with Little Lencha, were a tad dusty, so I found a rag and gave them a wipe, taking extra care with the delicate figurine. The bag of ashes was still there, so I made a mental note to take it out next time I threw out the trash.

I found myself talking to the small statue. "I really wish you were around, Lencha. I'm sure you could figure out who's behind all the pendejadas going on." *Pendejadas* being my favorite Spanish word for "bullshit."

Little Lencha began to glow. I was starting to get used to that, but it was still kind of alarming.

The cat broke the mood by scratching at the sliding glass door. With a sigh, I walked over and opened it for him.

"This is why we have a litterbox, my weird furry friend."

He darted out as usual but this time stopped in the middle of the garden and sat there, staring at me with his wide green eyes.

"What?"

He meowed once, then dashed around the side of the house. His claws scrambled over the side gate.

"Hey!" I called out, but he didn't stop.

In that moment, I wished I had given him a name. I couldn't exactly go around the neighborhood shouting, "Hey," without raising eyebrows.

A moment later, he was scratching frantically at the front door.

I stomped over and threw it open. "Seriously? What do you think you're doing?"

Instead of rushing inside, he pranced down the brick path leading to the street.

"Come back here!"

He ignored me and hung a left at the sidewalk.

Annoyed, I followed, picking up my pace when he also quickened his steps. In just a few seconds, we made it all the way down the street to the intersection.

"You come back right now, mister," I said, hands on my hips.

The cat stopped long enough to make sure I was watching, then sauntered across the street. He had never shown any interest in the outdoors before. It was obvious he wanted me to follow him.

Yes. Like the cat had a plan. He was acting unusual. And he had warned me about the big hummingbird…

Another few blocks and we'd be in Palo Verde. How far had he intended to go? I jogged after him, telling him to slow down while I tried to catch up. The cat glanced over his shoulder, taking it easy to make sure I was still following, then picking up his pace again.

It was getting late. If we didn't turn back soon, I wouldn't make it to my meeting with Stu on time.

We turned a corner onto a much busier street, and the cat suddenly broke into a sprint, weaving through parked cars and darting across lawns. I was huffing and puffing when we reached the road leading to Phantom's Pass.

My runaway cat waited until I caught up, then kept heading west.

—⟶·⟶· ⛩ ·⟵·⟵—

The cat moved with purpose all the way to Bishop, then turned up the street where Cora, Charlie, Hernan, and Pete Drury lived.

There was no turning back. And I really wanted to see what the cat would do next.

He stopped in front of Hernan Frias's gloomy-looking house, then darted down the wide side yard separating the property from Cora's. I nervously followed, automatically ducking my head when I passed the windows.

If I got caught, I would have a hard time explaining what I was doing. *Well, your honor, my cat wanted me to follow him onto private property. I'm sure he had his reasons.*

Luckily, Hernan's blinds were down, so my chances of getting caught were slim.

At the back of the house, a gate led to the backyard. The cat jumped it.

I stopped. Running through a yard, trying to catch my cat, was one thing, but going through a private gate was something else entirely. If Hernan saw me, what would I say? *Gee, I was just stopping by to ask for your vote to remove my PIP?*

But curiosity overcame my common sense. As quietly as I could, I unlatched the gate and stepped into the backyard.

Most of it was devoted to raised beds filled with herbs. Hernan seemed to love sage. Fruit trees—lemon and orange—lined the back fence. Tucked in the middle of the yard was a small wooden building with a thatched roof. The cat paced on the gravel path leading to the closed door, his tail flicking back and forth.

Someone moved around inside.

My heart raced. I peeked through a dusty window and couldn't believe what I saw.

Hernan Frias, wearing a black T-shirt and baggy jeans, was hunched over a table, cutting into a large square of red clay with a knife. He reached into an open bag of masa harina and kneaded it into the clay. I watched with disbelief while his hands molded a lumpy figurine, something resembling a rat with a long tail. Several similar figurines were lined up in a neat row, like an army waiting for orders.

My stomach did a little flip.

Hernan Frias—Chavez Ravine Association board member, defender of legacy stakeholders, descendent of a brujo with questionable skills, professor of mystical studies. And creator of supernatural creatures that terrorized his neighbors.

I should have known. Or at least suspected. He was just too hostile and mysterious. And for no reason.

I wondered if he was also behind my mysterious hex bags. Which would mean he wasn't just out to terrorize his neighbors.

He wanted to get to me too.

Chapter 40

I backed away from the shed and rushed down the side yard to the street, reeling with the knowledge Hernan Frias was behind the terrifying attacks. After fumbling for my phone, I called Cora. It rang once, and she picked up.

"Madeline! I don't have any updates for you. I'm sorry. The board hasn't met yet. No one was available until this evening."

I took a deep breath. "I'm not calling about the PIP. It's actually much more important than that. I know the source of the creatures that have been attacking our residents."

Cora inhaled sharply.

"This is probably going to come as a shock, but I'm absolutely certain what I'm about to say is correct. I've just come from Hernan's backyard. I saw him working in his shed. He's *creating* the creatures."

"Maddy, where are you? We should continue this conversation in person."

"I'm right outside."

Cora's front door opened, and she stepped out onto the porch, waving at me to join her.

"It's him, Cora. It's Hernan," I said in a voice bordering on a whisper. "Hernan is behind everything that's been going on in Chavez Ravine."

Cora stared at me. "Hernan? Are you sure?"

"Yes. I saw it with my own eyes. He's molding the creatures out of clay, then using black magic to bring them to life—"

Cora interrupted. "What exactly did you see?"

I described the shed, the significance of the red clay and masa harina, and Hernan making clay figurines I was sure he would later send to frighten residents.

"So, you were spying on him, and you caught him in the act." Her voice was heavy with concern. "Did he see you?"

"Yes, I caught him in the act. And no, he didn't see me. But Cora, why? Why would he do this?"

She took a deep breath and slowly let it out.

"I'm afraid I don't know. Hernan's always been very passionate about Chavez Ravine. Sometimes, he acts like he owns the whole place. And he's so determined to protect legacy stakeholders. I simply cannot imagine why he would do something like this."

"Protect legacy stakeholders..." I repeated. My mind started going a million miles an hour.

I remembered what Leo had said about Hernan Frias's proposed change to the rules. That he wanted to make it easier for relatives of the original Mexican American families to move in.

But if he was going to lure descendants of the original families to buy, he would need people to sell. People like Katherine Morris, Becca Tey, and Pete Drury. People with no family connection to the old neighborhoods. Who could make room for those Hernan thought were more deserving.

Hernan was trying to frighten away residents of Chavez Ravine, just like that witch on the city council decades before. He was no better than the racist politicians in the 1950s.

"Cora, I think I know what Hernan is doing." I explained my theory.

She tugged at her sleeves, straightening the fabric of her blouse while she listened.

260

When I had finished, she gave a long, sad sigh. "I'm very sorry to say this, but I think you're right. His proposed changes to our governing documents would make it nearly impossible for non-legacy people to buy into Chavez Ravine. The entire community would become Mexican American again. But the rest of the board wouldn't agree to such discriminatory behavior."

A car horn interrupted our conversation. Someone shouted, "Way to go, Maddy!"

I automatically waved in response.

"Hernan has always been so darn difficult. And now this!" After a brief pause, she was back to her usual, all-business self. "Your safety is a top priority, Maddy. Do not—and I repeat, do *not*—try to confront Hernan. We don't know what he might do."

"I won't," I promised. "But I will be ready for his next attack." I sure sounded confident.

"Good. It'll be hard not to wring his neck when I see him at the meeting. Wish me luck."

"Forget luck," I said. "You be careful too."

Cora gave a grim laugh. "My husband says my face has subtitles when I'm upset, so I'll try to watch it."

Cora went back into her house, and I began walking down the hill, with the cat several yards ahead. When a dusty SUV pulled up next to me and the driver rolled down the window, my alarm bells started going off. But they stopped when Stu poked his head out and smiled.

"Did you decide to walk to our date?" His blue eyes twinkled.

Date. He had just called our get-together a date.

When I didn't answer right away, his eyebrows lifted. "You're a little far from home. Did the Jeep break down?"

I eyed his vehicle. Definitely not what I expected Stu to drive.

"It's a long story, but I had some unexpected stuff to deal with, and yes, I'm walking home. In fact, I was going to message you and ask if we can meet at seven instead of six?"

"Yeah, sure. No problem." He jerked his head at the empty seat next to him. "Hop in. I'll give you a ride."

"That would be great."

I was halfway around the front of the SUV when the cat let out a loud meow. He was glaring at me, tail flicking. I couldn't just leave him.

Stu stared at him, eyebrows squishing together. "Do you know that cat?"

I cleared my throat. "That's another long story, but yeah. He's kind of mine."

"Kind of yours?" Stu tilted his head and scratched his chin. "So, what? You were taking your cat for a walk?"

"Not really, no," I stammered. "He got out, I followed him, and now we're walking back home."

Stu's voice rose in disbelief. "You followed your cat all the way from La Loma?"

"That's pretty much it." I didn't sound too bright, but better to admit to a dumb thing like that than try to explain the reality: the cat had led me to Hernan Frias's shed, where he was up to black magic and sculpting creatures out of clay and masa.

Stu shrugged. "Okay. Then why don't I take you *both* home?"

Easier said than done. I had never touched the cat, let alone tried to pick him up. We could end up in a bloody little power struggle, and Stu didn't need to see that.

"It's okay. Thank you. Really. I don't want to get your car dirty. He'll get cat hair everywhere."

Stu flapped his lips like a horse. "Are you kidding? This thing already has enough dog hair to knit a sweater."

I bit my lip and eyed the cat, who was now sauntering toward me. "You have a dog?"

"No, my daughter does, and this is the dog car—the one we take to the park, where he rolls around in the mud." Stu leaned across the seats and opened the passenger door. "Grab him and hop on in."

To my astonishment, the cat darted around the front of the SUV and leapt inside, clambered over the middle console, and disappeared into the back.

Stu laughed. "Okay, make yourself at home!"

There was nothing else to do but slide in next to Stu. He hadn't exaggerated. The leather seats were covered in long white hairs. I peered into the back seat. The cat was sitting in the middle, looking straight ahead and blinking slowly.

"Is that normal for a cat? To just sit there in a car like that?"

"I have no idea," I admitted. "I've never had one before. And I didn't ask for this one. He just sort of…appeared one day."

Stu's pine-scented soap mingled with the musty dog smell of the SUV. I buckled up and turned in my seat to scowl at the cat. He returned my gaze with an inscrutable expression. We had a bit of a stare off before I turned to give my full attention to Stu's profile.

"So, you have a daughter," I said.

The conversation had to start somewhere. That seemed as good a place as any.

"Uh huh. Clare. She's sixteen. And that's all I'll say at the moment because if I start talking about her, I won't be able to stop."

From his stony expression, I suspected things weren't well in Daughterland. He changed the subject before I could.

"Where did you learn to use a slingshot like that? I've...never seen anything quite like it."

"Lots of practice. It's my new hobby."

"You're kidding?"

"I'm not. I just happened to see some guys using them at an axe-throwing club in the valley and I thought, what the heck."

"You hang out at axe-throwing clubs?"

I couldn't help but laugh. "You make it sound like I go to dive bars or something. Julia took me. They serve fancy cocktails."

As we drove through Palo Verde, Stu told me about his coworkers' reactions to Bad Pete's viral video. Some had suggested he hire me, and so did one of his clients.

We reached my house. He gripped the steering wheel and bit his lip, staring straight ahead. Finally, he said, "I could come in. Wait for you while you get ready."

His suggestion caught me off guard, and I hesitated. Mostly because the act of getting ready was going to take a lot of time in the bathroom, and having him waiting around would be awkward.

His face turned red. "I'm sorry," he said hurriedly. "I shouldn't have asked."

Now it was my turn to be embarrassed. I liked the guy. He had asked to come inside, and now I had given him the wrong impression. The fact was, I hadn't felt awkward around a man since my twenties, and I had no idea what I was doing.

"No, no. Please, come in. Have some wine while you wait."

I flung open the door, but before I could get out, the cat scrambled over the console and jumped onto my lap. He was heavy, like a furry sandbag. I looked down at him, not sure what to do.

Stu stared at him too. "That is one really big cat. Is he part cheetah or something?"

"He's a Bengal." I stuck a leg out of the door and braced myself for whatever was coming when I tried to pick up the cat.

He suddenly went limp. I took that as a good sign and carefully lifted him, making sure to keep both of my hands around him until he was resting against my chest. His fur was soft on my skin and his body warm next to mine.

I'm going to survive...

Until Stu reached over.

"The cat and I can hang out while you get ready." He gently put his hand on the cat's head.

Big mistake.

The cat swatted at his hand, claws raking his flesh. Stu yelped in pain.

I leapt from the vehicle, bringing the cat with me. He squirmed out of my arms, jumped to the ground, and raced toward the house. A white truck driving past slammed on its brakes and parked at the curb, but I didn't pay much attention.

Stu's hand was bleeding. A lot.

"I'm so sorry," I cried. "Come inside. I've got a first aid kit."

Blood dripped onto his shirt and jeans. Stu grabbed a napkin from the glovebox and tried to staunch the flow. He managed a weak smile.

"Thanks, but I think I'll go home and get cleaned up."

I closed the door and hurried around to his side. "This is awful. He's never done anything like that before. Are you sure you're all right?"

Stu chuckled, though he sounded more pained than amused. "It's just a scratch. I guess he doesn't take kindly to competition." He tossed aside the blood-soaked napkin and pressed a fresh one to the wound.

From the porch, the cat meowed loudly.

"See you at seven," I said with a sigh. "If you're still up for it."

Stu snapped his head up. "Are you changing your mind?"

"Definitely not, as long as you survive without stitches." I smiled and patted his arm. "Seven it is. I think we both could use a drink."

I stood on the sidewalk and watched him drive away. The scratch had been unfortunate, but it also revealed a glimpse of Stu's vulnerable side. And his good nature too.

The cat was waiting for me on the porch when I walked up the pathway.

The white truck pulled away from the curb and into my driveway. It was a newer model coated in a layer of dust. The driver's side door opened, and a man got out. He was short and stocky, with a bald head and a broad chest.

The cat leapt up to the kitchen window and wriggled through the small opening. It was like he was being chased.

The stocky man, who appeared to be around fifty, was halfway up the brick path. "Is that my cat?"

My heart dropped into my stomach. I wanted to scream, "No!" But all I could manage was a weak, "Uh…"

The man stopped in front of the porch and glared up at me. He had the bushiest eyebrows I had ever seen.

"I don't think it's your cat." I sounded guilty.

The man crossed his arms in front of his chest, and his eyebrows lowered. "I just saw a red Bengal jump through that window. Red Bengals are pretty rare, and mine disappeared recently. I'm working a job up the street, and one day, he managed to get out of my trailer. I haven't seen him since." He jabbed a finger at my front door. "Why don't you bring him out so I can have a look?"

I cleared my throat. "And your name is?"

"Rory. I'm the developer building the new neighborhood up the hill. Who are *you?*"

"Madeline Madrigal, head of security for the Chavez Ravine Association."

"Is that right?" Rory's eyes narrowed. "Then I'd like to report a theft. I think you've got my cat in there. Why don't you bring him out so I can have a look?"

I leaned against the porch railing for support. "If that's really your cat, then you know picking him up and bringing him anywhere isn't going to happen. Or at least, not without bloodshed."

Rory threw his head back and laughed. "That's him, all right. That's my Hugo."

"Hugo?" *No wonder the cat ran away. What a stupid name.*

Rory shot me a dark look, pulled a phone from the pocket of his jeans, swiped at it, and then held it up. "All right, then. Take a look here. Is this the cat you've got inside? Because if so, I want him back. I paid a breeder three thousand bucks for him. I've got his papers and everything."

I forced myself to stare at the photo. The cat was sitting on top of a cat tree, glaring at the camera.

"Maybe. It's hard to tell in a picture." That was a total lie. The picture might as well have been a mug shot.

"All right, then." Rory snatched the phone away. "Where did you get your cat? Can you prove its yours?"

From his determined expression, Rory wasn't about to give up. As much as I didn't want to lose the cat, I didn't have a lot of choices. But I wasn't about to make it easy for Rory.

I opened the front door and stepped aside with a sigh of resignation. "The cat wandered in one day, and I thought he was lost. But if he's really yours, then go ahead. Go get him." I felt like crying.

Rory clapped his hands together. "Now we're talking. I've got a crate in the truck. I'll be right back."

Crate in hand, Rory barged into the house, cursing up a storm and shouting at the cat. I winced, wishing I had magical powers to make the annoying man disappear forever. From the screeching, the cat was putting up quite the fight. I stayed outside, not wanting to witness the violence.

Eventually, Rory stormed out onto the porch. He had scratches on his face and hands but a victorious look in his eyes. From the crate, the cat let out a furious meow.

"I'm sorry," I called after him.

With a heavy heart, I watched Rory heave the crate into the bed of the truck. He didn't bother thanking me for taking care of his cat. Didn't even say goodbye.

When the truck roared off, I whispered a silent thanks to the cat for bravely fending off the hummingbird and protecting me from the hex bags.

Which reminded me.

I still had work to do. While I wasn't giving up on the cat just yet, if Hernan was about to unleash a rodent infestation, I would need some supplies.

I caught Jo at the Occult Affairs command center just before the end of her shift and asked if I could borrow some equipment. When she agreed, I sent Brandon to The Dump to pick up a few crates designed for smaller entities. Those would do the trick, assuming we could figure out how to trap the rat monsters in the first place.

Then I called our contract security firm and arranged for extra patrols starting that night. I didn't think Hernan's batch of rats would be ready so soon, but I wasn't going to take any chances. Finally, I put Ron Mendez on standby so he could help me with our next incident.

Once all the arrangements were in place, I showered, shaved, and put on my makeup.

On my way out the door, a noise came from the back of the house. Surely, it was too soon for Hernan's rats to be on the prowl. I slowly walked through the living room.

Nothing.

I tiptoed past the ottoman and peered around the corner into the sunroom.

There, sitting next to Little Lencha like nothing had happened, was the cat.

He must have escaped from Rory, found his way back, and jumped through an open window. I could have found Rory's number and let him know what happened, but he didn't even say goodbye. He would figure it out soon enough.

"I have no idea how you knew about Hernan, but thank you."

It seemed perfectly normal to talk to a cat. He blinked at me with his huge green eyes.

I told Lencha goodnight. "If you sent the cat out on his mission today or if you helped him find his way back, thank you too. And if there's anything you can do to help me deal with Hernan Frias, that would be really, really great."

I half expected Little Lencha to glow or vibrate or something. But she just sat there, giving no indication she had heard me.

Maybe she was just a figurine after all.

Chapter 41

My date with Stu didn't exactly go as planned. As soon as I walked into Olga's Cantina wearing my bright gold trench coat, I was swarmed by a group of people who wanted to congratulate me and buy me drinks. Caitlin was at the bar, and when she spotted Stu, she made a beeline for him. He grinned when he saw her.

"Hey, kiddo!" He turned to me. "You've met my niece, Caitlin, right? She works for the HOA."

Well, that was a surprise. And a relief, if I was being honest.

I managed to nod, watching Caitlin place a hand on his arm.

"Uncle Stu here pulled a few strings. I was miserable in my last job, but I really like working for Cora." Caitlin leaned over to me and, in a low voice, said, "Maybe I shouldn't say anything, but when that whole PIP thing happened, it made me really mad. It just seemed so unfair. That kind of thing wouldn't happen to a man, you know."

I had really jumped to some unfortunate conclusions, but there was no time for discussion. Complete strangers wanting selfies with me pushed their way in, and my conversation with Caitlin was over. And any small talk with Stu was out of the question.

He was good-natured about the whole thing, but after it became clear people weren't going to leave us alone, Stu suggested we go somewhere quieter. I happily agreed. He looked especially handsome in a V-neck sweater that matched his blue eyes. One hand sported a sturdy bandage covering the wound the cat—*my* cat—had inflicted.

The restaurant at Bishop Plaza was even worse. Turned out, it was Bad Pete's favorite place, and the staff all knew him. So, when the diners weren't making a fuss, the servers did.

Then there were other interruptions.

Stu's daughter phoned to vent about a fight she had just had with her first boyfriend, so he excused himself and took the call out on the patio. Cora contacted me with the results of the board meeting, so I took my turn outside, where I learned the PIP had been canceled. The vote had been four to one.

"Eileen?" I guessed.

Cora gave a disgusted sigh. "No. Hernan."

"Hmm. How was Hernan? Anything suspicious?"

"No, everything was fine. He was more insufferable than usual, if that's possible. He didn't say why he voted the way he did. Charlie played the Pete Drury video at the start of the meeting, and Hernan just sat there, stone-faced."

I updated Cora on the extra security measures I had put in place, anticipating Hernan would unleash his next attack at any time.

"I hate rats," Cora said.

"I don't think you have much to worry about. It's not you he's after."

When I shared the news about the PIP with Stu, he was genuinely happy. I thought about warning him we would likely have some trouble in the wee hours one of these nights, but that felt presumptuous. It would also mean telling him about Hernan Frias, and the idea of explaining all that drained me. I just wanted to sip some wine and get to know Stu a little better.

The wine wasn't a problem—the free drinks were flowing—but privacy was impossible.

After we had finished our dinner, Stu leaned across the table. "How about we try this again soon? Between our busy lives and your fan club"—he gestured to a group replaying Bad Pete's video at the bar and fist pumping in my direction—"we haven't had a moment's peace. And my ex is driving Clare over because she's decided I need to take her to school tomorrow for reasons I don't completely understand. So, I can't even invite you over for a nightcap."

"Your daughter is lucky to have you." I hadn't meant it to sound so morose.

By the time we left, I was a little tipsy. It had been dumb of me to indulge. There was always the chance I would be jolted awake at three a.m. by a rodent crisis. Stu wasn't any better, so he called the car service exclusive to Chavez Ravine. Privacy issues, Cora had explained. Pretty nice for those who could afford it.

"Can we try this again next week?" Stu said in the dimly lit parking lot.

He was leaning toward me—so close I could smell his soap—and I responded by doing the same.

The door of the restaurant opened, and a drunken voice shouted, "Hey, I want some Madeline Madrigal too!"

Stu's expression turned from tender anticipation to total irritation in an instant.

The man stumbled closer, eyes glassy and breath reeking of alcohol. The guy was bigger and taller, but Stu stood his ground, positioning himself between me and the idiot.

"She doesn't want anything to do with you," Stu said firmly.

The man swayed on his feet and pouted. "I just want to make sure she knows where I live, in case I need saving with a slingshot. That's not too much to ask, is it?" He rattled off an address in Palo Verde. One of the swankier pockets of Chavez Ravine.

Stu held up a warning hand. "How about we let Madeline get home? Even a superhero needs time to recharge."

"Yeah! That's right. Madeline, you rest, okay, darling?" With a sloppy grin, the man stumbled back into the restaurant, and we were alone again.

For about five seconds.

A black car pulled up. A window rolled down, and a young man in a baseball cap stared when he saw me. "Whoa! You're my ride? My friends aren't going to believe this. Hey, would you mind taking a selfie with me?"

With a sigh, I nodded. There was a grand conspiracy preventing me from having a romantic moment with Stu.

He took the driver's phone and did the honors while I posed next to the window. The flash lit up the dark parking lot for a moment, revealing Stu's smirk while he snapped the picture.

I couldn't help but laugh at the absurdity of it all. In a few hours, I had gone from feeling like a failure to being a PIP-free local celebrity.

Stu began to laugh too. "Let's hope you don't need to take your slingshot out tonight."

I hoped not too.

When I climbed into bed, I tried to forget the evening's frustrations. I really needed to sleep, but between the cat prowling around and me worrying I would get a call about rats wreaking havoc, I couldn't relax. It was nearly midnight when I finally drifted off.

At two o'clock, my eyes snapped open. And then again at three.

I lay awake, my entire body tense, waiting for Hernan's black magic to strike. But the phone remained silent.

When my alarm went off at seven, I had slept three uneventful hours.

I retrieved my phone from under a tangle of sheets. The overnight reports I had requested were waiting for me in my inbox. The guards had made their rounds but observed nothing unusual.

Good news, but it was just one night.

Maybe the board meeting had interrupted Hernan's plans. Perhaps he had run out of time to do whatever dark things he needed to do. Or he was waiting for the next night.

I was already dreading tomorrow, and this one was barely over.

The problem was, I was stuck in react mode, and I didn't like it.

Now that I knew Hernan was behind the attacks, I needed to shift to offense and learn more about the man. I understood his motivation, but what about his weaknesses? Who did he trust? Who would be persuaded to share information? Or maybe there were clues in his past—secrets waiting to be discovered.

I fired up my computer and was just beginning to scroll through public records when my phone rang. It was Cora.

"Something's happened." Her voice quavered. "I can hardly believe it."

My heart leapt into my throat. "What is it?"

"It's Hernan. He was rushed to the hospital this morning. His granddaughter called me. She's not sure if he's going to make it."

My mind struggled to keep up. Just a few hours before, I had seen him in his shed, sculpting the next wave of creatures. And now...

The timing was just too weird.

"Was it a heart attack? A stroke?"

"They haven't said. The doctors are still running tests, but he can't speak or move. His granddaughter found him this morning. She was supposed to drive him to a doctor's appointment. We know he'd had leukemia, but he told me it was under control, and he expected to make a full recovery."

Hernan, the man behind all the chaos, was now incapacitated in a hospital bed.

I thanked Cora for letting me know, but my thoughts raced. Had Hernan miscalculated and his black magic backfired?

Could he still unleash his creations from his hospital bed? I couldn't shake the feeling he might still be dangerous, bedpan or not.

But I wasn't sure because I knew next to nothing about brujeria.

The only real bruja I knew was long dead, her clay statue sitting in my sunroom.

Lencha Bantacorte.

I had a dark thought. The night before, I had asked for Lencha's help. Was this her way of providing it?

I rushed toward the sunroom. When I rounded the corner, I noticed a faint yellow glow emanating from the figurine.

A couple of days earlier, I wouldn't have been able to say whether the glow was real or in my head. But now, I had no doubt. Little Lencha's eyes followed me when I approached. That had happened before, but this time, her head seemed to tilt slightly to the side. There was a rustling of her skirt, and I was definitely not imagining it.

Was I?

"Did you do it?"

Little Lencha didn't reply, but she answered another way.

The glow around her intensified, enveloping the entire room in a warm light. I watched, spellbound, while she emerged from the clay, like a butterfly breaking free of its cocoon. The light became so intense, I had to close my eyes. When I opened them again, a woman was standing before me.

Lencha, the legendary bruja herself.

She was stunning, a slightly built woman with dark skin and long black hair. But her beauty had an edge. Her features were regal but stern. She radiated strength and power.

Her fierce gaze locked onto mine, dark eyes piercing and unrelenting.

"Mi hija." *My daughter* in Spanish.

Those simple words brought tears to my eyes.

I raised my hands to touch her. She stepped back, eyebrows arched.

"Chingona. Nada mas."

The room went completely dark. From another part of the house, the cat howled. By the time my eyes had adjusted, Lencha the woman was gone, and Little Lencha the figurine sat quietly on the workbench.

I laughed. In fact, I probably sounded hysterical. But I couldn't help myself.

A long time ago, *chingona* had been an insult—a term men would use for women who were too assertive, a touch sassy, or just unconventional.

But women had reclaimed the word. Now, *chingona* meant competent, self-assured, living life on one's own terms. The spirit of Lencha Bantacorte had appeared with a stern reminder:

I needed to be strong, determined, and independent. And I needed to follow her path.

Chingona. Nothing more.

I smiled again, unable to imagine any advice being easier to follow. After all, I came by my inner chingona naturally.

But her appearance gave me a new sense of clarity. I could wring my hands over Hernan, or I could let my chingona flag fly and start digging.

After a quick shower, I dressed in black. Today would be a busy day. As would tomorrow, and every other day until I had solved the mystery of Hernan Frias and the creatures attacking Chavez Ravine.

I chose a trench coat in soft gray. The perfect color for inconspicuous detective work.

Chapter 42

I staked out the ICU until a young woman asked about Hernan Frias at the nurses' station. His granddaughter was his only living relative besides some far-flung cousins. I followed her into the hospital cafeteria. She wasn't much younger than me, with deep-set eyes and a weary expression.

I bought a cafe latte and sat at a table next to hers.

"Rough day?" I asked when she glanced in my direction.

She sighed. "It's my grandfather. He's in pretty bad shape, but I need to get back to work tomorrow. I can't afford to take any more time off."

"That's rough." I sounded sympathetic, and I was. Not toward Hernan, but I felt for his granddaughter. She was in a tough spot.

His granddaughter looked down at her untouched slice of apple pie. "It *is* rough. I live in Pomona, and the drive is a bitch. How about you? Are you visiting someone here?"

"A coworker." It wasn't exactly a lie.

"That's kind of you. I'm Valeria Torres."

I changed the subject quickly before she could ask my name. "Both my grandfathers died when I was a kid. Are you close to yours?"

She brightened. "I am! We weren't always, though. He had this crazy idea growing up that I should become a healer. And by that, I really mean a witch. Have you ever heard of brujeria?"

I nodded, and she continued.

"My grandfather is an international expert on magic. He swears it runs in our family. And he wanted to send me to some place in Mexico to learn all that stuff, which was crazy. But I've always wanted to have my own bookstore. My grandfather thought I was wasting my talents, but I bought a small store, and I've never been happier."

"Sounds amazing." I couldn't imagine anything more different than the career I had chosen—or the one that had chosen me.

"It's a tough business, but I love it."

"You mentioned your grandfather is known internationally?" I asked nonchalantly. "What's his name? Maybe I've heard of him?"

"Hernan Frias," she said, pride in her voice. "He used to teach at Occidental College. If you look him up, he's written a half-dozen books."

"Oh, wow," I replied, feigning surprise. "What's it like, having a famous grandfather?"

Valeria rolled her eyes. "Not easy, that's for sure. I love him, but he's a bit of an egomaniac. My poor grandmother catered to his every whim. I was worried he wouldn't know how to take care of himself when she died. I found him a lady from the church to do all the cooking and cleaning, and he was doing fine until this happened."

"So, when he gets out, you'll have him go to a convalescent hospital near you?" I asked innocently.

Valeria made a face. "I wish. The doctors can't figure out what's wrong with him. He's kind of a medical mystery, and they won't release him until he's fully stable. At least, that's what they're saying now."

I drained the last of my coffee, wished her the best of luck, and left.

Over the next week, I thought about how Valeria had described her grandfather's situation as a medical mystery.

Of course it was. No doctor would conclude Hernan Frias had been the victim of a spell. Lencha's spell. Which must have been pretty strong stuff. Hernan spent five days in the ICU before being transferred to a regular room.

In that time, there were no more supernatural attacks in Chavez Ravine. The respite meant I could stop playing defense and come up with a plan to end them for good.

I met Stu for drinks twice. We had a nice time, but his daughter was staying with him for a while, so that put a damper on things going any further.

I kept busy. *Very* busy. I had all the usual projects, like getting bids on a stone wall for the border along Elysian Park and responding to complaints about graffiti and car break-ins—the work of teenagers who had hopped our lousy wooden fence.

But I did my most important work in the Palo Verde library. There, I poured over Hernan Frias's books and articles. Somehow I had gotten the wrong impression about his work. Instead of practical studies into Mexican witchcraft, he was a big fan of Carlos Castenda and his exploration of the spiritual side of man's nature. Kind of cerebral for an actual brujo, I thought.

What he wrote about the practice of magic, I didn't think was very good. His works on shamanism and his ventures into inner space were lost on me, and like several academics pointed out, Frias's writings about sorcery weren't exactly original. *Ouch.*

But one essay made me break out in gooseflesh. He had written about sorcerers being able to transport themselves out of their bodies while in a trance state. That made me nervous. If Hernan was right, it might mean he could "spy" on us by projecting himself into my office and monitoring my private conversations with Cora.

The same essay claimed sorcerers could enter the bodies of their "spirit animals" and send them off to do their bidding.

When I read that, I remembered the huge hummingbird that had appeared at my window and set fire to Trini Duran's notebooks. The same one that showed up at Cora's, trying to eavesdrop.

I was beginning to understand the full extent of Hernan's power.

Two weeks after Hernan had been rushed to the hospital, Cora sent me a text.

Hernan's recovering. His granddaughter says he can't walk yet, but he's eating and talking. What are we going to do?

That was the million-dollar question. There was no telling how long Lencha's magic would last. Maybe it was already wearing off. He might be back in his shed, sculpting creatures, in no time.

As much as it gave me the heebie-jeebies, I had to confront the man in person. He needed to know I knew. And that I wasn't going to let him get away with his dark plans.

It was time to visit Hernan Frias in the hospital.

Luck was on my side. A nurse with curly black hair looked up from her computer when I asked about Hernan's condition.

"Oh, you must be Mr. Frias's granddaughter. I've heard all about you. I just checked on him, and he's awake. Go on in. Just don't stay too long. He's a bit tired out. He had more tests this morning."

She didn't have to tell me twice. I hurried down the hall, looking at the names posted outside each room. When I reached Hernan's, I took a deep breath and pushed open the door. He was lying in bed, looking gray but alert. As soon as he saw me, his lips curled in a snarl.

"You," he rasped. "Why are you doing this to me?" His voice quavered with anger.

"Me?" I crossed my legs and returned his glare. "Don't be silly. I'm not doing anything to you."

"Don't lie to me!" Hernan sputtered. "You're a Bantacorte." He said my family name like it was a dirty word.

If he thought I had skills, who was I to disagree? I decided to go with it.

I crossed my arms in front of my chest. "I am. I am a Bantacorte, and it's best you not forget that, Señor Frias. Not if you want to continue making a full recovery."

I sounded like the villain in a cheesy movie, but I didn't care.

"You don't know what you've done to me!" His lower lip twitched. "I'm dizzy all the time. I can't walk. I'm nauseous. My hands won't stop shaking. You have to take back whatever you've done. I can't live like this."

He tried to sit up but couldn't manage it. Hernan gave up and laid his head back on the pillow.

"Listen to me, Madeline." His voice was hoarse. "It's bad for the community for me to be in such a weakened state…" His voice drifted off, and he began coughing.

"Oh, I see. Care to explain?" I asked evenly.

He turned his head and stared at the wall. "I can't. You just have to trust me."

"Trust *you*?" I might have snorted.

A look of sheer panic crossed Hernan's face, and he clutched at his chest. The machine next to him began beeping loudly while he struggled for breath. He looked at me with fear in his eyes. The door burst open, and a nurse rushed to Hernan's side.

She checked his vitals, hit a red button, and called for assistance.

While chaos erupted in the room, I slipped out. The hallway outside was comparatively quiet. I made my way toward the exit and out to the parking lot.

Hernan obviously thought I was behind his troubles. But that was ridiculous.

It was, wasn't it? At most, I might have given Little Lencha some ideas, but I hadn't really *done* anything. Had I?

Hernan had said being in "such a weakened state" was bad for Chavez Ravine. Was that just a vague threat? Or was there more to it?

I had arrived at the hospital determined to confront him about his scheme, but I hadn't had the chance.

And I was leaving with nothing but questions.

Chapter 43

Funny thing about questions. Maybe it was the cop in me, but mine didn't just sit there quietly, waiting. They nagged at me and kept me up at night, jumping up and down in my head, until I found answers.

When I climbed into the Jeep, questions about Hernan Frias started forming.

Cora and I suspected he was trying to scare non-legacy people into selling their homes, but just how powerful a brujo was he? Was that line about staying healthy for the sake of the neighborhoods just bluster, or was there something more to it? Was he working alone, or did he have an accomplice? Did anyone on the board know what he was up to? Eileen Simpson?

She was, after all, a real estate agent who would rake in eye-popping commissions when properties started going on the market.

I parked the Jeep a couple of houses down from the Frias place and walked nonchalantly up the street. There was no sign of anyone, and a quick glance turned up no security cameras on nearby houses. I went up the side yard again, through the gate, and into the shed.

Maybe I had heard too many fairy tales, but I half expected to find a bubbling cauldron and a jar of newt eyes. I certainly didn't expect a man cave, but that's what the shed was, complete with a TV, refrigerator, and easy chair.

The place smelled of stale cigar smoke and mildew. It mixed with a sickly-sweet scent coming from a row of partially burnt candles. Several cardboard boxes filled a shelf. On a counter were a box of modeling clay, a bag of masa, tins of ground glass and salt, a spice rack with about twenty unlabeled jars, and a pair of socks.

My socks—issued by the LAPD.

Hernan Frias must have sneaked into my house and taken them, maybe while I was moving. But why would he want a pair of my socks?

I spent the next several minutes looking through tins, jars, and boxes. Behind one box was a small note pad. I stuck it in my pocket and took the box off the shelf. It was heavy and quite a bit larger than the others. I put it on the floor and opened the flaps.

Another surprise.

I reached inside and pulled out a replica of Chavez Ravine—a scale model, by the looks of it—made from what appeared to be paper mâché, with balsa wood buildings. The model was incredibly detailed. Streets, homes, and businesses covered the hills. The guardhouses were there, as was the fence along the border with Elysian Park. There were even tiny security cameras on it.

If Hernan had made this, the man had some skills.

I leaned down for a closer look at the HOA offices in Palo Verde Plaza, marveling again at the detail. There were even cars in the parking lot.

Including a Jeep.

From the fine layer of dust on parts of the model, it had been around for a long time, but the Jeep meant Hernan had added to it recently.

That's when I noticed a tiny red pin sticking out of the small vehicle. Another was on the roof of the Palo Verde community center, approximately above my office. And a third was poking out of the roof of my house.

The model was telling me something, and I needed to know what it was.

I went street by street, looking for something out of place. More pins—some white, some red, some blue. There were more than twenty in all. I noted the color and location of each and began to notice a pattern.

There were red pins in each of the places I had found a hex bag.

White pins marked the locations where we had faced clay creatures: the Morris's place, Becca Tey's, Bad Pete's huge compound, and party central, where the Simpson kid had freaked out. There were two other homes marked with white pins. I didn't know who lived in them, but those were probably where the giant rats would have appeared if Hernan hadn't fallen ill.

The blue pins were troubling. There weren't many of them, but I couldn't find a pattern. They were in seemingly random places in Palo Verde and Bishop. A small cluster was near the water company building in La Loma, and there was one on the hill leading down into Solano.

I took pictures of the model from several angles, with close-ups of the pins, then put the model back in the box and up on the shelf. After collapsing into the easy chair, I started going through the notebook.

Hernan might have been a talented model maker, but his handwriting was horrible. It took me a while to decipher his scrawl, but I was eventually able to make sense of his notes.

The first few pages were instructions for creating illness spells. The list of ingredients was familiar: salt, glass, cumin, brown paper bags, and a piece of clothing from the intended victim.

Check. One mystery solved.

Then came guidelines for sculpting and activating clay creatures.

While I deciphered Hernan's notes, it struck me how basic they were. Like I was reading from a child's textbook, not the journal of a master brujo. I couldn't imagine Lencha having to write down notes on how to create a hex bag. She probably didn't even need an article of clothing to make someone ill. Her powers alone would have been enough.

I kept reading. Hernan had apparently tried several kinds of spells. Some appeared designed to scare people, others to cause property damage, and still more to influence what people thought.

But obviously, the guy was a lightweight. He had successfully frightened people and might have done other things, but I got the impression his magic was fragile and rudimentary. Even Julia had been capable of defeating his fiercest creation with a rolling pin.

I continued thumbing through the notebook until I came to a page titled: "Tuck's Demons."

Several illustrations followed, including drawings that looked a lot like Dog Face Bride, the naked hairy guy, the Jumpers, and the giant birds. Obviously, these were the inspiration for Hernan's sculptures, but it wasn't clear where they had come from. I wondered if Tuck was the Irish witch who had sat on the city council in the old days. It would be easy enough to find out.

I snapped pictures of the drawings so I could take a closer look back at the office. Then I flipped through the rest of the notebook. I was about to put it back on the shelf when a familiar name jumped out at me.

Lencha Bantacorte.

I immediately stopped. Hernan's notes in this section had a different tone. They were no longer instructions or lists of ingredients, but instead contained his thoughts about something Lencha had done years ago.

It appeared she had cast a protection spell over Chavez Ravine to keep the monsters away, and he was trying to do the same thing. It also appeared he was not having much success. Hernan had had minor victories. He noted small accomplishments over the past few years, but he was still failing to do what Lencha had done.

When I closed the door behind me, a sound came from the fuchsia bush next to the shed.

A tiny, regular-sized hummingbird flitted from one delicate blossom to another.

Chapter 44

For the next two weeks, I was a machine. No 3:00 a.m. calls interrupted my sleep, and no clay monsters assaulted my neighbors. I got up each morning refreshed and ready to work through my to-do list, which I did with amazing speed.

Among other things, I compiled my recommendations for security improvements and sent them to the board. It included a stone wall topped with an electrified wire to replace the wooden fence along the border with Elysian Park, additional security staff so I could increase our regular patrols, a modern training program for all security personnel, non-lethal weapons to safely contain entities—just in case—and development of a rapid-response plan for all kinds of emergencies, from earthquakes to wildfires to entity invasions.

All in all, I was pretty proud of it. I didn't think there was much chance the board would fund the whole thing, but at least it would get them thinking about security priorities.

And, given my experience with Eileen Simpson, it would make the board responsible for any security shortcomings. I had given them my best advice, and if they chose not to follow it, it would be on them. They would no longer be able to blame their amazing and fashionable head of security if something went wrong.

I was productive on the domestic front too. After adding some knickknacks to my newly furnished living room, I bought some fancy dishes and glassware for the kitchen, spiffed up the bathrooms with new towels and mats, and even put in a wireless sound system so I could listen to Tito Puente in every room in the house.

But my greatest sense of accomplishment came from my work. I had solved the mystery of supernatural creatures and had devised a way to take them out. Plus, I discovered who had been pestering me with hex bags.

Still, even in my happiest moments, I knew this peaceful period would one day come to an end.

Hernan Frias was home, and he was slowly improving. I still didn't know what he was capable of. He believed I was responsible for putting him in the hospital, and I did nothing to convince him otherwise. But he was not the kind of man to accept defeat.

Hernan would continue to frighten non-legacy residents. Eventually, he would test me and try to find the limits of my powers. Of course, he would discover I had none, and when that happened, there would be nothing holding him back.

I worried about what he had said: Chavez Ravine needed him to be healthy. Though I still had to find out what that was about, when I did, I would have a whole new set of problems.

That was me. Couldn't be happy for too long. When I *was* happy, it just meant I hadn't discovered the bad stuff yet.

There was only one way to keep anxiety from driving me crazy. It was time to pay a visit to Señor Frias and somehow put a stop to his wicked plot.

—⟩·⟩·𝄞·⟨·⟨—

A cool wind was blowing when I got to Bishop. Palm trees swayed in the gusts when I pulled up in front of Hernan Frias's house.

A small, middle-aged woman with freckles and short brown hair answered the door. A caretaker, I assumed.

"Is Hernan home?" I tried to peer past her.

The interior of the house was dim as a dungeon, but I could just make out bulky dark wood furniture scattered throughout the living room.

The woman blinked rapidly. My question seemed to catch her off guard.

"Oh, yes, he's home. You want to see him?"

"That would be great!" I gave her my friendliest smile. "We work together. I was in the neighborhood and thought I'd stop by for a few moments to see how he's doing."

The woman shook her head. "Ay, he's so stubborn. He's in the backyard, doing who knows what. Because when I went to check on him, he told me to stay in the house."

I smiled again. "How about I pop back there and say hi? He can't very well get mad at *me*."

He definitely would, but oh well.

The woman's eyes flicked heavenward. "Okay, then. My name is Marta. I'm a home health aide, and he should be in bed, resting, but he won't listen to me." She lowered her voice. "He's been very hard to deal with."

Tell me about it, sister. "I'll just go around the side." I winked.

Marta nodded, but doubt began to creep into her eyes. After all, here I was, barging in on her patient. I hurried off before she could change her mind.

Wind had its advantages. With all the leaves rustling and tree branches scraping against the shed, Hernan couldn't possibly hear me coming. I pressed my ear against the door. Even over the wind, it was apparent he was talking to himself.

The breeze lifted my hair when I pushed open the creaky door and stepped inside. And there he was, standing in front of his clay rats. He admired his handiwork, presumably uttering words of magic to his nasty creations.

Hernan spun around, and we locked eyes. His surprised expression shifted to defiance. "What are *you* doing here?"

His silver-streaked black hair was disheveled and in need of a cut. Instead of his usual dapper outfit, he wore a worn flannel shirt and sweatpants.

I gestured toward the rats, noticing how they had changed since the last time. Their bodies seemed more defined, with longer tails that had spikes protruding from them. *Nice.* Despite his illness, Hernan had been a very busy brujo.

"This has got to stop. *You* have got to stop."

Hernan's chin came up. "You might think, just because you're a Bantacorte, that you understand these neighborhoods, but you don't. You're an outsider. I've lived here all my life. Your grandmother left when things got tough around here. *My* family stayed. *My* family resisted. They fought to save their homes. Their way of life. Their culture. And they won. Now, I'm preserving what my family fought for."

I could practically hear the violins playing. "By scaring away the non-legacy homeowners? By trying to change the rules so only people with legacy roots can buy property here?"

His dark eyes glittered. "I'll do whatever it takes so that my people—*our* people—have the advantage that was stolen from them all those years ago."

"Don't you try that 'our people' crap on me. You're no better than the politicians who tried to force everyone out back then! You're using your power to control what happens in Chavez Ravine, just like they did. You're not preserving anything. You want to kick people out, and that's not right. Legacy residents should understand that, of all people!"

Hernan's gaze hardened. "You don't understand the struggle we've faced to hold on to what is ours. You waltz in here, thinking you have all the answers, when you've never bothered to ask the right questions."

The man wasn't just stubborn; he was an egomaniac. Hernan Frias was obsessed with solutions to problems that no longer existed.

"You are *hurting* our community, not helping it, Hernan." My voice rose above the wind. "You're trying to create divisions that shouldn't exist in this day and age. It's got to stop." I pointed at the clay rats. "Either you destroy those things, or *I* will."

Hernan's nostrils flared. "You can't tell me what to do." He reached into his pocket and hurled something at my head.

I ducked, but it was too late. Something soft smacked me on the nose, releasing a pungent cloud of cumin in the air. A small fabric pouch fell at my feet. I stared down at it.

Hernan had just pelted me with a hex bag.

My knees went weak. Nausea rippled up in the back of my throat.

"Really?" I cried.

Hernan gave a cold little shrug and watched me expectantly.

Hell, no. There was no way I was going to be taken out by an old, sick man with bags of herbs. I reached for a rag on the workbench, used it to pick up the pouch, and marched outside into the wind. With one hand clamped over my mouth, the nausea intensifying, I tossed the bag over the back fence into the alley.

I gulped in some fresh air, grabbed the hose, and aimed the spray first at my face, then at the scattered remains of the hex powder. When I was done, I was dripping wet, but I felt better.

I grabbed a paper towel from a roll on the workbench and dabbed my face dry. It came away bloody, and for a moment, I was puzzled.

The hex bag had contained ground glass.

Hernan backed up against the far wall, clutching a chair for support. His eyes were closed, and he was muttering, his face scrunched in concentration. I couldn't make out the words, but I knew what he was doing. He was launching his clay monsters.

As he spoke, the clay rats on the shelf started to tremble, their eyes flicking open and glowing red. Outside, the wind began to howl, rattling the tin roof. A pressure built in the room.

I was done giving warnings. Done trying to convince Hernan to do the right thing. I reached into my front pack, pulled out the slingshot, loaded a pellet into the band, and released it.

Bullseye, right between a pair of little rat eyes.

The tail quivered, and then it toppled off the shelf and broke into tiny pieces.

I quickly reloaded and took another shot. One more clay rodent down. I moved fast, letting my pellets fly until there was nothing left but clay pieces and dust.

Hernan's expression was a mix of shock and rage while he watched his creations disintegrate before him.

I trained the slingshot on Hernan, just in case. He slowly straightened up, his chest heaving with anger.

"How dare you?" he snarled. He grabbed the small knife he had used to carve the red clay.

Was he really going to stab me?

He lunged toward me. But I reacted quickly and smacked the back of his hand with my slingshot. The knife dropped to the floor.

Hernan cried out in pain, pitched forward, and fell to his knees. The knife bounced away. I kicked it across the shed.

He was breathing heavily. I knelt beside him, wondering if it was safe to help him up. Sweat beaded on his forehead, and his face was pale and twisted in pain. He toppled over and lay on his back. Unseeing eyes stared up at the ceiling.

I grabbed my phone and called for an ambulance, then ran to the house to fetch Marta.

Chapter 45

Three Weeks Later

Chavez Ravine had once again become a peaceful refuge from the congestion and grime of Los Angeles.

The board and I worked on my proposals. As expected, I wasn't going to get everything I wanted, but they did agree to some of the bigger asks.

Rory tried once more to reclaim his cat but gave up after the cat bit a chunk out of his bald head. He was so furious he didn't even acknowledge my offer to pay him. Not the entire three thousand bucks, but more than I ever thought I would be willing to spend on a big furball with an attitude problem.

After nearly a week in the hospital, Hernan moved to a convalescent facility to recover from what had turned out to be a heart attack. With him out of the picture for who knew how long, it was finally time to celebrate with a small housewarming party. Nothing fancy, just some appetizers and wine.

But when I called to invite Julia, my casual little get-together turned into the event of the season.

The next thing I knew, Leo and Toby were scheduled to tend bar, Cora was bringing tamales, Becca Tey was making her famous kale and brie salad, and I even bought Julia-approved furniture for the backyard.

I installed French doors leading to the patio and arranged to have the inside of the house painted. Julia suggested bright colors to compliment the furniture, but I went for a tasteful cream and a few accent walls.

I stopped short of refinishing Liliana's workbench. Who knew what magical energy was embedded in the woodwork? Or whether Lencha would approve?

I hadn't even thrown out the remains of Trini Duran's notebooks. The bag containing the ashes was still sitting next to Little Lencha, just as it had been since that evening the hummingbird set them ablaze.

On the day of the party, I woke up early and gave the house a thorough cleaning. After that, I hung string lights in the backyard.

Everything looked perfect.

By early evening, the party was in full swing. I looked around and felt warm and tingly all over.

Jo was splayed out on one of the new chaises on the patio, glass of wine in hand, looking more relaxed than I had ever seen her. She was laughing at Becca Tey's latest tale of cosmetic surgery. Holly, wearing a lime green jumper over a sparkly black top, was in the living room, sitting on a floor pillow. The cat was on her lap, and she was massaging his neck while chatting with Stu about some new security technology. Stu held his martini with two olives with both hands, warily eying the cat.

Cora had brought enough tamales to feed a small army. There were sauces to go with them, and I had made chili beans too.

Charlie Perez was in attendance with his charming wife, Hilda, a teacher at an elementary school in Palo Verde. She took my hands in hers and said, "I'm so glad you're here, Madeline. Those terrible attacks have stopped, thank goodness. And that video! I feel so much safer with you here."

I nodded and smiled, but I couldn't shake the anxiety that crept in whenever I thought of Hernan Frias.

Several neighbors came too. The Connors were there—without their teenagers. So were the young couple across the street and Gerald, who was visibly disappointed when he learned Cora had a husband at home.

Eventually, the conversation turned to the housing development being built up the street. The developer was hoping to acquire more land and expand to the properties below. Which put us right in their crosshairs.

Everyone else had been offered a buyout. They had all refused, of course. Apparently, the money was fair but not enough to cover the cost of buying a new property. And besides, as Charlie pointed out, things had settled down, and my skills as a monster killer had spread far and wide. The demand for homes in Chavez Ravine had only grown, so property values were sure to go up.

"In fact,"—Charlie poured red sauce over his tamale—"there was a bidding war on the Morris house. It went for nearly a million over asking. A million! I heard if they hadn't already bought a house in New York, the Morris's would have stayed put and taken their place off the market."

"I'm sure the deal made Eileen very happy," Cora replied, dropping another tamale onto his plate. "She should thank you, Maddy."

I met her gaze and rolled my eyes. "I wonder why the developer didn't reach out to me."

We were sitting around the new, uncharred kitchen table.

"You're legacy," Charlie and Cora said at the same time, then laughed.

"That's something they don't want to mess with," Charlie added. "They know the HOA rules. If a legacy homeowner decides to sell, that's fine. But developers doing business inside Chavez Ravine aren't allowed to make unsolicited offers to legacy stakeholders."

Jo had joined us and was following the conversation with great interest. "I don't get it. Why not?"

"Because of the history here." Cora was at the stove, ready to dispense tamales from an enormous, steaming steel pot. "A long time ago, the city tried to evict the people living here—to build a housing project no one wanted—and then used dirty tricks to try and force out the people who resisted. There were protests, and the city changed its mind, but it was a very disruptive time for thousands of people. When Hernan Frias and his cohorts created the homeowner's association, that was one of the first rules they put in place. Legacy owners can never be bothered by outsiders suggesting they move."

"I wish they'd stop bothering us too." Toby held a plate out to Cora for seconds. "These guys started with emails, and now they're taping letters to our doors."

Hilda smiled slyly. "You should file a grievance with the HOA. No soliciting."

"It's better to start with the property management company," Charlie said. "That's the official way to go about it, and it gets on the agenda for the next board meeting."

Toby joined us at the table. "Developers, I can handle. I'm more worried about that vote to expand the definition of legacy."

"It doesn't really affect you," Hilda said, bristling. "If you decide to sell, does it matter to you that someone with a family connection to Chavez Ravine buys it?"

"It does if it means we won't be able to accept the best offer," Toby said evenly. "The way the new rule reads, we'd have to take the highest offer from a legacy stakeholder, and not just the highest offer, period. How is that even legal? It's like…socialism."

I was legacy, and even *I* didn't think that sounded fair.

Cora and Charlie exchanged looks. They were too discrete to weigh in, but they both thought the proposal was a bad idea.

"From what you've said, it doesn't sound like it will pass," Jo noted.

Toby sighed. "If all the legacy homeowners vote for it, it could."

The conversation turned to less serious matters, and I made a pot of coffee to go with the tres leches cake Stu had picked up from Muertos Café.

Stu was the last to leave. Just when I was about to ask if he'd like to stay awhile, a horn blared at the curb.

Stu's shoulders slumped. "Ah. My designated driver has arrived."

Clare Wells had impeccable timing. I was a little too tipsy to meet her, so I walked Stu to the door and waved from the porch.

"Hello, Madeline!" Clare called brightly, leaning out the driver's side window.

I got the distinct impression she was mocking me.

Cockblocked by a sixteen-year-old. Score one for Clare.

Chapter 46

I was too worked up to go to bed. Maybe it was the wine, but I was just anxious.

I decided to put the time to good use and started tidying up. We had used the fancy paper plates Toby had donated, so there weren't many dishes to wash. I collected the trash in a plastic refuse bag, which I carried into the sunroom to take outside in the morning.

Little Lencha was up to her old tricks. She was glowing again, a soft shade of purple.

I smiled, wondering at the significance of the color, when something caught my eye.

Earlier, there had only been two things on the rough wood of the sunroom workbench: Little Lencha and the bag of burned diaries.

Now, the ashes were gone, but an old wooden crate sat next to Lencha. I didn't recognize it. Had someone used it to carry food or supplies and then left it behind?

But I didn't remember anyone bringing it in.

I approached the crate and lifted the lid. A musty odor wafted out, and I sneezed.

Inside was a stack of cloth-bound journals. I reached for the top one and inspected it. It appeared to be made from old flour sacks. *Very* old.

My fingers itched with anticipation. Who had put this here? And where did it come from?

I opened the journal and read the title page.

Lencha Bantacorte. Spells and Recipes of Brujeria. Book 1.

I let out a little cry. The Lencha figurine seemed to glow a little brighter.

"You…left these for me!"

I held the journal close to my heart.

"Thank you," I whispered to the figurine.

There was no way in hell I was going to let anything happen to the journals. I carried the crate into my bedroom, far away from any windows and hummingbirds, until I could figure out how to protect its contents.

Afterward, I climbed into bed, made myself comfortable, opened the first journal, and prepared to read.

The cat jumped up and nestled against my hip, radiating warmth and contentment. His purring sounded like a small motor.

I felt like crying; I had a new home, new friends, and a new job I actually enjoyed. And a cat.

The cat. I couldn't keep calling him that. It was time to give him a name. He had earned at least that.

"Sam."

I hadn't meant to say it out loud, but when I did, his head snapped up. His eyes met mine. I smiled, sensing an almost electrical connection with this big red Bengal who had found his way into my life.

"All right. Let's see how smart you really are. One blink means you hate your new name. Two blinks mean you like it."

Sam blinked twice. I tapped him lightly on the head, and he closed his eyes.

When I began reading Lencha's first journal, I finally understood how I would develop my skills, how I would channel the legacy shared by the women in my family. Lencha would be my guide, teaching me in her own words, helping me realize the potential running in my blood.

I was going to be one badass chingona.

Author's Note

Most people know Chavez Ravine as the home of the Los Angeles Dodgers. Many also know it was once home to thousands of Mexican Americans who were evicted in the 1950s so the city could build a public housing project. The housing project never happened. My mother and her family were among the evictees.

One day I was talking with my dear friend Teri about a new story idea, and she suggested I set it in an alternative universe where the evictions never happened. I had already set several books of supernatural suspense in Chavez Ravine prior to the evictions, so that idea made perfect sense. That's why this book is dedicated to her.

I have always wondered what the neighborhoods of La Loma, Palo Verde and Bishop would be like today if the bulldozers hadn't arrived.

Imagine the gentrification that would certainly have happened, the original families cashing in with their equity and eventually, their inherited wealth. The story took off from there. Chavez Ravine evolved into a private, gated community with a Homeowners Association. And creatures, of course.

If you're interested in learning more about the history of Chavez Ravine, I have a list of recommended non-fiction books on my website at debracastaneda.com, including Eric Nusbaum's excellent Stealing Home: Los Angeles, the Dodgers, and the Lives Caught in Between. On my website at debracastaneda.com, you can also find a few photos of my mother and her family in Palo Verde, where my grandfather Julian Castaneda bought a home from a Pasadena developer in 1926. These stories are my way of keeping the memories of Chavez Ravine alive.

Thank you for reading this story. I hope you enjoyed it and will also try the other books in the Maddy Madrigal Mysteries series!

Keep Reading for a Preview of

MADDY MADRIGAL MYSTERIES BOOK 2

SOMEWHAT MAGIC

DEBRA CASTANEDA

Chapter 1

Spending a few years with the LAPD's Occult Affairs Division teaches one to expect the worst. Wrestling with Mexican fairies, being chased by trolls, and fending off attacking nixies develops a heightened sense of danger. One finds themselves looking for things that are out of place, for slight disturbances which might indicate an entity eruption is imminent.

And often, finding them is easy.

So even though I had been out of the force for months, I immediately recognized the little indentation in the field for what it was.

And that's when a soccer game turned into a disaster. Unfortunately for Clare Wells.

When Clare invited me to her game, it seemed to signal a turning point in our relationship: Stu's daughter had finally warmed up to me. Stu and I were sitting in the bleachers, watching the sixteen-year-old play. She was good—fast, nimble, and focused.

So centered that when the small hole opened in the middle of the field and tar started bubbling out, she didn't even notice. In fact, nobody did.

Except me. Also, we were just half a mile away from a recent emergence at the La Brea Tar Pits.

So, I wasn't the least bit surprised when a small head popped out of the black ooze, followed by bony shoulders and a twisted body.

I jumped to my feet and began shouting, "Run, Clare, run!"

Which did nothing.

People yell things like that all the time at soccer games. I had to try something else.

"Clare! Get off the field! Everyone, off the field!"

That worked.

Stu caught on first and rushed down the bleacher stairs.

The game gradually stopped. The girls stared at the rapidly expanding pool of tar.

More small shapes pulled themselves out of the pit, some rolling around and wailing in distress. Others lurched to their feet, arms outstretched in a Frankenstein parody.

And that's when the girls in their blue and gold soccer uniforms began to run, except for Clare, who had the bad luck of being closest to the pit.

One of the things hopped toward her and threw its arms around her waist. Right about then, Stu reached her and started to pull the creature off his daughter. I ran too. Straight for my Jeep in the parking lot.

It didn't take long to find what I was looking for: the entity smoke bomb I kept in my glove box. With the rubber pouch in hand, I dashed back to the field, where Stu was still trying to pry bony little hands from a shrieking Clare's waist.

The rest of the crowd was yelling and rushing for the parking lot at top speed. Only Stu and Clare were left on the field, surrounded by a growing mob of sticky, knee-high figures. The thing clutching Clare wasn't making any attempt to bite her, but it wouldn't let go either.

I threw the rubber pouch onto the ground and gave it a good stomp. A purple mist rose into the air. Humans were immune to the stuff, but the scientifically derived compound nicknamed "Smoke Bomb" had an immediate effect on most entities.

The tar-covered biped attached to Clare went limp and fell to the ground.

Her reaction was interesting. One minute, Clare was panting and screaming, trying to break free, and the next moment, she was furious. Fists clenched, she ran toward the slack form on the ground, screeching words I was surprised she knew. Stu intervened just before she kicked it. He wrapped his arms around her waist and pulled her away from the field.

I didn't exactly blame her for getting pissed off. The entity hadn't hurt her, but it must have been terrifying all the same.

In the distance, sirens wailed. It wouldn't be long before Occult Affairs officers rolled up. There had been no need for me to call the LAPD's emergency number; the heatmap tracking entity arrivals must have lit up like a Christmas tree, and since Jo was working, she had sent the cavalry.

I looked at Stu standing in the shade of a tree, his arm around Clare. She was sobbing. It was best to give them some father-daughter space.

Stu and I were still in the early stages of our relationship, and I swear Clare did everything she could to make sure it stayed that way. Which, honestly, was fine by me. Two months into my job as head of security for the Chavez Ravine Homeowner's Association, I was plenty busy, and Stu had his hands full running a security firm with a growing celebrity clientele.

So, for now, neither of us needed the distraction of a relationship. Still, I looked forward to the day when Clare would allow her father to stay out past nine o'clock without text bombing him.

A few Occult Affairs officers ran over, hands on the Smoke Bomb pouches dangling from their belts.

Bailey Nixon reached me first, which was no surprise. She was an avid runner and kept herself in good shape. As always, her copper hair was pulled back, and she wore minimal makeup, except for a shimmery shadow ringing her brown eyes. Today, it was a bright blue matching the clear sky.

"Hey, Mads! Surprised to see you here. What are they?" Bailey asked.

"Well, we won't know for sure until all that tar is cleaned off, but considering their size and beards, I think we're looking at goblins."

"Goblins!" Bailey echoed. "We haven't seen those before, have we?"

"Not for a long time. Fairies, the odd brownie, and the elves that appeared in that maternity ward during the nurse's strike…But very few goblins. Until now, if I'm right."

"Lucky you were here." Bailey turned to the approaching officers. "Hey, guys, Maddy's got it under control. How about bringing some crates? The medium ones ought to do it."

Bailey was the youngest officer in Occult Affairs, and she wasn't their boss, but that didn't stop her from taking charge. I had always liked that about Bailey. She stepped up and got things done.

"How's it going back at the farm?"

Bailey sighed. "It sucks. Except for Jo. I *love* Jo. But the chief? He's such an asshole." She paused, biting her lip. "When you left, it got me rethinking my choices. I'm going to start looking around. Life is too short to put up with that jerk. So, if anything opens up where you are, I'd…be interested." Bailey's pale, freckled face turned pink. She wasn't normally the blushing type, so that must have been hard for her to say.

"I just hired some security guards," I said. "But you're way overqualified for a guard shift. But I'll tell you what: if anything better opens up, I'm calling you."

Bailey brightened. "Awesome!"

I walked past officers stuffing sticky, dazed entities into crates and went to find Stu and Clare. They were in the nearly empty parking lot. Most of the other families had gone, but Stu stood next to his fancy SUV with tinted windows.

Claire was leaning back in the passenger seat, hands over her face, crying softly.

Stu slid an arm around my waist. "I'm not sure what we would have done if you hadn't been here," he said into my ear.

I wasn't sure either. It was fairly rare for a new arrival to grab a civilian, so there were no protocols for that. "Is she okay?"

Stu took my elbow and steered me away from the SUV. "She'll be fine," he replied in a low voice. "But ever since her mother and I split, any little blip seems to throw her for a loop. It's like she's three again, and if you give her the pink cup instead of the purple cup, she just sort of falls apart, you know?"

My own teenage years of living with a mother who was exploring her psychic abilities and her flair for PR had caused me overwhelming embarrassment and anxiety. Stu's wife had slept with Clare's best friend's father, which, arguably, was worse than having a self-absorbed psychic for a mother. Clare had earned the right to freak out.

"Stu, this whole entity thing is a lot scarier when it happens to you. She's in shock. Take her home, get her some pizza, and watch some sappy movies."

Stu's shoulders sagged. "You make it sound so easy."

True that. I wasn't her parent and all that came with it, but there was no reason for him to expect her to bounce right back.

Hell, even Occult Affairs officers got a mental health day after their first attack.

"Stu," I said firmly. "She's been traumatized, okay? A creepy-ass goblin slithered out of a tar pit and grabbed her. Take her home and baby her a little. She'll be fine. Come on, don't be a jerk."

Stu's mouth opened, then closed. A moment later, he laughed. "I guess I needed to hear that. Maybe if I'm really good, she'll even allow us to spend some time alone."

Without looking back to see if his daughter was watching, Stu leaned in for a kiss. A voice called from the car.

"*Dad!*"

Books by Debra Castaneda

Maddy Madrigal Mysteries

Monsters, mayhem, and Mexican food

Barely Magic

Maddy Madrigal lands a cushy security job in a gated community but must confront a supernatural threat and come to terms with her magical heritage.

Somewhat Magic

In the heart of Los Angeles, Maddy Madrigal battles legendary creatures and unscrupulous developers as an old protective spell begins to fail.

Desperate Magic

Maddy must unravel a web of supernatural clues and confront ancient predators to stop a string of brutal murders.

Mortal Magic

Something ancient and deadly is roosting outside Chavez Ravine, and Maddy's weapons, magic, and extremely agitated cat aren't enough to fight it off.

Dark Earth Rising
Themed novels that can be read in any order

A Dark and Rising Tide
When a massive storm surge hits the central coast of California, the ferocious surf destroys buildings, floods streets, and washes up something sinister from the depths of the Monterey Bay.

The Devil's Shallows
Eight miles of mystery. One night of terror. Residents trapped in a remote neighborhood confront the unimaginable.

Circus at Devil's Landing
Creatures that howl in the night, a mysterious circus, and a clash between a ringmaster and a woman determined to rescue her captured lover.

The Copper Man
Haunted tunnels. Unexplained deaths. Eerie sightings. Decades after The Copper Man killed her brother, Leah Shaw returns to the remote mining town of Tribulation Gulch where a lethal mystery awaits.

The Root Witch
A beautiful forest. A terrifying legend. It's 1986. Two strangers, hundreds of miles apart, grapple with disturbing incidents in a one-of-a-kind quaking aspen forest.

The Spore Queen
A charming reporter, an ailing tech mogul, and two strangers hiding secrets are brought together by a mysterious fungus, one that will either save them or destroy them.

Chavez Ravine Novels
Stand-alone novels set in Chavez Ravine, Los Angeles during turbulent times

The Monsters of Chavez Ravine
A 2021 International Latino Book Awards Gold Medal Winner! Before Dodger Stadium, dark forces terrorized Chavez Ravine.

The Night Lady
A rebel curandera, a plucky seamstress, and a young reporter are pulled into the investigation of a killer terrorizing Chavez Ravine.

The Haunting of Chavez Ravine
La Llorona is terrorizing people in the hills of Chavez Ravine, and a sassy curandera and her clever young niece must stop her.

The Christmas Cucuy
It's Christmas Eve, 1949, and Kiki's dreams are about to come true: she'll be singing at Palladium with her old bandmates. But when she threatens her rambunctious son with El Cucuy, her plans change.